EMERALD OBSESSION

A Novel

Carolyn Greeley

www.carolyngreeley.com

Library of Congress Control Number: 2015911428

ISBN: 978-0-9966002-1-7
ISBN: 978-0-9966002-3-1 (ebook)

Printed in the United States of America
First Edition

Cover Design: Sagaponack Books
Author Photograph: Luboš Šalomoun

DEDICATION

Immeasurable thanks go to the following. Without them, this novel wouldn't exist:

Jill Kruskal, for the kick in the butt that got me started.

Kristen Alia Garvey, *Cuzzie*, for the unwavering support, boundless love and subsequent butt-kicks that kept me going. They still do. They always will. I will miss you forever.

Natasha Foy, for the early read. And the late one, along with the encouragement in between.

Mom and Dad, Phyllis and Brett Greeley. When I uprooted my life to pursue my dreams, your unparalleled encouragement, optimism and love helped make so much possible. Dad, I wish I could have been your "rich-and-famous-author-daughter" while you were still with me to enjoy the ride. Heaven's the lucky one.

And my husband, Luboš Šalomoun. You add to my life every day, in so many beautiful ways.

ACKNOWLEDGMENTS

Writing a book takes a while. Making it as good as it can be takes much longer. So many people and groups have nurtured me and my story. Sincere and cheery thanks to everyone, especially these generous people, in no particular order: my family and friends; the Florida Writers Association, for their continuous offerings and advice; the Florida PWG critique group; Anne Dalton, Esquire; my editor, Beth Mansbridge; my beta readers; and Kimberly Sentek.

Also to: Jodi Sykes, Glen Roberts and Frank Linn, my St. Augustine critique compadres. If my writing is any good, it's because of their influence. "Thank you" is simply not enough, but I hope the words suffice.

And you know the saying … if something in here is wrong, the fault is mine. I'm sure that's true.

Chapter 1

"Buy them, damn it, Alexandria."

The woman pounded her wrinkled fist against the escritoire in her study, diamond rings glinting in the desk lamp's light. Paperwork crinkled under the marginal weight of her hand. "Those jewels belong to me, and I will have them one way or another. No matter the cost. You get yourself down there today and do whatever you must, but do not come back without them."

She drew herself up, imposing though she remained seated. "Those jewels are the key to everything I have been searching for."

Alexandria Nichols stood at attention in front of her eighty-six-year-old client. Her eyes widened at the vehemence echoing off the diminutive woman ... normally a sedate, dignified matron of Manhattan's Upper East Side society. *Wow, I can't believe she deigned to utter a swear word.*

In the ten years she'd worked as Claudine Lansing Stellery's jewelry buyer and designer, Alexandria had not once encountered anything but cool civility and courteousness from her client.

Alexandria, Lexy to everyone other than Mrs. Stellery, knew when to hold her tongue and when to give as good as she got, even with, or perhaps especially with, her officious, high-paying client.

"Mrs. Stellery, I realize this latest acquisition is of primary importance to you ... but are you out of your mind?" Incredulousness flooded Lexy's voice. "There're almost hurricane conditions outside."

"Nonsense, Alexandria. We are barely into August, barely hurricane season at all." A stretching of the truth, considering summer was the midpoint of the Caribbean hurricane season. Claudine Stellery inclined her silvered head at her. "That weather service you listen to is hardly worth their salt."

"I'll never get a flight out now." Lexy brushed her black hair back to fall in a light wave past her shoulder blades. "God knows if they'd be able to land in Nassau, or anywhere in the Bahamas, let alone shuttle me to Eleuthera by tomorrow. Because—despite your opinion of our local forecasters—I checked the weather on my cell phone on my way here, and the entire Eastern Seaboard is being slammed by this system. The Caribbean islands are half underwater."

Lexy dropped a skeptical, gray gaze on her client's sharp-featured face. "I can't toddle off down there to attend some estate sale in the hopes of finding you another cache of jewels."

Lexy's comments might have surprised some, but Lexy and Claudine had known each other too long to stand overmuch on ceremony. "In all honesty, Mrs. Stellery, what gives? What's so important about these particular stones that you'd have me fly into a gale to get to this auction?" Lexy shifted her stance, wondering if she'd get a straight answer.

"That is impertinent, Alexandria."

Lexy tilted her head, disconcerted as she realized the comment marked the first time Claudine dodged questions about an acquisition. *That's just great. Of all the times for her to start being cagey ... when this buy has more than its fair share of travel and expense. Danger, too.*

Lexy looked at the elements that pounded at the windows. She decided to wait out Claudine. A tense minute dragged in silence.

"It will suffice to say it is of the utmost urgency that you make your way to Eleuthera and that auction by tomorrow afternoon. Consider this carte blanche approval to use any means necessary to get there, as well as to procure those emeralds." Claudine blasted a steely look at Lexy. "*Any* means. *Carte blanche.* Now ... do I have your word?"

Lexy regarded the elder woman. Admiration and annoyance crisscrossed Lexy's face, and her mind raced for some logical rationale to explain Claudine's adamant position. Coming up empty, Lexy began to pace the hardwood floor. The tap of her heels punctuated her sincere, pointed words. "I'll do my best, Mrs. Stellery."

Lexy strode across the room and ticked off a quick to-do list. "I'll contact the airlines and will let you know what I find. And I have my guy Matt on St. Kitts, who should be able to help with local water transportation, if I can manage to get a flight to the Bahamas. It's a long shot, but I'll see what he comes back with. Or maybe this other fellow I know, Lucas, can be of some help …." Her voice trailed off as she turned to study Mrs. Stellery. "I'll reach out to the Edwards estate manager for the auction details and to let them know I'm coming."

She heard the whisper of an almost-covered sigh escape Claudine, and Lexy's eyes flickered over her client. Curiosity burned. "If you're absolutely sure …."

"Indeed I am, Alexandria."

Claudine Stellery's jeweled hand sparkled again as her thrusting forefinger accentuated her words. "Those jewels—and having them in my possession as soon as possible—are vitally important. Now, move along with your plans, and be certain to keep me apprised of your progress." The words resounded, then dissipated into the air like the trailing notes of a symphony's coda.

Lexy glanced around the immaculate, classically decorated study and took her leave. "Well then, Mrs. Stellery, off I go to do your bidding." A trace of sarcasm edged the words when they left Lexy's lips. "I'll be in touch once I have my travel details arranged."

She headed toward the mahogany den doors, which silently opened from the hall, as if her departure had been imminently expected. "Wish me luck."

"You will not need luck, Alexandria."

Lexy stopped and turned to face Claudine. The woman's sharp blue eyes conferred an unexpected and startling prescience. "You will need only savvy. See that you take it with you."

The cryptic comment rang in Lexy's head, and she frowned as the butler escorted her out. He preceded her down the curving oak staircase, into the front foyer. Her eyes roamed the vast space. She marveled, as she often did, at its utter oppositeness from her own

Manhattan home. Rich oil paintings hugged the silk-dressed walls. Gleaming Louis XVI consoles held aloft Ming vases. Fresh-cut ivory roses adorned antique marble pedestals. Nary a dust mote floated about the silent hall to mar the pristine surroundings, faint with the tangy scent of some cleaner less gauche than Forever-Pine Disinfectant.

The butler returned with her Kate Spade trench coat, ready to assist. As Lexy donned the overcoat, her mind wandered. *What the hell, Mrs. S.? You already seem to possess everything material that could make you happy. What's with this crazy desire for yet another collection of jewels? Should I be worried about this trip?*

Never before in their association had Lexy experienced such fervor from Mrs. Stellery. Still, she was a valued—and well-paying— client. One whom Lexy appreciated not only for her pocketbook, but also for her keen eye for beautiful things, her impeccable knowledge of gems and her drive to obtain them.

Now, that's something I can get on board with. Lexy smiled to herself. *Guess I'll have to wait and see what all the hoopla is about.*

The butler held open the door and handed over her teal blue umbrella.

"Thank you, Charles."

She stepped out, opened her umbrella against a sudden gust and inhaled the scent of summer rain. *Here we go again ....* She ducked her head and forced herself into the wind tunnel known as East Sixty-Third Street.

Behind her, the butler closed the heavy door with not even the ping of a dislodged doorknocker.

*****

"Charles?" echoed down the stairs from the study.

The butler hurried to his mistress, found her staring down through the window sheers at the sodden street. A pale, jeweled hand parted the curtain and tightened a moment, wrinkling the otherwise perfect drape. She stood pole-straight, garbed in a vintage Valentino suit, her casual posture belying the taut fingers.

"Yes, ma'am?" he inquired.

Without turning from the view, Claudine Stellery spoke. Her voice quavered as she struggled to contain her anticipation. "Indeed, Charles ... the game is now afoot, is it not?"

She didn't wait for his reply—knew none would be forthcoming—and turned around. Her crisp, silver-blue gaze sought his. "Everything I have been searching for is within reach. I can feel it, Charles. In a matter of days, the jewels will be mine. Along with their secrets. Soon, the past will be revealed."

She beamed a cool, sparkling smile. "And," she said, "the world will know the truth."

Chapter 2

Outside, Lexy debated the fastest way to her Tribeca apartment: subway or taxicab. She decided to hoof it toward the nearest station, the F train at Lexington, and see if she lucked onto an empty taxi before she got there. *Yeah, me and the rest of Manhattan trying to catch a cab in the rain. Fat chance.*

Her brain shifted gears as she walked. *The sooner I get home, the sooner I can sort out my travel plans. I can't imagine what has Mrs. S.'s panties in such a bunch.*

The smell of drenched concrete wafted around her as she hurried along. The mellow scent reminded her of warm playground days, caught in the drizzle, playing with her friend Claire. The memory teased out a brief smile before anxiety fluttered through her. *This weather is not gonna make for an easy trip south.* Nor for a guaranteed flight, she realized, no matter what her bankroll could cover. She sighed and sidestepped a puddle.

Glancing backward, she stepped to the curb and strained to see whether an oncoming cab was available. She squinted through the rain and mist that rose off the passing traffic. The cab sped past her, splashing a muddy spray of water across her body. Too late, she jumped back and skidded on the wet sidewalk, barely keeping her balance.

"Son of a bitch!"

She looked up in time to curse the cab and the dark-haired man who watched her through the rear window.

"Damn son of a jerk." She spat the words at the retreating taxi and flung a rude hand gesture its way, knowing the act was pointless, yet feeling better for it.

The cab stopped at a traffic light, and Lexy wondered why the guy still stared at her. Wondered if he was mentally—or physically, with his cell phone—taking a picture of her face so he could stalk her later and make her pay for flipping him the bird.

Oh, Lex. Don't be so paranoid. The entire city is not populated by psychos just because you've had a few wonky experiences. The internal chat calmed, as it always did.

"Damn and …. Damn, already." Grouchiness lingered, but the heat left her voice. Resigned to riding the subway, she continued toward the station.

Doing the duck-and-weave of a lifelong Manhattanite, she skirted several slower-moving pedestrians and scooted into the terminal. *C'mon, trains. It's midday Friday, let's make this quick.* Ten minutes later she boarded, squeezed herself between a chattering Alabama tourist and a guy smelling like McDonald's fries, then rocketed downtown.

After changing to the A train at West Fourth Street, she continued toward Chambers. She exited and walked the remaining blocks to her apartment, rain pounding her as she headed northwest on Hudson Street. Lexy plodded home, dodging the smelly, dingy-looking puddles. *Why on earth did I wear open-toe heels today?* A left turn onto Harrison Street and a short walk toward the Hudson River, visible and frothing in the distance, brought her to the front door of her townhouse.

Lexy climbed the worn stone steps, keyed the lock and swung open the squeaky oak-and-etched-glass door into the downstairs hallway. The muted light cast by the old-fashioned wall sconces threw the entry into a familiar mellow pattern of light and dark, and Lexy immediately unwound. The homey décor, punctuated by walls of deep pine wainscoting and buttery yellow paint, soothed away the tension of the world outside. She took another deep breath.

Maybe I was born in the wrong century. Of everyone I know, I'm the only one who feels more comfortable with a book instead of a Kindle, a landline instead of a cell and this wonderful, old-fashioned apartment instead of one of those luxury high-rises going up every other week.

"I love this place. Coming home is like a tonic, good for what ails me. If I could bottle this, I'd be freakin' rich." She shook her head as she noted the empty hallway. "Wow, I talk to myself too much."

Lexy grabbed the newel post and trod upstairs to her third-floor apartment. One, two, three locks and she pushed the door open. *Home, sweet, tiny Manhattan home.* She threw a reflexive look over her shoulder, went inside and bolted the door. She'd never call herself truly paranoid, but growing up in Manhattan meant being cautious. As long as that didn't interfere with having fun.

Let's face it, it ain't always easy to pay attention when you're stumbling home drunk at four in the morning. I know that's when I should be most alert, but what's a girl to do when she's out and about, having a good time?

"It's not like I can be on guard 24/7; I have to relax sometime, don't I?" She stood in her apartment and paused. "Damn! There I go again. If anyone caught me talking out loud, they'd think I'm nuts. Not that they'd be wrong."

She went into the bedroom and ditched her work clothes and bag, then wandered back to her couch for a quick respite before calling the boutique. *Something's missing.* She popped up and headed to the kitchen for a glass of wine. The layout of the tiny space, par for the course in Manhattan, perfectly suited Lexy; she had room to fit a substantial wine rack and a tattered folder of takeout menus.

She peeked out the window at the rain-spattered streets and wondered again whether she'd get a flight out. *Five minutes, then I'll call. Just five more minutes.* Carrying a glass of chilled white Rioja, Lexy settled on the espresso-colored couch. She inhaled the wine's tangy aroma, sipped and closed her eyes.

Designing for an exclusive SoHo boutique gave Lexy opportunities she thought no other job could rival. The prestige of their clientele ensured continual travel to the world's most exotic locales on the client's dime. The big budgets meant first-class travel, five-star hotels and dining and procuring priceless gems and jewelry from around the globe. She came home from every trip with at least a trinket to adorn her home, a fabulous story to relive or a memorable meal to salivate over. For Lexy, pure heaven.

Except all that travel has been wearing me down lately. It's been great for so, so long, but these days? It feels like every time I turn around, I'm heading to the airport. She inhaled slowly and fortified herself with a swallow of the crisp, tart wine. *C'mon, Lex, you know you can do this. For a little while longer, at least. It's all part of the plan.*

She turned her head and gazed about the calming blue tones of her living room. Along one wall, memorabilia from her sojourns, with the rare holiday memento thrown in for good measure, festooned the mantel of the wood-burning fireplace. Lexy padded across the rug, glass in hand, and fingered the perfect conch shell she'd uncovered on the beach in Cameroon. Her eyes lit on the coral she'd smuggled off the Great Barrier Reef on one of her dives in Queensland, Australia. Her hand grazed the uncut emerald she'd found while touring an excavation site in Peru, scouting the operation for Mrs. Stellery.

The deep beauty of the gem went unnoticed by her visitors. *Ha-ha, as if I'm ever home long enough to have visitors. I really crack myself up sometimes.* Those who saw the nugget thought it was a rock. Plain and lumpy. *Silly people. Missing the beauty hidden beyond mere eyesight. Don't they realize there are deeper ways of seeing? More important things to see?*

Lexy knew the brilliance that lay below the stone's rough, unpolished surface. Years of training and experience had honed her skills, sharpened her perception and helped her see with more than eyes alone. That insight taught her, more so over the recent months, to appreciate the beauty and the value of all she had in New York, in her hometown, in the place she loved best and saw least.

Poor me, right? Like it's such a hardship, traveling and dining and playing with fancy jewelry. Still, the words felt hollow, the rebuke empty. *I know twenty people who'd kill for my job. I just have to remember there's a reason for all this craziness.*

She slid her fingers along the mantel, then left it behind as she grabbed her purse and settled at the sleek drafting table that passed for a desk. Rummaging in her bag, Lexy produced her cell phone and her old-school pocket calendar. She tapped the digits for the shop, determined to waste no more time being melancholy over the unexpected trip. *Hell, at least I get to go to the Bahamas for a few days, even if it is freakin' August.*

The office manager, William, answered and put her through to their travel department. The challenging nature of the boutique's affluent clientele demanded a staff of three agents to accommodate the buyers' travel needs. The necessity spoke to the nomadic and lonely aspects of a job that had held a great deal more appeal in previous years. In Lexy's opinion, the need for such a large group yelled louder than ever: "Too much traveling."

Maybe I'm getting old. Her mind wandered as her agent and good friend, Stacey Dallen, looked up Lexy's preprogrammed details in their online system. *Though thirty-eight doesn't seem quite over the hill yet.* She blinked. *Damn me, did I really think that?*

Stacey's perky "So, Lexy, what can I do for you today?" interrupted Lexy's internal conversation.

"I have to get my ass down to the Bahamas tonight, if you can believe that trick. Courtesy of Claudine Stellery, which I'm sure won't surprise you."

Though Lexy enjoyed working with Mrs. Stellery, the woman's last-minute demands, often requiring long treks and short notice, were the most wearing of all of Lexy's clients. Lexy gave her friend a rundown of her client's latest mandate.

"So, Stace, you've met her a few times …. Does this sound weird to you? I know she can be difficult, but this is stretching it. She acted really … odd. Plus, she gave me the barest of information about the jewels or the auction. What the hell, right?"

"Yeah, Lex, that does sound a bit extreme, even for Mrs. Stellery. You sure she's not going to send you information once you arrive?"

"I'm not sure of anything at this point. She's never been this secretive before. It's really strange."

Silence filled the line. Then Lexy said, "But I've still got to go. You know the damn drill. Help a girl out, will ya?"

Stacey, well-seasoned to Lexy's casual speech, took the comments in stride. Lexy could hear the clickety-tap of Stacey's fingers on her keyboard as she searched the company's travel program for flights.

"Let's see now …."

Lexy heard a lot of tapping.

"Looks like there are still a few scheduled flights for today that haven't been canceled because of this lousy weather. Here's one leaving LaGuardia at 8:45 p.m. You could make that, of course, but if the rain doesn't let up, who knows when you'll get there."

Lexy heard more clicking and caught a faint curse. "Damn, Lex, I'm sorry. I'm not finding anything that's going all the way to Eleuthera. Looks like that one is stopping at Freeport. I can also get you on a 6:05 p.m. that'll take you to Nassau, but none of the airlines are going to the Out Islands in this weather. There are advisories and bulletins streaming across my screen. No one's taking chances in this mess."

Lexy heard the worry in Stacey's voice. "Except good ol' Mrs. Stellery, clearly." She didn't bother hiding the sarcasm. She rose from her desk and started pacing. "No worries, Stace. I still have Matt operating out of St. Kitts. He'll hook me up. He knows everybody and their brother down there, so water transportation in the a.m. shouldn't be a problem. Especially since money isn't an object, per Claudine." The barest hint of a snicker accompanied her remark. "Get me on that flight to Nassau, and I'll give him a shout when we're through."

More tip-tapping sounded, and Stacey replied, "Right on, Lex. Nassau it is. Leaving Newark at six oh five. I'm emailing your reservation details as we speak." A snarky chuckle slid over the line. "And don't forget your passport, would you please? That was a total pain in the ass trying to get you back into the country last time." She laughed. "By the way, make sure Matt hooks you up with something that doesn't leak, okay?"

Lexy burst out laughing. "Damn straight, girl! You remember that? God, I thought my arm would fall out of its socket, I pumped so much friggin' water out of the bilge. And in that heat, too."

She laughed, but as she thought about it she reminded herself to stay on top of Matt Aldridge and his potentially sketchy transportation options. *And to keep Lucas's number in my back pocket, if need be.* "Thanks for the brain jog," she said with a touch of soberness.

A few minutes later, Lexy had the travel arrangements on her cell. Her employer had a straightforward operation: The buyers and designers worked with certain clients, at their beck and call. As such, the staff needn't answer to the owner of the shop for last-minute travel plans like those ordered by Mrs. Stellery. Lexy left a voicemail on Christian's phone, letting her boss know she'd be traveling at her client's request. End of story.

Glass in hand, she went into the bedroom and pulled out her overnight bag. The six o'clock flight gave her thirty minutes to gather everything. She'd long ago learned to keep a travel toiletry kit ready, along with a second set of her jeweler's tools, so packing on the fly was no longer a haphazard event. Travel requirement number one: Never leave home without contact lens solution, tampons and Imodium. *God forbid I forget any of those things ever again.*

Lexy opened her lone closet and sorted through the clothes. The only potential obstacle to her speed-packing was whether or not she had done the laundry. She sniffed to make sure. *Lucky for the islanders.* She eyed the rack, trying to guess what would look appropriate for a weekend Bahamian auction. *Like I'm supposed to know what would work?* She held up a dress, replaced it and slugged another mouthful of wine. *Well, winging it usually turns out alright.*

She sifted through her outfits and made an executive decision. *Okay ... dress, skirt and top, jeans, tank tops, shorts, bikini, strappy heels. Done!* One after another, she packed the items into her luggage. She zipped up the bright orange bag and hefted it, testing its weight.

Not too bad. Besides, a girl's got to be prepared for anything.

Chapter 3

While she waited for the car service, Lexy sat and flipped through her calendar. "Shit!" she cried. "I can't believe I forgot."

She stared at the scrawled Saturday plans that had been made far in advance to accommodate a couple of hectic schedules.

"Oh, fuck. Claire's gonna kill me," she moaned, head falling back against the couch cushions. "Hell, I'd kill me, too. Of all the weekends for Mrs. S. to spring this trip. How on earth can I cancel our girls night?" She leaned forward, dropped her elbows onto her knees and covered her face. The thought of ringing Claire to break plans—again—squeezed her heart.

Claire McEvoy and Lexy had been best friends since first grade. Lexy followed Claire to the Central Park swings after the second day of school, to the consternation of Lexy's nanny, who'd lost her in the shuffle of the after-school pickup line. Mrs. McEvoy noticed the tagalong when Lexy punched a rascal bullying Claire. By the time Claire's mom located Lexy's distraught nanny, the friendship between the girls had been cemented with skinned knees and jump-rope rhymes.

Their friendship remained true to this day, thirty-odd years later, despite the lapses instigated by separate colleges, careers and boyfriends. Lexy and Claire were sisters by choice; their close bond meant the world to Lexy, but that didn't mean she didn't screw up now and again.

Shit! I know she loves me, but she'll still want to strangle me for canceling on her. When I get home.

Their plans, a late-afternoon pedicure followed by dinner, were Lexy's attempt at quality catch-up time. Claire's month-old engagement to Mike Ramsey and Lexy's work schedule had wrought havoc on their girl time. *How could I have forgotten our plans? God, what kind of friend am I?*

Now she had to cancel. Because of work, *again*. "Fuckin' A."

Lexy pushed off the sofa and paced. Postponing meant coordinating schedules again and, worse, breaking the news to Claire. *I can't even make up an excuse. She'll know it's work-related no matter what I say. And she'll tell me she understands, which is even worse. Damn it! I hate bailing on our plans. I hate friggin' bailing on my life.* She stalked around the room, a scowl wrinkling her face.

Her cell vibrated on the coffee table, announcing the arrival of her car. Lexy grabbed her papers, bag and trench coat, then locked up and hurried downstairs. She shoved her belongings into the backseat of the sleek Lincoln Town Car and slid in before the driver could assist. She caught his profile when he closed the door against the downpour.

At least I didn't have to hail a cab. She looked up as the driver entered, hustling to get out of the rain. "Hey, Jimmy, I thought that was you. How're you doing these days?" Lexy perked at the sight of Jimmy Moran. He'd been her usual driver for the last eight years and had accompanied her on many travels … to and from the airport.

"Ah, Miss Alexandria, 'tis so good to see you again," his Irish lilt sang out. "And in such fine form too, despite this nastiness we're havin'."

His smile reached the backseat, charming Lexy as usual. *I do love a man with an accent. And a familiar face is a good way to start this trip.*

"'Tis rainin' something fierce out there, now isn't it?" Without waiting for a reply, he said, "And where'll you be headin' off to this time? And on such a day as this?"

"Now, Jimmy, you know duty calls. Frequently and annoyingly."

Lexy said it with a smile, and Jimmy tossed a laugh over his shoulder. Jimmy reminded her of hanging out at her favorite Irish bar,

McHale's, where she never met a stranger. Good old-fashioned—or perhaps it was old-world—kindness permeated everything he did.

"I'm off to the Bahamas, but only for two or three days. Can you believe that? Yet another drive-by." Saying it aloud made her blue again. "I'm getting sick of those," she mumbled. She gazed outside, oblivious to the rain pelting the window.

"What's that, miss? I didn'a hear ya over this bloody rain."

"Sorry, Jimmy. Don't mind me and my nonsense," she replied. "Wondering when I'm going to stop all this crazy traipsing around the globe. Mrs. S. sprung this trip on me earlier today. Sometimes I can't believe I'm still jumping at the drop of her hat." Lexy grimaced. "I guess I've got a little pseudo-midlife crisis going on."

Jimmy gave a "Pshaw" of disagreement. "Now, Miss Alexandria, you're far too young to be havin' such thoughts. Why, you're not even halfway to keelin' over! What ya might need, however, is to be takin' one of these tropical trips of yours for purely entertainment purposes … if ya be catchin' my drift." He glanced at Lexy through the rearview mirror. A horn blared, and he shifted his attention to the traffic.

"I appreciate the thought, Jimmy, but you know the deal." Lexy overrode his attempt to cheer her. "This lifestyle is getting to me, but I've got to hold out for a while longer. I know, I've said that a million times the past couple years. You must be sick to death of hearing the same shit." She gave him an apologetic look through the mirror. "But I promise there'll be an end soon." She smiled, but Jimmy had his eyes on the road.

Before he could respond, she tried to divert the conversation and added, "So, Jimmy, if you truly love me, make sure you have the proper medicine for me on Sunday, would ya? I can't believe you didn't stock the bar today." She waved a hand in the direction of one of the car's compartments. "No biggie, I guess, but don't forget on Sunday. A good-sized tot of Bushmills will suffice. The sixteen-year single malt, please." Her tone left no room for argument.

Jimmy frowned, then focused on the road. "Alright, miss, if that's what you'd like …."

Lexy's head leaned against the plush leather seatback as she mulled over the frequency of her "woe-is-me" talks with Jimmy. *Too often, probably. But there's no one else I can talk to, really. Sure, Claire, but we hardly ever get to see each other, and I hate dragging her into my mess every time we do.*

The swish of the wipers melded with the splatter of the rain and cocooned her from much of the outside madness, giving a bit of solitude. She closed her eyes.

Jimmy's awesome. He's a great listener, and—usually—he comes with a well-stocked bar. But I need to remember he's a captive audience. I should keep my mouth shut sometimes. He means well, but his poking and prodding reminds me I have a loose tongue. I know I need to make changes in my life, but it's not as easy as he seems to think. It's not like I can flip a switch and automatically "be happy" somehow. These things take planning.

Lexy's fingers drummed a beat on the seat, and she stared at the back of Jimmy's head. A half-smile inched up one side of her mouth. She realized that despite its shortfalls, their friendship had grown into one of her closest and longer-lasting relationships.

So remember who you're mad at, Lex. It's not Jimmy. Stop making excuses and suck it up. Remember what your brother used to say: "Either change your situation or change your attitude; if you can't do one, do the other, but do something." Ha, if only he knew how hard it was to simply start doing. I could use a little more advice, big brother. If only ....

Unwanted memories squeezed into her head before she could stop them. Lexy's life had changed in the span of a phone call. The call from the state police telling her her only sibling had died in a car crash. The searing pain rushed over her again. *Not now. I can't do this.*

She expelled a deep, pent-up breath and forced her mind away from the past. After several slow inhalations, she directed her thoughts back to the problem at hand, but she knew the answers, the actions wouldn't come today. She rubbed her temples for a few moments, and then spoke.

"Jimmy, hope you don't mind, I'm going to zip up the little divider window thingy to call Claire. I've got to cancel our plans, and you may not want to witness the massacre. Not that she's a screamer." She chuckled dryly. "But I might have to do some very loud apologizing."

Jimmy snorted. "Bah, you know better than to expect that from Miss Claire. Do tell her I said hello, if you would, though. I hope she and her young fella are gettin' on well and all these days."

"Will do. And yes, those two are getting on like a house on fire." A touch of jealousy flared, and she muttered, "Damn lucky, engaged bastards."

The partition slid up, and unease trickled through her as she speed-dialed number 2. A quick click of the window button cracked it open. Hoping for fresh air, instead she inhaled the putrid mix of northern New Jersey industry and acid rain. *Niiiice, that'll make this call better ....*

"Hey, Lex, whatcha up to?"

Claire's cheery hello tweaked Lexy's already dinged heart. She smothered another sigh.

"Oh, the usual, I guess … depending on how you look at things." She tried forcing liveliness into her voice, hoping Claire wouldn't hear how low she sounded. "I've got some bad news, though." Her fingers fiddled with the strap on her bag, worrying the leather. "I'm really sorry, I have to cancel tomorrow; I'm in the car now, headed to Newark for a flight to the Bahamas for Mrs. S."

Static crinkled over the line. "You're going to the Bahamas now? In this storm? It's hurricane season!" Claire's words came fast. "Is she crazy? Why on earth is she sending you into this monsoon?"

Claire was more-than-passing familiar with the whims of Mrs. Stellery. The friends had laughed and cursed her demands through the years. Lexy waited, the silence heavy.

"Please tell me you're quitting this nonsense soon, Lex. And you'll slow down, start living a life you actually enjoy."

Leave it to Claire to focus on my issues, despite me canceling our girls night. She's too good for me.

"Ah, shit." Lexy fumbled for words. "I know. I *know*, but there's nothing I can do about this right now." Even to her the comment sounded lame, but she went on. "Really, though, you know it's not always like this. And when I secure this buy, my commission will be huge."

"Uh, duh. Aren't you the one who keeps saying money isn't everything? Is this worth the crazy life you're living?"

"Come on, Claire, cut me a tiny bit of slack, please. You know what a big-ass commission like this means. I'll be one step closer …."

Lexy let her mind quickly skim the familiar dream.

There'd been nothing as enticing to her five-year-old self as the gems display in the American Museum of Natural History. From her first visit, nosing around the darkened Halls of Gems and Minerals, sneakers scuffing the worn brown carpet, dim lighting casting spooky shadows about the room, Lexy was captivated.

Hooked by the glitter and sheen of the spotlighted diamonds and the Star of India sapphire. Hooked by the hush and reverence of the surroundings. Hooked by an earthy scent and the brush of her young hand over smooth-worn iron meteorite.

Young Lexy knew she'd one day work with those most rare and exotic of the earth's treasures. And the adult Lexy grew into a practical version of the teenager who wandered unsupervised through the halls, exploring everything.

These days, one simple fact held true: any—all—commissions she earned meant money in the bank toward her dream, toward financing her own jewelry boutique.

The thought tugged her to the present. Her eyes focused on the spattering rain. "Sorry, Claire, guess I spaced for a second …."

"Yeah, I hear you, Lex. And I agree you're right to keep at it with Mrs. S. for a little while longer. Still, I worry, you know?"

Lexy did. Even now, Lexy pictured Claire in her West Village studio apartment, fidgeting at her desk chair, eyeing the pelting rain. "You know what they say, 'Another day, another dollar.' Or some bullshit like that." Though she tried to brighten the mood with her usual off-color language, her false cheer didn't fool either of them.

"Anyway, this job *is* intriguing." Lexy told Claire about the carte blanche mandate and the vague information. "I haven't had time to research anything on my own. I kinda can't wait to see those gems and find out why Mrs. S. is so hot to get her hands on them. But damn, I hope my flight's not canceled."

"Be careful, Lex. The more you tell me about this trip, the less I like it. Make sure you come home in one piece. Okay?"

"I promise. Don't worry so much. We're almost to Newark, so before I flitter off, can we pick a new date to hang out?"

The limo's brakes squealed as Jimmy pulled into the departures lane for United Airlines ten minutes later, the women still chattering. His knuckled interruption on the back window chased away Lexy's grin. Jostled from her good spirits, she hung up and scowled at the still-driving rain.

"So sorry to be botherin' ya, miss, but now's about the time I be kickin' ya out."

"Ah, Jimmy, you're a hard one," she teased. The banter was their farewell routine; Lexy could hardly leave the country without it. It was practically her good luck charm. "So, 'tis off with me, is it? Are ya sure about this, laddie?"

"Aye, I'm sure. But you be certain to make your way home safe and sound." A stern look accompanied his words.

"Of course, Jimmy." His comment, out of character, made her pause. "There's no need to be concerned. This trip is no different than a hundred others I've taken."

His eyes locked on hers, and Lexy squirmed. *Bizarro.*

"What was that, Jimmy?"

"What was what, miss?"

"That weird sensation. Didn't you feel it?" His blank look said no. "I got the strangest feeling ...." She looked over her shoulder, trying to figure out what had pricked her senses. She didn't see anything unusual and turned back to find Jimmy staring at her.

It must've been my imagination, but still .... And, great. Now Jimmy looks like he's even more worried about me. She shivered and looked around again as the unusual sensation clung.

Jimmy hovered with his umbrella, then escorted her under the overhang. "My return flight's due Sunday night around seven fifteen. I'll see you then?"

"Aye, lass, I'll see ya Sunday. Farewell and safe travels." He backed away with a tilt of his head, then folded himself into the car.

With her mind fixed on the strange sensation that had overcome her, Lexy sped through check-in and found the gate. After a swift perusal of the departures board, she gave a low "Son of a bitch." Delayed one hour. "Curses," she grumbled. "Damn weather."

She stood, idle and annoyed, letting people flow around her for a change, and took in her immediate surroundings. To the left, she saw nothing but wailing kids and harried travelers grabbing a last-minute cardboard burger in the garbage-littered food court. To the right, success! In the form of a neon sign announcing draft beer specials and "every game in town." The ubiquitous airport sports bar, Lexy's home away from home.

"At least the Yankees are in L.A. today," she murmured. "Maybe I can catch part of their game."

First things first. Better clue in Mrs. S. to the delay, or she might get agita if she doesn't hear from me. Before Lexy left the city, Mrs. Stellery had reiterated her instructions, insisting they keep in touch. *She's positively neurotic about this trip, and it's rubbing off on me. But she certainly made her point clear.* Lexy pulled out her cell and made the call.

"Absolutely, Mrs. Stellery, I'll ring when I land in Nassau. Stacey's arranged to have a car waiting, and I've got a room not far from the marina. I spoke with Matt Aldridge. He's been watching the weather, and the boating conditions look to be decent by morning." *Thank goodness. I don't care how many air miles I rack up, I'll take a boat ride any day. Flying is definitely not my thing. Especially those puddle jumpers. They scare the hell out of me.*

She paced a path in front of the bar. *At least I can ease the pain with a preflight cocktail. Or two. Always helps.*

Focusing on Mrs. Stellery, she said, "I'm on track to be on Eleuthera no later than twelve thirty tomorrow. Plenty of time to scope out the competition before the auction begins at four thirty."

As Mrs. Stellery droned on, Lexy craned her neck to see the Yankees-Dodgers game through the bar's window. Home run, Teixeira. "Yes!"

"What was that, Alexandria?" The strident tone registered in Lexy's ear.

"Oh, just agreeing with you, Mrs. Stellery. Yes, everything's set for tomorrow. No worries."

"Be careful, Alexandria, and keep your eyes open for anything unusual. This buy is absolutely vital. See that you return without delay."

They hung up, and Lexy wondered again at Mrs. Stellery's behavior, but decided not to worry. She didn't want to bring herself down before boarding a potential death vehicle. *Kidding, Lex, just kidding.* She went into the bar and settled at a seat with a good view of the action—the game and the guys.

After one additional weather delay, two scores (by the Yankees, not Lexy) and three pricey-but-expensed beers, Lexy boarded and storm-hopped her way to Nassau.

Chapter 4

"Jackson, are you there? Hello?"

The tinny, piercing voice crackled through his outmoded answering machine. "If you are, child, pick up at once."

The command in his aunt's voice rang through, despite the miles and archaic technology of the equipment. *Hell, I must be the only American in a two-hundred-mile radius who still owns an answering machine.* The thought brought a smile to Jack Hughes's face.

Jack loved his aunt, so he stifled his minor irritation at the late-night interruption. He'd expected to hear from her earlier, and her overdue call had begun to make him wonder. He muted ESPN's highlight coverage of the Yankees-Dodgers game, reached over the crinkly arm of his leather recliner and grabbed the cordless handset.

"Hey, Aunt Claudine. It's about time you called." He put a smile in his voice as he teased her. "Thought maybe you'd fallen asleep. Got an update for me?"

Jack pushed down the footrest and grabbed his bottle of Hoptical Illusion before ambling onto the covered deck that overlooked Morning Star Beach. The short lag across the phone line gave him a moment to take in the vast meteorological show battering the bay.

For as long as he'd lived on St. Thomas, which encompassed most of his forty-three years, the weather in his small corner of the Caribbean continually impressed him. Stark, blistering sunshine, blinding lightning and slashing, powerful storms … the extremes that occurred during a typical August only left more to love. Even now, as the clock eased past 11:00 p.m., the sodden air lay heavy on him. A deluge pelted the ground. He could make out red hibiscus strewn about the grass as if decapitated by a samurai's sword. The gusting wind lashed palm fronds with a high-pitched buzz, and the scent of crushed, soaked greenery saturated the air. *God, I love this place. I probably shouldn't be on the phone outside, though, in the middle of this.*

He stayed put.

"Indeed I do, Jackson," his aunt replied. "Good news for the auction. Alexandria has arrived in Nassau, despite the foul weather inconveniencing all of us. She has water transportation set for nine o'clock tomorrow morning to bring her to Eleuthera." There came a laden pause. "You do understand what that means, of course, don't you?" Static again engulfed the landline.

Jack did a mental once-over, holding the handset away from his ear to scowl at it. He hesitated, slightly put off that his aunt felt the need to question him. *Yeah, I get it, Aunt Cee.*

Stories of the jewels, now up for grabs at the auction, had peppered his entire life. Stories of those gems and so many other lost treasures. As a child, tales of ancestors' fortune-hunting antics had dominated the conversation at family gatherings. These days, with no family left in his native St. Thomas, he continued to hear the stories when he visited his aunt in Manhattan.

"You bet I do, Aunt Claudine," he replied after a swallow of his favorite beer. "It means getting my ass out of bed at the crack of dawn to fly through this crummy weather, so I can get decked out in a monkey suit and keep an eye on her and those jewels at the auction tomorrow."

"Honestly, Jackson."

He heard his aunt's huff as clear as if she stood next to him.

"Some days I do find you as cheeky as Alexandria. One would think you would approach this situation with a modicum of gravity. Do you realize how long it has taken me to find those jewels? Believe me when I tell you it is of great importance to our family to obtain them."

Jack wondered at her comment. His aunt hadn't shared the jewels' full story with him, or what she planned to do with them, so he could only guess at her motives. He believed their family's old treasure stories were more fluff than fact, but maybe there was more to them than he realized. *I don't like being kept in the dark, Aunt Cee, but I'll let it go. For now.*

"Aw, come on, Aunt Cee, you know I'm pulling your leg." He enjoyed messing with his favorite, and only, relative. "I can't resist. I'm the only one who can get away with teasing you. Besides, it keeps you young, of course."

Claudine couldn't see his smile, but it was no less genuine for that. Despite a three-day stubble, the grin showed off his dimples; Jack called them his "face cracks." Women, Jack knew, called them killer.

"Oh, child, you do drive me to distraction on occasion."

The admonishment sounded mild, and Jack relaxed at the softening in his aunt's voice. *Good. She needs to mellow out about this treasure-hunt stuff. It used to be a hobby, but these days she's obsessing over her search. Even when I try to distract her. If anything happens to her because she's so fixated, I'd never forgive myself.* He shook off that somber thought and took another swig of beer.

"Then my job this evening is done. And it's on to bigger and better things. Which for you, young lady, means getting yourself to bed already." He felt compelled to chide his eighty-six-year-old aunt. "Where the hell is Charlie that you're still up making phone calls at eleven o'clock? Why isn't he keeping an eye on you?"

Jack loved the old butler but wished the man had more of a say in his aunt's activities. The two had outgrown the butler-employer relationship and blended it into one of mutual companionship after Jack's uncle Jonathan died. *Though Aunt Cee clearly still runs the show—at least when it comes to searching for these jewels.*

"Do not be daft, Jackson. Charles is a help, but he toddled off to bed ages ago. Besides, you knew I would not sleep until Alexandria arrived safely. Now that she has, and knowing you are prepared for tomorrow, I should be able to settle down for a few hours."

Jack shook his head in admiration. *A few hours? I never feel right without a solid seven. And even that's pretty rare.*

"Aunt Cee, all I can say is it's good to hear your voice and know you're still up to your old tricks." He heard a mild scoff. "I'll call you tomorrow when I land on Eleuthera and get the lay of Powell Pointe and the Cape." Jack went inside and watched his muted television, the game's highlights long over. "I'll get on the horn with Pete to confirm the flight plan, so I'd better run. Say hi to Charlie for me. Love you."

"Good night, Jackson. See that you keep me promptly informed tomorrow. And remember, Alexandria is not to know a word of our association." A subtle cough sounded, then she added, "I love you too, dear."

Jack dropped into his recliner, guzzled the remaining beer and dialed his longtime friend Peter Lambert. Jack had to chuckle. The TV remained muted, and if there hadn't been a storm howling outside, Jack would've heard Peter's phone ringing. He lived twenty-five yards away, in the guest house on Jack's property.

Since the phone's shrill ring didn't relent, Jack walked back onto his porch and bellowed across the intervening space: "Yo, jackass, pick up the damn phone. It's me!" That got a response.

"Hey, Jacky-boy, that you?"

Jack knew Pete loved to yank his chain.

"What's up, man?"

He heard Pete's scratchy voice and guessed his friend was about twelve cigarettes down. A good day for him.

"Pete, you lazy shit, don't you think it's a good idea to answer your phone when you know we're flying out at the crack of ass tomorrow?"

The two knew each other well enough to see through their nonsense, so the question needed no answer.

"I'm confirming it's a go." Jack sank back into his chair with a squeak and volumed up Sports Center. "Are you set with everything?"

"Dude, totally."

People often thought of Peter as nothing more than a sun-worshipping slacker. He had a beaches-and-rum charm, but that covered about half of his eccentric personality. Another quarter embraced cigarettes and tequila. And the last part … that was all whip-smart pilot.

"As long as I've known you, Jack, you're seriously asking me if I'm ready to fly us? Man, you break my heart." Peter erupted into raucous laughter, followed by a coughing attack.

At that, Jack laughed hard. "Yeah, alright, I know, man, but I had to check in. Got the call from Aunt Cee. Figured I'd touch base, make sure the ol' gal was ready for takeoff." His fingers itched over the remote, flicking restlessly, and then raked through his shaggy, sun-streaked brown hair. "You sure about flying through this weather, though? I don't want to puke in your copilot's seat. I have an image to maintain."

Jack, not much of a flier, preferred to sail, but the stormy waters and distance to Eleuthera prohibited him from piloting his 33-foot Silverton. He'd miss the auction if he cruised to the island. The details from his aunt had come in the day before, so Jack considered himself damn lucky his friend had a cancelation for his charter service and could fly him north. *Who knew what the major airlines would fly in these conditions, if anything.* Jack wasn't looking forward to the flight, but he did have faith in his friend's skill.

"Sure thing, bro. I've flown through hurricanes before. This is nothing compared to that crap. We'll be aces, no problem. Besides, the weather's supposed to clear out 'round five thirty tomorrow morning."

Peter's voice eased his worries.

"But I gotta say, you're lucky as shit with your timing. What's up with this crazy, last-minute trip for your aunt?"

"Yeah, right? You know Aunt Cee. She got a bee in her butt about this auction and really wants my eyes on the buyer. I'm glad I can help out, if it means some peace of mind for her. Appreciate you flying me."

"Sure thing, Jack. And no worries, man. Good chance we'll be smooth flying."

Jack inhaled, relieved. "Awesome, Pete, that's what I like to hear. Alright, call if anything changes. Otherwise I'll come knocking at eight thirty. Be sure to answer the damn door."

A snarky laugh echoed before Jack's ear buzzed with the dial tone.

Chapter 5

"Son of a …!"

Lexy slammed the snooze button on the hotel alarm clock, and a bouncing, plastic crash followed. "Agh, how could it be morning already? This sucks," she groaned.

She almost collapsed onto the pillows before she realized breaking the clock probably meant "snooze" wouldn't work if she fell asleep again. *Mrs. S. would skin me alive if I go home without the jewels. I'd better get my butt moving.*

She tried to talk herself awake as she squinted in the darkness. "Seriously, how do morning people do this? All the freakin' time?"

The alarm had gone off at 7:30 a.m.—not early by the standards of a large segment of Manhattanites—but Lexy rarely appeared at work before ten.

She slid from between the eight-hundred-thread-count Egyptian cotton sheets and melted onto the floor. Her slide left her tangled in the comforter and propped upright against the mahogany poster bed. Now to lever herself up.

"Ugh. Effort."

Soon she rose, propelled more by curiosity over the morning's weather than a desire to move. A short stumble, and Lexy yanked aside the room darkening drapes. She shouted as shafts of brilliant sunlight shot into her eyes. "Shit!" She flung the shades closed and flopped back onto the silky duvet. "Ow, that hurt. Serves me right. But I guess that means the weather's blown out. At least the ride this morning should be decent."

With a full day ahead, Lexy trudged into the bathroom to pull herself together. She had a vague sense of the distance between her hotel and the marina and didn't want to be late. So much hinged on getting to Eleuthera on time.

When she looked presentable, she covered her tired and slightly hungover eyes with dark sunglasses, checked out of the hotel and settled into an idling cab.

"Hurricane Hole Marina, please."

Off they went. *Though not quite like "off to the races," huh?* She patted herself on the back for leaving more than enough time to get to the dock, noticing how the cab meandered through the streets from her Cable Beach hotel. The driver's conversation meandered, too. He kept up an amiable patter in his lilting patois while they wended their way along West Bay Street and through the heart of downtown Nassau.

"You see, lady? D'e Christ Church Cat'edral, beautiful lady, is down d'at a-way. And d'ere we passed d'e pirate museum. Very fun, lady, right, yes? D'ere you can see d'e Parliament Houses ... so very lovely ...."

The drive continued, with her personal, personable tour guide pointing out the highlights along the way. "Don't forget d'e Water Tower at Fort Fincastle, lady. You be getting a great big view of d'e island from up top. Don't forget, now." He drove on. "Here we coming to d'e bridge, you check out d'at big Atlantis hotel. So massive, it is."

They crossed over Island Bridge, and she gazed around, taking in the mammoth cruise ships in port, the mega hotel Atlantis and the infamous blue-and-yellow Bahamas Fast Ferries docked below the bridge. The cab angled down the off-ramp and curved around the service road that brought them into the marina.

"Slip number forty-two, please, or however close we can get."

The cabbie pulled up in front and pointed out the dockmaster at the entrance to the marina. "D'ere you go, lady. You should be all set."

Lexy paid and said, "Sir, that was one of the most enjoyable cab rides I've had in a good long while. Thank you. Maybe I'll catch you on the return. Chowda."

After giving him a smile and a wave, Lexy made her way to the dockmaster, who directed her through the maze of slips. She approached number forty-two and saw a dark head, sprinkled with gray, surface from the boat's interior. Her heart kicked in an extra beat.

She called out, "Leave it to you to dock this wreck in a place called Hurricane Hole. You're a lucky son of a bitch that the sun's shining, or I'd accuse you of trying to jinx me."

"Lexy, luv! You're near to breaking my heart, speaking ill of the *Kelsi*. Don't be cruel, woman."

As Matthew Aldridge turned to face Lexy, the glittering sun illuminated his winking, sage-colored eyes, and Lexy inhaled fast. The quick tug in her gut reminded her how she lusted after this Brit. *Girl, get a hold of your hormones, would you? It's just an accent. And a damn fine face. Atop a rock-solid body .... Damn, I have it bad.*

She tried to wrestle herself into a work mindset as she approached the boat's starboard side. *Come on now, this is business.*

Oh, but I wouldn't mind being in his business, the devilish, half-hungover, sex-starved side of her brain countered.

Ugh. I am not prepared for this without at least two more cups of java, the sane part of her brain weighed in.

Matt tilted his head and shot a confused look her way. "Come again, luv? You're not ready for this trip? That's unlike you."

Her toe caught on a plank, and she almost tripped onto the boat and into Matt.

"Christmas!" She caught herself before she fell. She couldn't believe Matt heard her gaffe. "Sorry, Matt." *How embarrassing that my vocal cords took over my brain!* "You know me, jabbering because I haven't had enough caffeine to know when to keep my mouth shut." Lexy downplayed her slip. "The storms delayed my flight, and I'm not the best of fliers, so I had maybe one cocktail too many, and it's time for another coffee fix." *Stop rambling, Lex.* She took a deep breath. "No worries, though. I'll have my sea legs soon enough. But have you got a cuppa you can spare for your old friend?"

"Always, luv. Here now, let me stow your bags below and set you up right."

Matt grasped her hand to assist her over the gunwale, and Lexy felt shivers from the contact shoot along her spine. She squirmed. *This is so not cool.*

Determined not to let her wayward thoughts distract her, she moved forward and eyeballed the cabin. "Damn, Matt, I've gotta say, this is quite the upgrade from the last bucket you put me on." Her gaze roamed about the galley, the small head and the forward bunks. "And I'm shocked you're sailing me. I feel so honored. If I'd known earlier you'd be taking me yourself"—she sniggered inwardly—"I wouldn't have bothered reaching out to my backup contacts. How lucky am I?" She turned to smile and found him standing directly behind her.

"Well, Lex, luv, I felt so bloody awful about that last bloke I sent you with …. You recall, pumping out the bilge and all that shite? Of course you do." He hung his head. "For the record, I've tossed his lazy self to the roadside. I wanted to set things right, so I decided to sail you meself. Now you've had a look at me new honey of a ship, be honest. Tell me what you think of her."

Green eyes stared into gray, and Lexy's brain veered into thoughts having nothing to do with their conversation. *I really need not to have this massive crush on you is what I think, damn it.*

Aloud she said, "That rocks, Matt." She broke eye contact, tried to will away a blush and glanced at the rest of the quarters. "She's lovely. Beautiful lines, excellent layout for the bridge. And she seems to be seaworthy." She winked. "I'm finally starting to look forward to this trip."

"Right, then, let's get you that coffee and get under way. We're due for calm seas for the rest of the weekend, lucky you, so we should make the Cape Eleuthera Marina in around two hours, give or take. Time enough for you to make your auction."

Though Lexy hadn't seen Matt for four or five months, the two eased into their familiar onboard rhythm, tossing lines and maneuvering into the open waterway. They kept a steady pace, with Paradise Island sliding past their port side, then kicked up the twin diesels when they exited the bay and headed into the Middle Ground and Exuma Sound.

Lexy stood in the bow, wind whipping her dark hair, sea spray coating her limbs. She inhaled the sea air. Cobalt water clear enough to see a hundred feet below surrounded the boat. She could scarcely believe the 180-degree turnabout in the weather, so she simply enjoyed it. She glanced back to where Matt had the helm and saw his cockeyed smile light on her. *Peace at last. As we sail toward an island called Freedom. Pretty damn cool.*

Lexy had read a brochure about the Out Island before she left her hotel that morning. The pamphlet had supplied the Greek origin of the name Eleuthera, which means "freedom." A fine idea, in her opinion, given its history of being inhabited by peoples in search of a more peaceful place to call home.

The ride to the island jounced the friends, but despite some lingering chop, they passed through the sound with ease. The undemanding trip left Lexy ample time to stare at Matt and to review the map and estate literature Mrs. Stellery had given her. Since she hadn't supplied copious amounts of information, Lexy reviewed the material within minutes. *It's so unlike Mrs. S. to be stingy with details. Why does everything feel different this time?*

Before traveling, Lexy would normally receive a mini dossier on whatever project or acquisition Mrs. Stellery had lined up. Thinking about her sole in-person briefing and the lack of a thorough report churned her stomach.

Maybe because this trip's so spontaneous, she didn't have time to pull together anything more. A lock of hair flew into Lexy's face, and she brushed it away. *Nah. It's easy enough for her to get her hands on whatever info she wants quickly. She didn't even give me a heads-up. And she must've known this was coming down the pike, because estate auctions can take eons to set up, once a person croaks. Well, depending on the property and items being liquidated. So, what gives, Mrs. S.? What have you gotten me into, chasing after these gems?*

"Land ho, luv," Matt called from his perch. Not that their course kept them long out of sight of land. "Come up for air and have a look at the cape as we approach. You've never been, have you?"

Lexy scrambled to the flybridge and goggled at their surroundings. "No, never been. Not to this island. It's magnificent ...."

Matt eased the engines back to idle so Lexy could soak in the view. Then he glanced over and saw her lips curve upward. The boat glided forward, quieter now, entering the shallow waters outside the marina at Powell Pointe.

This is nothing like Nassau ... I can hardly believe I'm still in the Bahamas.

Lexy loved the color blue. She'd decorated her apartment in shades of the color. But that blue is a one-casino town; Eleuthera blue is Vegas on steroids. Sailing the waters between the Bahamian Out Islands gave a whole new meaning to the word. Even with a color wheel emblazoned on her brain, Lexy awed at the variety, the range of azures, teals and turquoises that engulfed them sea and sky. She had no words. Dark to light, and the clearest waters of anywhere she'd ever been. From the second-story bridge she could see fish darting around their boat, scores of feet below the surface.

"Wow, Matt, I'm blown away."

Still ogling, they neared the jetty that opened into the harbor. A narrow strip of beach appeared along the starboard side. As they edged closer, Lexy spotted woven hammocks tied between rustling palm trees. *Heaven on earth ... every one of them empty!*

She pointed. "Check that out, Matt. This place is practically deserted. Unreal. I could sooo get used to this!" She peered again. "And swings! Hell, Matt, they've got swings under that big old tree. I'm never leaving."

She threw a wide grin his way and laughed at the expression on his face. *He's probably never seen me this animated about anything. Well, now he knows what'll do it for me.* She chuckled at the thought.

That and a couple other things ... like maybe him beside me in the hammock. She laughed again. *Right, Lex, dream on.*

A head shake brought her back. She noticed the two-story, yellow-shingled house jutting out on the peninsula north of the hammocks.

"That's the owner's place," Matt said. "You're likely staying in the townhouses on the far side of the marina, right? There's not much else 'round here in the way of lodging."

"Right you are, sir. And I guess I've had enough daydreaming for now. At least until we land, and I can check in and get settled. Let's get this show on the road, shall we?"

Matt piloted them through the no-wake zone into the marina, where he docked the *Kelsi* with barely a bump against the wooden landing. The two clambered around the deck, and then Lexy jumped onto the pier to tie in. A short woman with lean, ropy arms and a local tan strolled down the planks and gave them a hand with the lines. In quick fashion, they tied fast to the pilings, and Lexy met their helper.

"Melody's the name. I'm the resort's concierge. And deck hand and dishwasher and any number of other job titles they can foist on me." A massive grin accompanied the comment, belying the bite of the words. "You must be Alexandria Nichols, eh?" she asked with an accent that sounded more South Boston than South Eleuthera. "You're the only newbie we're expecting by boat today. Here for the big auction."

"Yes, ma'am, that's me. I gather that means you're putting up the other buyers. Cool, I can check out the competition beforehand." Lexy shared a mischievous smile with Melody, getting a good vibe off the older woman.

"We sure are. And a bunch of stiffies they strike me as, too." She snorted, and Lexy smothered a laugh. "But you'll soon see for yourself. Why don't we check you in, and you can get the lay of the land before the big to-do later." Melody lifted Lexy's suitcase and strode toward the main entrance.

Lexy shook her head with a smile. "This sure has the makings of an interesting trip." She faced Matt. "Here I go again."

"Very true, m'dear." He chuckled with her. "Right, then, I'd best be getting back now, luv. You look to be in good hands here, and I've got me an overnight charter this evening, night fishing off Andros. Should be a right laugh. I'll be back tomorrow to return you to Nassau." His green eyes dug a little deeper than usual. "You sure you'll be alright here, luv?"

Lexy did a double take and hesitated before she answered. "Alright? Matt, how long have you known me?" She smirked at him, covering up the smidge of doubt that intruded. "Of course I'll be alright. This place is amazing, and as soon as I figure out where I'm headed later today, I'm going to conk out in one of those hammocks for an hour or so. Seriously, Matt." But his inquiry had touched a chord, and her reply sounded forced. "This is heaven."

"Right, then, luv. If you're all set, off I go." He gave her a quick hug. "I'll see you back here at 11:00 a.m."

"Happy trails, Matt," she said as he swung aboard his boat.

He powered up, and she tossed him the lines. As he eased away from the dock, she called, "I hope you catch some Zs somewhere along the way. I don't want you asleep at the wheel when you come back for me." She caught the deep rumble of his laugh and his quick wave as the *Kelsi* motored away.

A lonely pang sneaked up on Lexy in the wake of his departure. The feeling surprised her, and it annoyed her because it *had* surprised her. This was a place she wanted to share. A casual, pristine beauty called to her from every direction. She knew she'd rather enjoy this place with someone special than putter around on her own, as she always did. *Oh, well.* She shoved the thought aside. *There's nothing I can do about that now, so I may as well appreciate as much as I can.* Resolve in place, she took off after Melody and her bag.

Fifteen minutes later, her room attendant, Sa'naa, escorted Lexy to her townhome. The large space housed a gourmet kitchen and great room downstairs and two well-appointed, luxurious bedrooms upstairs. Sable-colored rattan furniture decorated the home, tossed with plump batik pillows and tropical throws. "Jeez, Louise, get a load of this place."

She stepped onto the covered balcony, its ceiling fan swirling, and took in the gorgeous vista of the marina visible beyond the palms that framed her view. She recognized the scent of wild frangipani as its aroma drifted up from the garden. "Hmmm," she sighed. "I gotta hand it to you, Mrs. S. Nice digs."

After Lexy unpacked, she decided vegetation of a different sort—her own—topped her agenda. The auction began at 4:30 p.m., with dinner and music to follow, which left ample time to grab a sandwich from the snack bar and unwind in one of the hammocks. She could hear them practically screaming her name. With nothing but a couple hours of me-time on her mind, she changed into her standard-issue, black Vicky's Secret bikini and twisted her peach sarong into respectability. She searched out a beach towel, and—in deference to the client footing the bill—she tucked the auction paperwork into her tote before leaving.

Lexy scoped out the grounds as she walked. The resort was small and self-contained, so a quick stroll brought her to the shop-restaurant that served as the hotel's main dining area in the summer season. The space did triple duty as a registration center.

While she waited for her turkey and Swiss on whole wheat, a stray gust blew in two new arrivals. *Two rascals, if my intuition even remotely works in this sapping heat.*

From her seat in the corner, she watched the taller of the two bestow an ain't-life-grand, come-play-with-me devilish grin on the clerk. Lexy scanned his lean body, taking in muscled calves, faded olive shorts and a brightly obnoxious, '80s-era, purple Hawaiian shirt that covered pretty much everything else. She caught sight of striking amber eyes and a scruffy cheek in profile when the man leaned over to flirt with Melody. Who, Lexy saw, wasn't swayed by it, but who flirted back freely, used to such over-the-top, friendly attention from the customers.

Lexy gave the second fellow a similar once-over and discovered his deep brown eyes staring back at her, full in the face. She darted her eyes away, unnerved that he'd seen her checking him out. She was a New Yorker, after all, and they didn't get caught staring for more than a split second, lest they get mugged on the spot. Looking everywhere but at the men, she tapped her fingers on the table and wondered what was taking her sandwich so long. *Ah, yes ... don't forget you're on island time now, Lex.*

"Here you go, lady."

She popped up to grab her sandwich from the counter at the same time the two men headed past her. The taller one bumped into her side.

"Oh, excuse me, ma'am." A teasing smile crossed his face.

Wow, killer dimples. Then a small furrow creased her brow. *And, dude, "ma'am"? Come freakin' on ... I'm not that old. Yet.*

"No worries. Sir."

Take that, you old fogie. She added a killer grin of her own. Though he didn't look old. And he didn't have much gray flecking his blond-and-brown streaked hair. "If you'll excuse me, I'll be on my way. Chowda." The word slipped out.

"What's that, girlie?"

A correction. *Better.*

"Did you offer us chowder?" The lean man looked at her, perplexed.

"Oops, sorry. Holdover from time spent in Boston. I meant 'so long.' You know, like '*ciao,*' c-i-a-o, only it's 'chow' like food, like chowder, only New Englanders don't say their r's, so it sounds like 'chowda.'" She looked him in the eye and blushed. "Yup ... way too much info there. Okay then, gotta run. I'll let you fellas get to your room. See ya."

She tried to beat a hasty exit after that sparkling gem dribbled out of her mouth. But the lean man and the shorter guy blocked her way. They looked at each other and burst out laughing.

"Jeez, guys, it wasn't that funny," she mumbled as she none-too-gently pushed past them. Not offended that they laughed at her, she still felt embarrassed. *That tall one is pretty hot up close and personal, with those amber eyes. Those and the dimples are enough to make a rational woman spew verbal sludge. Clearly.*

"Okay, off I go to find me a hammock." She tried again. "Enjoy your stay." *Damn, now I sound like Sa'naa. I'm such a dork.* She succeeded in squeaking past them, and she and her sandwich escaped in search of a quiet patch of beach.

*****

The men's laughter subsided. Pete nodded his head toward Lexy's retreating figure. "So, Jack, wasn't that your aunt's buyer?"

Jack nodded.

"She sure is one hell of a looker, ain't she?"

Hell, yes. Jack agreed 100 percent. His aunt had emailed him a photo of Alexandria so he could keep his eyes peeled for her. But one fuzzy digital picture did not necessarily do a body justice ... any experienced online dater could tell you that. And the body he could barely glimpse as the sarong swayed away could give a guy a full salute.

Shit, this is gonna be more fun than I thought. But to his friend he gave a simple "Down, boy." And a small chuckle. "Don't forget we're here on business. Keeping an eye on Alexandria during the auction comes first, so save your daydreaming for after we get back to St. Thomas."

With a last glance toward Lexy's receding form silhouetted against the Eleutheran beach, Jack and Pete hoisted their bags. Their smiling hostess met them at the door and preceded them out. She led them to their rooms, another townhouse a short distance from the shop.

As they unpacked, Jack thought about the evening ahead of him. *I wonder what other surprises are in store ....*

Chapter 6

Mmmm, now this almost makes up for canceling on Claire.

Lexy stretched, let out a huge yawn and shifted, easing the bite of the hammock's weave. *Thank goodness the weather cleared, so I can enjoy this trip a little.* The nap she'd taken smoothed away the dregs of a rough night and early morning. A cooling breeze carried the earthy scent of palm fronds mixed with salty sea air. She wiggled again, then leaned over to grab the paperwork she'd wedged under her sandal before falling asleep.

Time to get to work.

She spent the next fifteen minutes flipping through the pages. *I don't know why I keep rereading the same stuff. It's not like any new info will miraculously appear. Unless I think my non-hungover brain will catch something ....*

She learned nothing more, though, about either the owner or the jewels and how he'd acquired them. *This is weird. Not having any real details makes this whole trip feel a little shady.* She shivered despite the warm sunshine that filtered through the leaves and toasted her skin. Since she'd only heard about the project yesterday, Lexy had no time to dig up information through her own resources. She often did that before a big buy so she'd be as prepared as possible. She sighed and started to gather her things, when she sensed someone nearby.

"Hey there, girlie, you enjoying yourself?" The lean man from the shop loomed over her, cutting off the slanting sunlight.

Lying down left Lexy feeling on edge, at a disadvantage. The tall man appeared even taller.

"I *was*. But that was when these hammocks were deserted." She gave him the evil eye through her sunglasses. He missed her point, or ignored it.

"You know, I watched you for a few minutes while you slept," he said, unnerving her. "You were conked out so hard, you looked like you were sleeping one off." His dimples flashed when he chuckled.

"Excuse me?"

She shot up in the hammock and fell straight down again when the wobbly bed bested her efforts to sit upright. That marked two times—in a too-short span—that Lexy looked less than her best in front of this guy. It irked her.

"Look, buddy, I don't know you from Adam, so how about you keep your pithy opinions on my sleeping habits to yourself, okay?" She attempted a sneer and almost pulled it off as she elbowed herself into a half-seated position.

The guy laughed at her again. "Now, how about we rectify that? My name's Jackson Hughes, though pretty much everyone calls me Jack." He thrust out a hand.

Hard-pressed to do anything else, Lexy grabbed it and shook once. She felt a zing course through her body. Alarmed by her instantaneous and potent reaction, she dropped his hand and flopped into the hammock. She eyed him again from behind her shades, as she would a used car salesman.

"So nice to meet you, Jack. My name's Lexy." She deliberately left out her last name. "What brings you to this little island paradise?" She considered his name, wondered why it felt familiar. *That's it! It sounds like that tax prep firm, Jackson Hewitt. Ha-ha-ha. Dork.* She giggled to herself.

"Oh, me and my pilot, Pete, the other guy in the shop, we flew in for a private event tonight. There's an old manor house that still sits way back on the edge of the resort's property. One of those grandfathered estates. They're having the shindig there."

So much for him being a dork. Humph. His own pilot, and he flew in for the auction. He's either filthy rich or doing the legwork for some posh client, like I am. I wonder ....

"Oh, how nice."

She made a subtle move to cover the papers in her lap. She couldn't pinpoint why, but her gut told her not to let this guy know who she was or what her plans were until she couldn't avoid doing so. "I'm sure you'll have a great evening." She glanced at her cell for the time. "I've got to run along now. Don't want to get too much sun my first time out."

She shimmied out of the hammock and wiggled into her Reef flip-flops. Jack stood a good four or five inches taller than her five-foot-nine frame. His presence felt too big, too compelling, too … everything, even with the scruffy cheeks and loud shirt that should've made him seem comical. She backed away and saw a grin ease up one side of his face, as if he knew he flustered her.

"See you around, Jack." After she put space between them, she turned and strode away.

In her room, she showered and prepped for the night's festivities. Usually quick to get ready, Lexy spent a few extra minutes layering on a coat of mascara that offset her light gray eyes and adding larimar-and-silver jewelry. *When in Rome ....* She twisted in front of the full-length mirror, checking to make sure her gauzy white dress didn't reveal too much. *All good and right on time. I wonder who else from here is going with me—and Jack Hughes—to the auction.*

The proprietor had arranged a limousine to chauffeur the attendees from the resort. Lexy's curiosity went beyond piqued as she tried to figure out who else she might know; her nap had prevented her from seeing the other guests. The high-end jewelry-buying world could be small at times, and it wouldn't surprise her to run across a fellow buyer from New York, even given the last-minute nature of the trip. *I wonder if anyone else got more info than I did. Guess I'll find out soon enough.*

Locking the door behind her, she hastened down the narrow path by the calm marina waters and went into the shop. The four occupants were dressed for a summer evening out. Her eyes drifted over each one—three women and one man—none of whom she recognized. She shared a smile with the room, got one in return from the man and took a seat as she waited for the car.

One body remained noticeably absent as four fifteen rolled around. While the group mingled and began boarding the limo, Jack Hughes showed up, looking like a different man.

Lexy, one strappy heel perched on the running board, stopped and turned at his approach. She did a double take. *Really? Is that Jack?* Balanced halfway into the car, she full-on ogled him, taking in his combed-back hair, shaved cheeks and well-cut summer-weight tan suit. *Wow.*

"Hello there, Lexy. Don't you look lovely."

So, no more "girlie" tonight, huh? Guess there's a new persona in town.

"Here, let me help you."

He assisted her into the back, and tingles spread along her spine. She couldn't stop the shiver that trickled through her body. He sat himself next to her on the banquette. His face showed no trace of reaction to her presence.

The driver bounced over the bumpy dirt road that led to the 1700s plantation house where the auction would occur. And bump Lexy and Jack did, into each other, for the next ten minutes. Lexy stared at the driver through the length of the car and wondered what she did to deserve such torture. *Curses!*

Upon arrival, the group made their way past a rickety gate and through an overgrown yard. Lexy, at first surprised at the property's state, remembered Mrs. Stellery's literature mentioned the owner had let the house go. The inside fared better, though, and she followed the crowd into a shabby-chic main parlor. There they joined the other buyers and got ready for the sale, picking up their assigned paddles and taking seats.

Jack landed in the chair nearest her. "So." He glanced at her. "You didn't mention earlier you were part of this little soiree." He let the comment hang out there.

"I didn't?" *Don't think you can weasel any info out of me with that line, mister.* "It must've slipped my mind. All that sun … it can frazzle the brain, you know."

The auctioneer's gavel sounded twice.

"Shush now, it's starting."

The docket included fifteen lots that evening, but only one held Lexy's interest. Throughout the sale, she familiarized herself with the auctioneer's tactics, as well as her fellow bidders' strategies. One other person, the dark-haired man who had traveled from the resort, still hadn't bid on anything. During their ride to the estate, she learned his name, Evan Maxwell, and that he had seemed agreeable enough. Which she supposed could soon change since as the evening wore on, the chances increased that they would bid on the same items.

Lot thirteen came forward in the hands of a well-muscled security guard dressed in a beige uniform.

The jewels. Lexy breathed in, at last setting eyes on them. At once she understood their enticement.

The guard lifted the display. Seeing the gems from three rows back could not diminish the fire the emeralds shot out. A massive faceted teardrop pendant dangled from a gold link necklace. Matching wide cuffs of oversized emeralds, intermingled with brilliant diamonds, rested on a black velvet tray. A set of matching emerald, tear-shaped drop earrings, set in gold, graced the center of the display.

Wow, those are incredible. I can see why Mrs. S. was adamant about getting her hands on them. But I have a feeling she's going to pay dearly.

The sale took off with the gavel's pound. All but one person joined the competition. The price rose and bidding escalated. The frenzy intensified while the players struggled to remain calm and confident. Lexy noticed couched glances darting around the room. Soon only four remained: Lexy, Jack, Evan and another man whom Lexy had not met.

Not a chance, boys. Not even one one-hundredth of a chance. Lexy raised her paddle once more and tried to hide as she wiped her sweaty palm on her skirt. *Mrs. S. wants these jewels. Well, by damn she'll have them. Thank God for carte blanche.*

Evan pursued the gems as if his life depended on it. The other fellow stayed full-on in the hunt.

They've got to kill their bankrolls soon. I know what Mrs. S. said, but damn!

Bidding rose over one million dollars.

The unprecedented nature of the entire trip began to eat at her. Typically, thorough research and an examination of the items for sale preceded any buy. Never before had Lexy been forced to rely on secondhand information about a product of such immense value. Regardless, she couldn't leave Eleuthera without possessing the jewels.

The gavel smashed again. A headache throbbed behind her right temple. Evan tweaked his paddle, and the second man followed suit.

Damn them. Ah, fuck it, here goes nothing .... "One point five."

Gasps arose, then silence.

Even the auctioneer looked flummoxed. He recovered, banged the gavel once, twice ... finally he said, "Sold! To the lady in white."

Whew! Lexy gulped air and tried to brush off her shock at the stunning amount she'd cost her client. She looked around and saw mingled disbelief, admiration and anger on the faces of the other bidders.

A chill crawled up her back, and she felt vindictive vibes waving over her. She eyed the room again, but the sensation sped away. She couldn't be certain where it had come from. Or even if she'd imagined the feeling.

In the break between lots, she went to inspect her prize—at last—in the back room that doubled as the staging area. Hesitant, she entered the darkened room. Then she saw the guard waiting with her purchase. *Thank goodness someone's keeping an eye on them.* A relieved breath escaped her. She crossed the space, right hand extended, and introduced herself to the guard, Romel.

"God, these are stunning." She looked up from her initial scan of the stones and smiled at the guard. "I bet you don't get tired of watching over these pretties, do you?"

Before the auction commenced, the estate manager had informed the group that the security staff would remain through the final sale of the property.

Romel offered a wide, bright grin. "Yes, d'ey are lovely indeed, miss." The brightness dimmed a fraction. "Though Master Edwards, d'ese past years, he rarely showed d'em off. I t'ink he was a bit afraid d'ere'd be too much talk, if folks saw d'em."

Curious, Lexy prompted him. "Too much talk? I can totally understand wanting to keep your privacy intact, but what would be so bad about a little chitchat?" She waved a hand over the jewelry. "Most people would want to brag about such a possession."

Lexy carried the tray of jewelry under the lone light source, an ancient-looking banker's lamp, and pulled out her tools. With the loupe to her eye and the lampshade angled for the best view, she gazed on emerald perfection. Literal purity. She couldn't find flaws in any of the gems, and all the pieces sparked with unusual fire and clarity. Inclusions were common in emeralds, but Lexy found none, a striking rarity and more precious for it. She also couldn't detect oils or other resins that might have been used to fill in fissures, another widespread, though unethical, practice to cover up an emerald's flaws.

She leaned back, awestruck. *My God, Mrs. S. ... how on earth did you find out about these stones? We'll need a complete spectroscopic exam when I get back to the States, but as far as I can tell, these babies are the real deal. I can't wait to hear what she has to say about them.*

Romel cleared his throat. "Now, I do not want to gossip, and d'e late Master Edwards was very good to me, but surely you've heard d'e rumors?" He dipped his head as she shifted her gaze to his dark, friendly face.

"What rumors?"

"About d'e curse."

Lexy inhaled sharply, watching the guard.

He leaned forward, dark eyes intent. "Some say d'e jewels been cursed for centuries. D'at blood be on d'em from all d'e deaths surrounding d'em. Some say Master stole d'em and brought d'em 'ere in secret."

"Edwards stole the gems? Do you believe that, Romel?"

A pause, then he straightened. "Ah, no, miss." He laughed at her confusion. "I know Master Edwards bring in d'ese gems from a man on Briland." He laughed again. "But it's a good tale to tell, no? Adds some spice to your purchase, no?"

Lexy took the ribbing with a good-natured chuckle. "Damn, Romel, you had me good for a second there." She bent over the luminous gemstones, absorbed. "Maybe I'm letting their beauty and mystery get to me." Her words faded into a whisper. The stones winked and sparked, calling to her as if alive.

"Extraordinary, aren't they?" A low voice sounded near her ear. She jumped and knocked her head on the lampshade. As she rubbed her forehead she turned toward the trim, dark-haired man standing at her shoulder. Evan Maxwell.

"Yes, indeed. I'm lucky to have them," she said. "You put up quite the financial fight."

He gave a grim chuckle. "Perhaps. But you're the victor walking away with the spoils."

She studied him but couldn't tell if the radiating anger she'd felt after the buy had come from him. If so, perhaps he'd come to terms with her success.

"I have to say I'm a big fan of winning. And its spoils." *Not that I want to goad him, merely gauge his reaction.* Apart from the barest tensing of his jaw, which he quickly smoothed into a smile, she felt nothing out of the ordinary. *Thank goodness. At a sale of this caliber, with so much money on the line, I could imagine us coming to blows over the gems.* A subtle breath of relief escaped as she recognized his peaceful overture.

"So, apart from my desire to steal five minutes up close with those stunning beauties …" Evan shifted his intense, dark blue gaze from the stones to Lexy, "… I thought I'd see if I could steal this stunning beauty and escort you to dinner in the main hall." He held out a tanned hand, and then frowned when she burst out laughing.

"God, what a line, Evan. Really, I quite like that one. Sure, you can escort me. After that bidding war, I'm totally famished."

Lexy exchanged a few words with Romel, who would guard the gems until she sailed the following morning. Grateful for the added security, she promised to check in before she returned to the hotel.

Then she turned to Evan and said, "Alright then, on to dinner, shall we?"

Evan grasped her hand, set it in the crook of his elbow and led her out, sending a swift, perusing eye over the dim room.

The two strolled through the downstairs hall, creaking over native Braziletto floorboards. Lexy smelled the must of closed-up air. She noticed painting after painting of what appeared—upon closer examination—to be the works of masters. She wondered what would happen to the rest of the items displayed throughout the house. The entire place epitomized dichotomy. Lexy said as much to Evan.

"You know, I got almost no information about this place before I came. The house and grounds are half-falling apart, yet the items inside are worth a fortune. This Edwards fellow must've been some eccentric guy."

They paused in front of a Waterford clock. She said, "Even when I arrived and spoke to the resort owner about this place, all I got were trifles about how the estate had existed on this edge of the resort's property for so long, they couldn't locate the written deed to the land. Apparently, Edwards and his antecedents predated the resort by close to a century."

They resumed walking.

"And I guess the poor guy—"—Lexy chuckled—"you know what I mean. I guess he didn't have any heirs, so the proceeds from the auction will go to the Eleuthera Historical Society. Talk about your generous freakin' bequests." She shook her head. "What about you, Evan? What nuggets of information were you able to suss out?" She cocked her head and stared him down. "Obviously you wanted the stones and were prepared to spend lavishly. Care to share?"

Evan faced Lexy as they stood in the doorway to the dining room. His deep eyes probed hers. She wondered what he looked for and what he found.

He said, "Well, if you haven't heard yet, you'll soon discover quite the fanciful story behind the late Mr. Edwards." He edged closer. "He was a thief."

"What? You too?" She laughed. "Where did you hear that? Romel told me a story that floated around the island about the jewels being stolen, but he said it was a tall tale. Local color."

One corner of Evan's mouth lifted. "Don't quote me as pure fact, but if you ask around—and I don't mean to the staff, as they're partial to their dear, departed tenant—you'll encounter more than a few yarns about him and his potentially ill-gotten gains."

Lexy raised an eyebrow at him.

"Really," he said. "If you have time before you leave, ask the locals. They'll tell you. And by the way, don't be surprised at the jewelry's provenance, or lack thereof, when you pick up your purchase."

The stories swirling around the gems caught Lexy off guard. Still, she wasn't completely gullible, especially after Romel's tweaking. She started to retort when an "Ahem" sounded from the corridor behind them.

"Excuse me, are you two heading in to dinner?" Jackson Hughes's husky voice flowed over them.

Lexy wondered how long he'd been listening. She didn't want to argue with Evan, so she let go what she'd planned to say.

To Jack she replied, "We are. Please, lead on."

Jack hesitated, and his whiskey eyes slid over her face, flashed to Evan's with a lightning frown, then cleared. A wave of uneasiness washed over Lexy; she shuddered in the warm Bahamian air, but brushed off the sensation, feeling ridiculous.

"Gentlemen, let's go, shall we? Dinner awaits."

The remainder of the evening proved uneventful, which suited Lexy. The considerable travel, coupled with the aftereffects of her huge adrenaline rush, exhausted her. After a flavorful dinner of native Bahamian conch and succulent lobster, spicy peas and rice and perhaps one-too-many fruity and very rummy Planter's Punches, she looked forward to a solid sleep. *What happened to wine with dinner? Whee.*

Before returning to the resort, she planned to check on her purchase to confirm everything would remain under lock and key until the next day. *Thank goodness the estate is managing security for everything until we leave the island. I'm so glad I didn't have to work out coverage here, in the middle of nowhere. That's a huuuge load off.*

The thoughts floated through her brain as Lexy wove out of the room where the guests enjoyed after-dinner cocktails. She sauntered down the hall, aiming for a last chat with Romel to square away the morning pickup. She found him standing guard, firearm holstered, in the same back room she'd left him in earlier. Several of the sold-off lots lay about the room, and Romel stood at attention, hand on his gun, wary of her approach. She stepped into the muted light, and a wide grin sliced across his face when he recognized her.

"Hi, Romel," she said brightly. "I'm checking in before I scoot back to the hotel. I wanted to make sure everything's set for the a.m." She smiled. "Anything else you need from me?"

"No, miss. We'll take good care of everyt'ing 'ere." He nodded at her. "Time for you to be gettin' back to d'e resort."

Leaving Romel with a grateful look, Lexy heard the other guests talking and clattering through the hall as they headed out and prepared for the bouncy return trip.

She glanced around while walking through the semi-decrepit mansion. *God, I feel like I'm in the Twilight Zone or someplace wonky like that.* A little shiver sneaked up her back. *I wonder what the place was like when Edwards lived here, surrounded by these crazy-valuable collections, with no one to share them, no one who appreciated them or knew their origins or worth. How sad.*

Her thoughts soon drifted away as three rum punches took over. She ambled outside and met the others on the porch. The women, sated by food and mellowed by drink, chatted together, happy with their purchases. But near the car, Lexy witnessed a terse exchange between Evan and Jack. *Wonder what has them in a snit. Maybe my new jewelry.* She snickered, then shifted her attention back to the ladies. They headed to the limo and climbed in, slurring their words and giggling. *Definitely time to head back.*

The brief ride jostled them home. When they arrived, the resort owner, Sabine, bustled out to meet them with a tray of full champagne flutes. "Welcome back, everyone," she called in a melodious French accent. Despite the late hour, she made no attempt to lower her voice. "Please, come join me for a celebratory drink, to congratulate you on your evening."

She beamed a huge smile at the group. Her silver bracelets jingled as she offered the tray. The women tittered like first-time drunken teenagers and they—Lexy included—reached for the sparkling beverage.

How can I say no to champagne?

The men declined with thanks. Each offered their version of "Thanks, I'll pass," "Off to bed" or "'Night, all" before making their way to their respective rooms.

"Come, then, ladies. Let us sit on the deck, and you can tell me all about your evening." Sabine herded them onto the patio overlooking the darkened marina. "What did you think of the house and all its amazing treasures …? Surprising, no?"

Before Lexy realized, 3:00 a.m. had come and gone. She and the other women had chatted and drank for hours.

Agh! I have to get my ass to bed. I'm so friggin' wiped. Gathering her dulled wits as best she could, she said her good-nights, thanked her hostess and tottered off to her townhouse.

As she poured herself into bed, she heard a light, tinkling crash on the walk beneath her window. "Uh-oh," she giggled. "Looks like someone needs to replace Sabine's champagne flute." She giggled again.

With that, all coherent thought fled.

Chapter 7

The creak of a worn floorboard shocked the silent night into awareness. Both intruder and occupant stilled, listened.

Waited.

Leaned into the darkness to hear, to feel what would happen next.

Plotted.

A security light gleamed down a distant hall, but its ineffectual glow gave laugh to the term "security." Everywhere loomed shadows, shifting shapes and intensifying darkness.

The room's sole occupant hesitated, strained for the sound's direction. He eased into the hall.

Waited.

"Who's d'ere?" he called. "D'ere's nothing for you 'ere. Leave. Leave at once!"

Silence.

He turned back into the room, ears playing tricks. The old house settled around him.

From behind, the light slip of a shoe sounded in the small, dim room. Before he could turn, something glinted in front of his dark eyes. A hand gripped his wrist, twisted his arm back and pinned him. A gleaming flash subdued him before he felt the prick at his neck.

The biting steel.

"Where are they? Where are the jewels," a throaty whisper rasped. The pressure of the blade increased. "They're mine!"

"No!"

The two struggled. Elbow to sternum missed its mark.

The steel blade slashed, found a soft, slippery home in the flesh of the neck. Blood spurted as the body fell.

"Damn it, where are they!" The intruder tried to muffle the strangled cry. The shadow hovered over the body writhing with spasms, and the antique blade was poised to strike the most vital place. "Answer me!"

"Never." The single word slipped out on a splutter. "D'ey don't belong to you …." His voice faded, dying away. "Not yours …."

"Damn you! They *are* mine!" the voice repeated, rising tones shattering the night air.

In a fury, the sword plunged straight into the guard's heart.

"I'll have them, whatever the cost. Damn you! Damn those jewels!"

Chapter 8

Bam-bam-bam!

The staccato rapping invaded Lexy's fuzzy brain after several minutes. *Oh, dear God.* She rolled over, buried under the floral duvet. *What the hell is that?*

The noise continued, growing louder and more insistent as she passed through degrees of wakefulness, until she reached "mostly with it." An eye creaked open and noted the time, eight thirty-seven. In the morning. *Shit.*

When she realized the pounding came from the front door and wasn't going to stop, she dragged herself out of bed and staggered downstairs. She squinted through the side window and bolted upright, then grimaced as pain radiated through her skull. On her front step stood an imposing dark-skinned man outfitted in the white tunic and traditional pith helmet of the Royal Bahamian Police Force.

"Shit, shit, shit," she muttered. "What the hell did I do last night?"

The pounding ceased, and a somber voice called, "Miss, I can see you behind d'e glass d'ere. If you'd open up, please."

Dumbfounded and embarrassed, Lexy did as requested. "Morning, Officer." She shaded her eyes against the blinding sun, winced and noted that several police cars had pulled onto the grounds. "What can I do for you?"

"I'm afraid d'ere's been trouble at d'e Edwards estate last night. We're questioning all guests as to d'eir whereabouts."

"Trouble?" Alarm zipped through her. "What sort of trouble? Is everybody okay? Are my jewels okay?" she asked, knowing how Mrs. Stellery would react.

The officer ignored her questions. "Where were you early d'is morning? Between d'e hours of two and four?" His piercing hazel eyes exacerbated her nervousness and her hangover.

"Between two and four?" *Duh, that's what he just said, Lex. Focus.* "I was at the shop with the rest of the ladies. Or, um, I should say, I was on the back deck with them. We had all been—us guests, I mean—at the estate auction earlier last night. When we returned, Sabine—she's the owner—" *Again, duh, I'm sure he knows who Sabine is. Stop blathering.*

"Anyway, Sabine had opened some champagne for us, you know, to celebrate the sale and our buys, and the bunch of us sat outside drinking and talking until after three. I actually got back here about three fifteen or so, and the rest of the women were packing it in then too. You know, it'd been a pretty long day, traveling and the auction and all. I just hit the hay from there. Uh, I mean, went to bed …." She decided to stop there, instead of offering the policeman further mush from her depleted brain.

He kept his eyes on her. "Please give me d'e names of d'e other ladies who were present at d'is gathering."

Though polite, his tone demanded an answer, and Lexy prattled off the names of the other female guests. She fidgeted, nerves twanging like an out-of-tune guitar. The officer scribbled the details in his notepad as she watched.

I can't believe this is happening. What do I say to Mrs. S.? Why won't this guy tell me what's going on? I can't believe I'm involved with a police investigation! In a foreign country. Thank God they speak English, or I'd really be freaking out. My God, this hangover sucks! I can't think straight. Lexy's thoughts rattled around her brain like loose change dropped in an empty jar as she struggled to concentrate.

"Officer, really," she pleaded, "can't you tell me anything about what happened? I'm in the Bahamas representing my client, Claudine Stellery, and we shelled out a massive amount of money for those jewels last night. Can you at least say if they've been stolen?"

Without giving him time to answer, Lexy rambled on. "When we left the estate, I checked in with Romel, the security guard on duty, and everything seemed okay." She shifted from foot to foot when she realized the officer had looked up from his notes to focus on her. "He told me—Romel, I mean—that they'd lock everything away after all the guests left. Officer, do you know if the auctioned items are safe? Please, what happened last night?"

She stood still and looked at him straight-on. She imagined how pitiful she must look: bloodshot eyes in a pasty face, hair in every direction. She hoped her appearance wouldn't work against her. *Please say something*, her eyes begged, though her voice remained silent.

Watching for her reaction, the officer said, "Well, miss, I'm afraid Romel was murdered d'is mornin'."

Lexy's hand clutched her stomach, and she heaved out a deep breath, fighting the onslaught of nausea.

"Slashed t'rough d'e 'eart wit' an old pirate cutlass, d'e one sold at auction, an eighteenth-century relic." He didn't mince words. As he offered the details, he studied her for any indication of prior knowledge.

"No!" she cried, hands thrown wide in disbelief. "That's not possible. I spoke to him before we left. Everything was fine, and they were getting ready to lock everything up." She had never before been this close to violence, to murder. "It can't be possible." She shook her head. "No way."

"I'm afraid it's true." He gave her a few moments to compose herself and stood by as she paced the front hall.

"God, this is awful," she whispered. "I hope it was quick and he didn't suffer." Bare feet slapped the hardwood floor. "Shit, I can't believe this is happening." Her disjointed thoughts sent her on a tangent. "This is the Bahamas, for Pete friggin' sake!" She turned back to the officer, still at attention on her front stoop. "Stuff like this isn't supposed to happen here."

When her pickled brain kicked in once more, she asked, "Who could have done this to him? Is my client's property safe? I bought the jewels on her behalf. Was this also a robbery? Was anything stolen?"

The officer leveled his hazel gaze on her from underneath the bright white brim of his helmet.

I must make for one helluva sight: ratty hair, disheveled pj's and bare feet. Great. Real trustworthy.

Regardless, he answered her. "No, miss, not'ing appears to be stolen, and your jewels were found secured in d'e mansion's main vault."

Somewhat comforted, Lexy exhaled, knowing at least she wouldn't have to explain away the loss of the jewelry. *Though I could be stuck in the Bahamas because of a murder investigation.* That thought disturbed her and brought to mind another question. "So, Officer …? I'm sorry, I didn't get your name."

"Inspector MacPhearson, miss."

"Oh, an inspector? Wow, okay then." Clearly the brain waves still struggled to compute. "So, anyway, now I'm wondering, what does this mean for me and my purchase? Am I allowed to leave the islands? And can I bring the jewelry home? Do I need a lawyer?" The questions poured out as her hangover began to lessen. "I'm not sure what I should say to my client about this situation. And she's expecting me back in New York this evening."

She tried to level her own iron gaze at the policeman. Not that she figured it would help her get off the island any sooner, but because she wanted to establish some sort of credibility with this man.

"We should not need to detain you, miss," he replied. "I do 'ave corroborating alibis from Sabine Rot'coate and d'e other female guests as to your whereabouts. I do 'ave several more questions for you, though."

The inspector ran Lexy through the typical cop-questioning gauntlet of what she had observed at the auction, her opinion of the other guests and auction-goers, if she had seen or heard anything out of the ordinary either at the hotel or the mansion. She replied as best she could, considering her diminished state. Recalling the crash of glass early that morning below her window, she recounted what she'd heard.

The officer wrapped up his questions. Lexy circled back to one of hers that he hadn't answered: Can her prize purchase leave the island with her?

"You will need to discuss d'at wit' my superintendent." He extended a printed card to her. "You should speak wit' him directly about d'e jewels and when you may take d'em from d'e islands."

Lexy palmed the business card. *Why can I leave but the jewels can't? What's that all about?* The inspector's stern expression shot down her attempt at further questions. "Okay, well, then, thank you, Inspector. I guess." A little out of her element. "I'm glad I've got the all-clear to leave, and I'll ring up your boss to check about the stones." Still floundering, she added, "So, if there's nothing else …? Well, good luck with your investigation. I hope you catch whoever would do such an awful thing."

Inspector MacPhearson gave a half-bow. "A safe journey to you, miss, and t'ank you for your assistance."

Lexy watched as he paraded toward the main house, back straight and pith helmet gleaming in the brilliant morning sun. *This is unreal. And God, my head is killing me. I guess rum punch and champers don't make the best combo.*

She closed the door and started to walk away, only to shuffle back and throw the second lock. *Unreal.* Then she headed upstairs for her Advil and her phone; next order of business: brain-pain help and a call to Mrs. Stellery.

The following hour and a half blurred by with calls, headache and gossip. The headache disappeared first. Next she dealt with Mrs. Stellery and the Eleuthera police. The efforts proved successful; the gems would return to the States with her. *The incomparable Claudine Stellery to the rescue, once again. I shouldn't be surprised her influence reaches all the way down here.*

After Lexy had retrieved the jewelry from the police, she went to find Sabine and the other late-night partiers. She wondered what they knew, and she wanted to find out more about Romel and the progress of the police investigation. The clock neared eleven, and she had little time before Matt arrived to sail her back to Nassau.

Walking down the path adjacent to the marina's turquoise water, she loped up the trio of steps and pushed open the door to the shop, nosing around for Sabine. She saw the woman through the office doorway and called to her. "Hi, Sabine. I was wondering if you have a minute before I leave?"

"But of course, my dear." Sabine, glamorous in white capris, a crimson beaded tank and matching sandals, pattered out. "My dear, how are you holding up? What a dreadful morning, no?"

"I should be asking you that question, Sabine," Lexy replied. "After all, you must've known Romel quite a while. I'm so awfully sorry for what happened."

Sabine acknowledged her with a head tilt and a murmured *"Merci."*

"And I wondered … do the police have any leads yet? Do they know anything at all about why he was murdered? I can hardly believe that such a horrible thing happened right here"—she swept her arm around the room—"while we were laughing and having fun. I feel terrible that there's nothing I can do to help."

"No, no, dear, do not feel that way," she admonished. "There is nothing any of us could have done last night. And now the police are investigating, and I have every confidence they will catch this horrid person."

"I certainly hope so. I'm glad they've cleared me to return home. My friend will arrive in a few minutes to take me to Nassau. Though, of course, I had to give my contact information to the police in case they have further questions." Lexy slid her worried gaze around the room. "I hope things calm down for you after all of us are gone."

"Oh, I am certain they will soon enough. Though not everyone is leaving the island yet." Sabine sent her a troubled glance. "The inspector let me know they are keeping Mr. Hughes here for more questioning."

Lexy spun around to gawk at her. "What?"

"Yes, that was my reaction as well. But apparently he does not have an alibi." Sabine shuddered delicately. "He has said he went for a walk, alone, at the time of the murder, and he has no witnesses." Her telling was glum, unbelieving. "I would never have thought. He seems such a likable man."

Lexy stared, gathering her flying thoughts. "I know, and I agree with you. Jack seemed …. He seemed so laid-back. Mellow, unconcerned about anything." She turned on her flip-flop–clad heel and recalled the unsettled, tingly feeling she'd gotten when they met. "Definitely not the killing kind." She grimaced at Sabine. "Not that I have the remotest idea what that would be or why I said that. Sorry, Sabine, my brain has a mind of its own. It really hasn't fully kicked in this morning."

Sabine gave a small chuckle, and a moment later the two women were laughing hard, a welcome release after the crazy, scary events of the morning.

"'Ello, ladies, is this a private party, or may anyone join?"

The smooth English tones sneaked between the women's laughs and soothed the rough edges of their worry. Lexy turned and saw Matt Aldridge leaning against the open door jamb, dark hair windblown and cheeky grin in place.

"Matt, you're here," Lexy said, moving in to give him a quick hug. "We didn't hear you motor in. God, what a morning this has been. Wait till I tell you."

She turned back to her hostess. "Sabine, I guess that's my cue to scoot." She grasped the older woman's hands in hers. "I'm sorry things ended so terribly, but please know that this is a delightful place. I so very much enjoyed yesterday, the beach, the exquisite scenery, our laughs last night. I hope everything works out okay, and soon, very soon." She gave a light squeeze to Sabine's hands.

"Thank you, my dear. The pleasure was truly mine," Sabine replied. "I do hope you will come back sometime. Perhaps stay a bit longer, have some time to truly enjoy all the good things this lovely island has to offer."

After the two women exchanged a heartfelt hug, Lexy and Matt left to gather her belongings.

Matt toted her overnight bag as they headed to the *Kelsi*. Lexy carried the waterproof, steel safe Mrs. Stellery had provided, now heavy with the jewels.

The wind whispered as they walked, and Matt raised an eyebrow and asked, "So, luv, care to tell me what that was all about?"

Lexy ran her fingers through her hair and said, "Matt, you're never gonna believe what happened here …."

Chapter 9

Lexy and Matt were well under way by the time she finished telling him of the weekend's events. Disbelief had him shaking his head.

"Lex, luv, are you certain you're alright? What a dreadful thing to experience. And it's shocking this happened on Eleuthera. It's typically a peaceful island." His troubled eyes found hers, and his hands flexed on the wheel as he sailed through the sound.

"Yes, I think so, but thanks, Matt," she replied. "I'm so glad you were here to pick me up."

A shiver crawled over her despite the hot summer sun blasting down. She reached for her well-worn Yankees baseball cap to shield her face. Edgy, she paced as far as she could in the tiny open area behind the cockpit.

"I still cannot fathom why someone would kill the guard," she mused. "Especially when nothing was stolen. It's not like I knew the guy, but Romel struck me as cool and sharp and likable." Sad eyes found the back of Matt's head. "Why on earth would anyone kill him, if not to steal Edwards's possessions?"

She corrected herself with a wry twist of her lips. "Or I suppose I should say, the former possessions of the late Reginald Edwards. Now that he's dead and his things are sold off, they're not exactly ol'

Reggie's anymore, are they?" She let out a dry chuckle that got lost in the wind.

The name, however, landed square in Matt's ears. "Did you say Reginald Edwards?"

He swiveled around on the pilot's seat and took them off-course in his haste. Readjusting smoothly, he half-turned to Lexy for her reply.

"Yeah, Edwards. The sale took place at his estate. Reginald Edwards … the fourth, I think. You knew him?"

"Knew of him, actually," Matt answered. "If he's the same Reginald Edwards I'm thinking of." He frowned. "I hadn't realized your trip involved him in any way. Or, for that matter, that he'd been living on Eleuthera." He drummed his fingers against the wheel. "I can't imagine there being too many fellows around who could be confused with him, though. Not based on some of the stories I've heard."

"Oh, really? What sort of stories?" Intrigued, Lexy grabbed a handrail and inched forward as the boat pitched over a high swell. She angled for a better view of Matt's profile.

"You'll get quite the kick out of this, I'm sure, though I don't have many details. One of the more infamous theories about Edwards swirling through these parts claims he was a descendant of the pirate, Calico Jack Rackham." Matt slid his gaze sideways for her reaction.

"What?" she exclaimed. "Descended from pirates?" A sharp burst of laughter rang out. "You're kidding, right? I mean, come on. All those guys must've died off years ago."

"Not necessarily. Lots of pirate by-blows could still be floating about the Caribbean. There certainly were plenty of pirates marauding around the Bahamas a few centuries ago. God knows they could've planted themselves anywhere." He spared her another glance. "That's by no means the strangest tale I've heard since I've inhabited these parts.

"And here's another rumor for you, luv. This one supposes ol' Reggie, as you called him …" he winked at her "… stumbled upon a stash of pirate treasure somewhere near Harbour Island and made off with it, without reporting anything or obtaining salvage rights for the find. Figure this: the treasure is said to be cursed."

Lexy scoffed at him. "Are you serious, Matt? The next thing you'll say is that my jewels are part of the cursed bunch Edwards is said to have stolen. Or wait, maybe the old man really had pirate blood in him, and he just took back what was rightfully his. And he happened to die without cluing anyone in as to what was fact and what was fiction. Come on now, get real.

"Anyway, I already heard the one about the cursed treasure he supposedly stole. In fact, Romel told me that rumor last night." She paused, and clouds of sadness filled her eyes. "He told me it was a story to add some spice to the sale of the stones, harmless. Besides, Romel said Edwards got the gems from a man in Briland, not Harbour Island."

"I've news for you, luv. Briland is the locals' name for Harbour Island."

Lexy paused and stared at Matt. "Come on, you're starting to worry me. You don't really believe the jewels I bought for Mrs. S. are cursed, do you? Tell me you're just having a go at me." She hugged herself, trying to warm against the chill that had settled on her.

"Ah, of course I don't believe that, luv." He grinned. "But remember, where there's smoke …. Or in this case, a rumor …." Matt's thought floated off and made her wonder what he really believed.

Skeptical, Lexy stared at him for another minute, then beyond him as she took in the changing scenery off the boat's starboard bow. *Looks like we're getting close to Nassau. Hmm, not sure how I feel about that. Mixed emotions, for sure.* She inhaled a deep, pungent breath, tangy with salt on the air. *Well, Eleuthera's been quite the adventure. It'll be good to get home, turn the stones over to Mrs. S. and get back to reality.*

Matt, silent as he eased off the engines and angled the boat into the marina, soon spoke. "You know, Lex, luv, I believe there's a museum in town devoted to those pirate fellows. If you're interested in learning more and you've time before your flight out, you may want to have a look."

Lexy turned toward him, thoughtful. "You're right. I'm pretty sure my driver mentioned that yesterday on my way here."

She let her eyes rove the marina as Matt navigated toward his slip. "God, can that've been only yesterday morning? It feels like a lifetime ago."

She sighed at how jumbled she felt after the events on the island. The combination of lack of sleep, worry over the murder and residual dissatisfaction with her life left her low and questioning. The doubt Matt raised about the gems added another layer of tension. These days she felt like nothing could go right.

Needing a distraction from those thoughts, she turned to the clock on the cockpit dash. "Christmas! It's after one. If I'm going to check out that museum, I've got to get my butt off this boat and into town."

She leapt onto the dock as they approached. Tied lines here and tossed baggage there, and Lexy was ready to leave. Matt joined her on the pier, and she gave a fast hug to her favorite Caribbean lust-object / transportation-aficionado.

Matt sent her off with a smile. "Ta, and be sure to miss me and all that, Lex, luv. Keep in touch with your adventures and stay safe."

"Will do, Matt." Then she tweaked him. "And thanks for not drowning me. So glad I didn't have to call in Lucas for a last-minute assist."

"Ah, luv, you wound me."

Lexy snorted. But as she stared at him, something flickered in his eyes. The look fled in a moment.

"Besides," he added, back to his cocky self, "you know Lucas hasn't one-tenth my charm *or* contacts." He winked.

"Cheeky bastard."

She laughed with him and said goodbye. After she left the marina, she found a cab and sped into town. They headed straight for the pirate museum off George Street. As the taxi drove along, her mind wandered to the emotion she thought she'd glimpsed in Matt's eyes. *Was it sadness? Dinged pride? Ha, as if I could ever wound him ....*

Her ride pulled up in front of the museum. She shifted her focus to the task at hand and went inside, thoughts of Matt relegated to the recesses of her brain. She roamed the musty space, clearly set up to entertain the cruise crowd that counted Nassau as a port of call. Regardless, she dug up interesting and eye-opening facts about piracy in the Caribbean during the 1600s and 1700s. Not previously interested in pirates, she admitted the extent of her working knowledge came from watching the *Pirates of the Caribbean* movies.

Yeah, that's cool. You can't rely on a Johnny Depp film to educate you on the ways of the eighteenth-century pirating world. Pirates in eyeliner. Nice, Lex.

Keeping an open mind—and reading with an eye on the time— she gleaned a few pertinent details.

Details such as: The Bahamas sat in the middle of the Spanish galleons' shipping route from the New World to Europe, through which they sailed ships laden with jewels and ores to the mother country.

And: The pirates knew well the shallows and shoals around the Straits of Florida off the Bahamas and would lie in wait for their prey to founder in the low waters. Once they did, the pirates plundered their ships and made off with their bounty.

And: Calico Jack Rackham called the Bahamas home, and he used Nassau as his base of operations.

And: Pirates had sex, often with many partners, and they left bastard children scattered throughout the Caribbean. *No shocker there, I guess.*

Along with the occasional hoard of hidden bounty. *Hmm, now that's intriguing.*

Those last bits of information stuck with Lexy as she zipped around the exhibit, flip-flops flapping on the wooden floors.

I wish I had more time before my flight. She hadn't expected the museum to offer her details about Edwards or the jewelry, but after her conversation with Matt she'd hoped to learn something more about Eleuthera and its history. Maybe something that could explain why Mrs. Stellery ordered her to a remote island in the middle of a tropical storm to buy jewels with a questionable provenance. *Yeah, fat chance I'll find anything relevant here.*

Lexy rifled through her purse to check the time on her cell. *Damn, I've got to get going.* She had time enough to fly through one last dusty room before she had to depart for the airport.

The final room captivated her in an instant.

She moved forward in the shadowy space, sandals slapping softly in the silence. Spotlights danced on jeweled displays, highlighting treasures the museum had obtained. Shimmering gold and silver coins and trinkets beckoned to Lexy. Brilliant gems sparked, and their fire drew her in, much like the displays from her childhood visits to the Museum of Natural History. The exhibitions cast a spell, enthralling her.

She hovered around the cases, quickly reading about each of the items. She tried not to get lost in the majesty of the simple room's display. The glowing exit sign caught her eye and reminded her of the time. As she walked toward the door, an exhibit attracted her attention. On the wall hung a brutal-looking Jolly Roger flag—crossed cutlasses below a grinning skull on a field of pitch black. She leaned in to read the placard. This particular design and its popularity were attributed to Calico Jack. Curious, she read on.

Not much information existed about the plaid-wearing pirate. But Lexy discovered another notable fact about Mr. Rackham; he had allowed women on board his vessel, a notorious taboo of his day, and one that few pirates admitted to. He had counted as crew two ferocious pirating women: Anne Bonny and Mary Read.

Lexy read on, eager for more, but learned little else in the short time she could spare. She dashed out of the museum, frustrated and still curious, but with a book on Caribbean piracy tucked into her bag, a fast purchase from the gift shop.

She sat in the back of the cab, and the driver chattered in a friendly fashion. She gave him half an ear while her mind drifted over the events of the past two days. *Wow, I'm really glad I'm going home. This has all been a little TMI for me, especially in such a short time.*

She glanced at the heavy-duty lockbox sitting on the seat next to her. *Well, you guys, looks like you'll soon be meeting your new owner. I think she's going to be very excited to see you.*

The cab deposited her at the airport, and Lexy made her way through customs with ease, regulations allowing her to clear in the Bahamas instead of the States.

Within short order, she nursed a Dark 'n' Stormy in first class and flew homeward, open book on her lap. She stretched and began to scan the text. Her focus waned as tiredness pressed down on her.

The last thing she read before fading into sleep was something about Jack Rackham's cursed and still missing Bahamian bounty.

Chapter 10

"Ms. Nichols, we're preparing to land." A soft nudge dented her shoulder. "I'm sorry to disturb you …."

The rest faded for a moment as Lexy tried to wave away the pesky irritant. *Damn it, why won't anyone let me get a solid bit of rest these days? This's really irking me. Grumble.*

"Ms. Nichols?" The sugary voice grew louder, nearer her ear. Harder to ignore.

"Yes, yes, I'm awake," she mumbled. "Coming upright, or whatever the hell it is you want me to do."

Ugh, I don't mean to be a total bitch, but this glorified flying waitress yanked me from an awesome dream: me and Matt doing the horizontal tango with me decked in a fabulous set of emeralds and nothing else. That's cruel.

Despite the disruption, Lexy shot an apologetic grimace toward the flight attendant and elevated her seat. *Heaven forbid I'm lying back comfortably if we happen to crash land and die in a burning wreck of metal.* Lexy caught herself before the lingering, tired snarkiness could make its way from her brain to her tongue. She slid up the window shade and peeked out. Flying into Newark International Airport, she couldn't see the city from her seat, but she had a clear view of the sun beginning its slide westward.

I'm so glad I'm almost home. I can't wait to tell Claire and Mike about my weekend. Especially the bits about the murder and the cursed pirate treasure. So crazy. Hmmm, maybe I'll ring her when I land, see if they can swing by my place, and we can order in.

The Boeing 737 slid a neat dive along the tarmac, and Lexy smiled, glad to reach New York in one piece. The flight attendant gave the "free to move about the cabin" speech, so Lexy scooped up her belongings and pulled out her cell, eager to call Claire with her dinner suggestion. As soon as she switched from airplane mode, the persistent tinging beep of her waiting voicemail sounded. Three messages. A slow sweep of dread niggled up her spine, and Lexy hit "1" on her speed dial as she exited the aircraft.

"Alexandria, this is Claudine Stellery calling." *As if she needs any introduction.* "Call me as soon as you land." *Gee, thanks for that complete non-explanation.*

Number two: "Alexandria, I am awaiting your immediate phone call. Be sure you ring promptly." *Ah, joyousness abounds, weaving through your dulcet tones, Mrs. S.*

Number three: "Alexandria, you should have landed by now." *Because it's my fault the flight was delayed by congestion into Newark. Hello, it's the international airport for a major freakin' city.* Lexy's inner monologue grew more annoyed with each message. "Call at once." *Ma'am, yes, ma'am. Charming and persuasive as ever.*

She hung up, mulling over the messages. Though beyond tempted to ignore the summonses, she knew she'd make the call. Professional pride and responsibility dictated it. *Besides, I wonder what the hell the issue is now. Better to find out and deal with it as soon as possible.*

Before she'd left, she and Mrs. Stellery had set up a plan for safeguarding the jewels. Since she returned on a Sunday evening and Mrs. Stellery's bank was closed, Lexy had arranged to deposit the jewelry in her boutique's vault, where it would be formally appraised first thing Monday morning.

Confused and a tad concerned, she dialed her client. "Good evening, Mrs. Stellery," she chirped. She could chirp when she felt it necessary. "I've landed at Newark, and I got your messages. What can I do for you?"

"Alexandria, I have made other arrangements for the jewelry's transport."

"Really? I thought we were all squared away with keeping everything at the shop. I've got the lockbox with me as we speak."

"I should hope so. However, I want them now."

Shocker.

"I have chartered a helicopter to bring them directly to the heliport at East Thirty-Fourth Street, and my driver and I will pick up the jewels there."

Lexy began spluttering as she juggled the phone and her things. "Okay, Mrs. S., I truly do understand how anxious you are to get these jewels, but there's no way—I repeat, no way—I'm getting into a helicopter and flying in a teeny-tiny metal gas can just so you can get your purchase ten minutes sooner than crosstown traffic allows."

Indignant and taken aback by the unusual request, Lexy pounded her feet along the lane outside the aircraft's gangway as she fought for space between the departing passengers. "I respect this is your purchase, but there's absolutely no way." She stomped her flip-flop, wishing her client could see her putting her foot down.

"Calm down, Alexandria." The wry voice carried across the line.

If I didn't know better, I'd say Mrs. S. sounds amused. Or what passes for amused in her world. But I don't find this funny at all.

"I recall your fear of small aircraft, so I have taken the liberty of hiring an armed guard—" *Armed guard?* Lexy's eyes popped. "—to meet you in the ground transportation area and fly the gems to me."

Lexy pulled up in the middle of the concourse, forcing traffic to shuffle around her, garnering grumbles and stares. Stunned, she could do little else than agree to the plan, so she continued toward the pickup point while her client ran through the details of the exchange. Lexy would meet the guard in the baggage claim area, a series of phone calls among the three parties would confirm the transfer of the gems, and then Lexy could meet her driver and go home to Manhattan. The phone call ended, *fait accompli*. She hoped it would be that simple.

Bemused by the lightning-fast turn of events, Lexy shook her head at no one in particular. *God, can this trip get any odder? Tropical storms, murder, pirate progeny and now a last-minute helicopter flight. All for the sake of some—admittedly very, very pretty—jewels.* She shook her head again and scanned the baggage area for her two meet-ups.

The first to catch her weary eye made her lips curve in a slight smile. Jimmy Moran, timely and faithful as always. She edged her way through the crowd, and he moved forward to relieve her of her suitcase.

"Jimmy, my hero." She laughed as he assisted her. "There's been a change of plans."

Lexy filled him in on what details she could, ending with the good news that he now had simply to bring her straight to her apartment. "And I sure as hell hope you stocked up on that Bushmills, because have I got a story for you."

But before they could go anywhere, the small matter of turning over the jewels remained. Lexy wove between the passengers, letting her gaze sort through the series of black suits that lined the airport exit. She found her name on a placard, and her silver eyes bore into those of the stocky man holding the sign. She tried to read his trustworthiness in them but felt completely inept at doing so. She sighed to herself. *Well, this is what Mrs. S. wants. I hope she's thought this through.*

After making the requisite confirmation phone calls with Mrs. Stellery, Lexy inhaled a huge breath and relinquished the reason for her existence these past forty-eight hours.

"Don't worry, Ms. Nichols," the quiet man said. "The jewels will be in good hands all the way to Mrs. Stellery."

Lexy couldn't be certain of that, but she respected her employer's decision. *And let's face it; I'm just glad I don't have to fly in a helicopter over the Hudson River. That sure as hell relieves some stress.*

"Come on, Jimmy. It's time to go home." Hefting her heavier-by-the-minute shoulder bag, she donned her shades against the setting sun and followed her driver to the car.

With Lexy and her bags stowed, Jimmy left the airport and began the trek into Manhattan. The quick and dramatic turn in the weather left plenty of weekenders heading back to the city with them. Lexy relaxed into the leather seat and swirled a tumbler of amber whiskey before taking a sip.

"Thanks for this, Jimmy," she said. "It's been one hell of a trip."

Lexy decided against calling Claire and instead regaled her driver with tales from the weekend. Jimmy, a multitasker like many chauffeurs, had eyes on the road and ears in the backseat.

He listened with a frown as Lexy recounted her story, but he kept his thoughts to himself.

Chapter 11

The *fwump* of the Bell 407's blades buffeted the air. The quiet man sat in the helicopter, lockbox secured beside him, alone aboard the luxurious craft save for the pilot. Systems checked and walk-around completed, they lifted off the helipad and nosed eastward toward Manhattan. He leaned back and settled in. *May as well enjoy the ride. This'll be quick. It has all the appearances of a cake assignment.*

He heard the pilot on the radio, but couldn't distinguish any words because his headphones were tuned to a different frequency. The guard saw the pilot's hand fly up and a hurried glance thrown his way; it looked as if the pilot was arguing with someone. Unease slithered through the guard.

Was that "Now what?" I heard?

He shook his head, certain he'd misread the situation. *I'm sure everything's fine. We'll be on the ground in less than ten minutes.* Angling toward his side window, he watched the approaching Hudson River. It grew nearer, silver-peach and undulating in the setting sunlight.

He absorbed the changing scene around him, appreciating the unique view. Massive skyscrapers grew out of the tiny parcel of land like shards of crystal exploding from quartz. He gazed at the setting, mesmerized.

Then he noticed a variation in the pitch of the engine. The radio silence of the pilot. *Wonder what's going on. We're not at the heliport yet.* He looked toward the pilot and settled his right hand on his holstered gun. *Best be prepared, just in case.*

He leaned as far as his seat belt permitted and glanced at the pilot's seat, to the left and forward.

His jaw dropped. *Not so cake after all.*

The barrel of a 9mm Beretta pointed at him.

"What the hell?" he yelled.

"Hold it right there, buddy," said the pilot, hiding behind dark shades and a baseball cap. "I'd think twice about popping the guy with the gun on you. Might mess with my flying this rig."

The words flowed out calm and easy-sounding through the crackling headset, but the guard detected a tremor in the pilot's gun hand.

Negotiate first.

"Alright, man, let's take it easy with the gun, okay?" The guard held his hands palms up. "How 'bout you put that thing away and tell me what you want."

"Don't be a jackass," the pilot snapped, jiggling the joystick. He struggled to keep the craft on its trajectory while keeping the gun aimed at the man in the backseat. "I want the jewels, obviously. And you're going to do exactly what I say if you want to live through this flight."

How the hell does this guy know what's in the safe? What's going on? The guard's mind raced through multiple scenarios. *Gotta stay calm. Stay focused.*

The call for the job came in an hour before he made the pickup in Newark. Minimal information had been supplied for the assignment; his duties were simple. He'd been told he would transport gems only so he could verify their existence upon arrival at the airport.

"Sure, man, sure. Whatever you want," he said to the pilot.

Have to lull him into complacency. Be agreeable. Wait for an opening.

"There's no need for guns, though. You're in charge. All the way. Tell me what you want me to do."

Placating the pilot seemed to work; he lowered his gun an inch, and the guard breathed in, dropping his hands to flex them against his thighs.

From the corner of his eye, the guard saw they flew directly above the Hudson River, heading northward on a parallel. The helicopter suddenly dipped, cruising so low he could see sunbathers on the downtown piers, lingering in the dying rays of the day. Thoughts sped through his brain. *Damn! What the fuck is this guy planning?*

"Alright, here's what you're gonna do."

The pilot turned his head, thrusting the gun at the guard, trying to keep him strapped in and unable to maneuver. "Slide open your window," he commanded.

The man did as directed. A fury of sound pummeled the interior of the craft.

"When I say so, you're gonna toss the lockbox out into the river."

The pilot flipped his gaze between the water and the guard.

"Got it?"

I get it, alright. But it doesn't make any sense.

The helicopter zoomed on.

"If you want the gems, you can't do this," the guard yelled over the wind flooding the aircraft. "We're too high up. If I toss the safe from here, it'll be destroyed ... like dropping it on concrete."

The guard's attempt at reason was to no avail.

"That's why I'm going in lower, jackass." But the pilot's hand shook on the stick as the copter skated downward.

Lower ....

Lower ....

The guard knew they couldn't fly like this for long without repercussions. Air traffic regulations around Manhattan remained strict. He guessed they had mere moments before being joined in the sky by the NYPD. He wrestled with impatience, flattening his hands against his legs again, and waited for the opportunity to strike. His seat belt still bound him, and time flew by.

The pilot twisted again and jabbed the gun in the guard's face. The movement scuttled the helicopter. "Now!" he ordered. "Dump the box!"

The radio squawked with a burst of violent static.

That's it!

The distraction the guard needed. One hand gripped the box and launched it at the pilot, slamming his head sideways with a sharp blow.

"Son of a bitch!" the pilot cried out, reeling from the punch.

The guard grappled to unbelt himself as the helicopter shuddered and tilted downward. The pilot still gripped the pistol and struggled to fight off the guard and control the listing craft.

The guard grabbed for the pilot's gun, no chance to reach for his own. The copter yawed as they fought. The lockbox dropped to the slanting cockpit floor and slid, unnoticed, out of their reach. The Hudson River loomed frighteningly close. Water filled the view out the cockpit window.

"Give it up, man!" the guard yelled. "Drop the gun! There's no way out of this."

But the pilot wouldn't give up. He twisted to get a better angle on the guard, and his hand left the throttle. He found the trigger.

Two shots burst out. A hole shattered in the fuselage, spewing smoke. An acrid smell lanced through the cabin.

"Goddamn!" Pain filled the guard's shout.

A bullet sliced through his shoulder and blood spurted, covering them in slippery, metallic-smelling syrup. He lost his grip as his blood poured out. "Damn, you son of a bitch! Get the controls, we're gonna ditch!" he screamed.

His blurring vision caught the onrushing river. *Too close. Much too close.* He lurched toward the stick. He had to get control of the helicopter or they'd smash into the river at full force.

The pilot tried to stop him.

"What the hell are you doing?!" yelled the guard.

He lunged past the pilot, reaching for the throttle, ignoring the pain, ignoring the flailing gun. The pilot snagged his jacket, jerking him backward, and the guard's fingertips slipped off the joystick. The two fell to the cockpit floor.

A high-pitched whine filled the air. Smoke blasted its way through the interior of the craft, and the smell of burning fuel singed their noses and made them cough.

"You son of a bitch!" the guard screamed, glancing toward the cockpit window. "You've killed us both!"

He landed a weak punch to the pilot's chin and looked up.

The river's blue-gray strength decimated the rotor blades on impact. They cracked like surfboards in a tsunami, sounding like thunder, and hurtled into the distance. Metal fragments sliced through anything in their path.

The cockpit window imploded. Water crashed in.

Shards of glass speared the guard, pulverizing him.

Metal and water smashed their bodies, snapping bones with ease.

The force of the crash upended the helicopter. The chassis flipped and skipped along the Hudson, the pressure of the collision obliterating anything recognizable about the craft and its occupants. It careered northward, end over end, scattering the evening's river traffic. Shrapnel flew off the copter, and debris traveled in its wake as its progress slowed.

The copter bobbed for a few minutes, like a child's overused bathtub toy. Then, after releasing the last of its air bubbles, it sank. Downward it plunged, the remnants of two men lost in its watery confines.

The prize they fought over, that small, watertight lockbox, nestled into the river bottom like a turtle's egg, buried near the helicopter's final location.

Chapter 12

"What was that?"

Lexy leaned forward, pushing a lock of hair behind her ear. "Sorry to interrupt, Jimmy. Would you please turn up the radio? Sounded like there was an accident on the Hudson." A worry line traced across her brow. She elbowed the cushion and scooted to the edge of the seat so she could hear. They caught the end of the special news bulletin.

"... low-flying helicopter crashed into the Hudson River north of Chelsea Piers moments ago, with no apparent survivors. Emergency responders are on the scene, engaging in search-and-rescue operations. Unconfirmed reports claim the Bell 407 helicopter flew from Newark International Airport and appeared to head northeastward before ditching in the Hudson. Eyewitness statements describe the helicopter as 'tilting and weaving' immediately before plunging into the river. There is no official word this evening as to the cause of the accident, nor is there information about the aircraft's occupants. We'll bring you live updates as soon as details are released, so please stay tuned."

Lexy sat back, aghast. "Jimmy, do you think ...?" She faltered, her mind blank for a second. "Do you think it's possible that's the helicopter Mrs. Stellery hired to transport the gems?" Her voice feathered out, hollow sounding, and her eyes questioned Jimmy through the mirror.

"Now, Miss Alexandria, I'm certain that couldn't possibly be the same fellow we saw off. Why, how could they have gotten so far so fast? T'wasn't enough time, I tell ya." Doubt crept into his voice, belying his words, and Lexy's eyes widened.

"I've got to know. We're almost through the tunnel. Come on, drive us along the river, or as far up the West Side Highway as we can. I need to find out if this had anything to do with the jewels."

"Are ya sure, miss?" He darted a look over his shoulder. "I canna' figure how close we'd get, what with such madness going on. You're not likely to get any good information that way. Mightn't you be better off going home and getting your updates from the news?" He tried again. "Truly, now, it's going to be a horrible mess, I'm certain of that."

"Jimmy, I totally agree with you," she replied, "but I've got to go. I have to find out who crashed and what happened to the jewelry."

They exited the Holland Tunnel and Jimmy, following orders, nosed the Lincoln northward. Straight into the mayhem.

Lexy fidgeted as they crawled through traffic. She stared out the window into the dying daylight, and her mind wandered. *Christmas! Were these past three days for real? God help us if Mrs. S.'s stones were lost.*

Exhaustion plowed over her like a semitruck in that moment. Overcome, she almost dropped her tumbler. *Whoa, take a deep breath, Lex. You can handle this.* She snatched the bottle of Irish whiskey and topped off her glass. *Though maybe another finger of this tasty treat will take the edge off.* The hint of a smile crept up her face. *If nothing else goes right, at least I can enjoy this.*

A frown displaced her smile, though, when she heard the latest newscast. "Police and rescue workers are searching for possible survivors, along with the aircraft's black box, which could hold clues as to what transpired before the crash. Police are cordoning off the West Side Highway between Twenty-Second and Thirty-Third Streets," the reporter said. "All motorists are advised to avoid the area and look for alternate routes. To bring you the latest on that situation, I'll turn it over to our traffic reporter. Michele …?"

A groan rolled out of Lexy. "Son of a bitch! We'll never get close enough to learn anything now. Damn it."

A minute of silence ensued. Jimmy waited, listening to the rustle as Lexy shifted positions.

"I guess we may as well get out of here."

She gulped back the rest of her Bushmills. Her rueful glance found his eyes through the mirror, and she cocked her head. "Time to go home."

"Aye, miss, I'm all for that."

Jimmy swung right at the next available corner, then cut right again to head south on Ninth Avenue. Lexy located her cell and speed-dialed Claire, needing to sound off about the weekend's craziness. *And at this point, I may need Claire to reaffirm my sanity. Whatever's left of it.*

The phone trilled into Claire's voicemail. "Hey, girl, it's me." Lexy twirled a tendril of hair, soothing herself. "I'm mostly calling to let you know I'm home, s & s." The friends had used their own lingo for "safe and sound" their entire lives; nobody guarded Lexy like her best friend, and vice versa, even if much of it was done via text and voicemail. "Of course, you know me, so naturally you know I've got massive, crazy, who-could-believe-it stories to tell you."

She pulled her cell away and glanced at the time. "It's almost eight forty-five, and I'm heading home with Jimmy … should be there in fifteen or so, hopefully." She let out an accidental sigh, which she hoped hadn't gotten recorded. "If you get this soon, give me a shout. Miss you, love you. Chowda."

With a quick click, she disconnected the call and melted into the seat, content to do nothing more than await her arrival home. The car jostled over the cobblestone street as they pulled up in front of her place. She hauled herself and her bag out of the car, then gave Jimmy a big hug and a larger-than-usual tip, in part as a thank-you for the potent backseat addition.

As she waved goodbye and started up the steps, she realized that said "potent addition" had had its way with her. She stubbed her toe and stumbled over one of the steps, nearly falling. *Yeah, that, plus my total exhaustion from the weekend.*

She managed to navigate her way into her apartment and past her multitude of locks. As she drove the last one home, her cell phone plinked out the calypso ring that meant Claire was calling.

"Hey, girl," she said as she flopped onto her couch. "How are you?"

"How am I, asks the world traveler." Claire laughed. "I should be asking you. How was your trip, and what're all these stories you've got for me, huh?"

"Christmas, girl!" Lexy heaved out a huge breath. "I don't even know where to begin. This has been one first-class, seriously effed-up weekend, that's for sure. How much time've you got?"

"Really, Lex?" Claire heard the tension in her friend's voice and moderated hers. "What happened down there? Are you alright?"

Lexy realized her loose lips had worried Claire. "Yeah, Claire, I'm totally fine, absolutely." She straightened on the couch, trying to sound alert and more like herself. "I'm just wiped from everything, but otherwise, really, I'm cool. No worries."

The false note was apparent, but clearly her friend was alive and well, mostly, so Claire didn't push. "Okay, you're alright, but you've obviously got stuff to tell me. It sounds like you had a bizarro trip." Claire paused. "I'm coming over, and you're gonna tell me all about it," she said in an iron voice.

Lexy knew better than to argue with her. Nor did she want to. Claire's rush to help, to be there with undivided attention, soothed her bruised self. After the madness of flying through the storm, gouging *(I hope not)* her client's finances on the largest purchase of her career, being questioned by the Bahamian police about the murder and potentially losing that largest purchase of her career, well, Lexy had had it with putting up a brave front. Her ears tuned back in to her friend.

"You haven't eaten yet, right?"

A mumble on Lexy's part meant "no."

"I'm calling in an order to Green Ginger Thai. I'll pick it up on my way over." Silence on the line told Claire her friend needed serious friend-therapy, since Lexy failed to insist her favorite spring rolls be included. "Sheesh," Claire said. "Must've been some weekend. I'm on my way, Lex. See you soon."

Lexy blew out another long breath. Then she hauled herself off the couch and attempted to stow her travel things. Not that her friend would mind the mess, but accomplishing something, however trivial, might give a semblance of order to the weekend.

She dragged her overnight bag and purse into her bedroom and dove in. Within minutes, she'd dumped the bulk of her clothes into the hamper, had stored her toiletry kit and tucked away her tools. She grabbed her pocketbook and rifled through it. Her hand encountered a large, rectangular object. She withdrew it and stared at the pirating tome she'd bought dashing out of the museum in Nassau that afternoon. Hefting it, Lexy left the remaining unpacked bits scattered about and wandered into her living room.

She paused in front of her hall mirror. *God, is that what I look like?* Her face wrinkled like an old peach as she frowned. Gray, crescent-shaped bags appeared below her eyes. Typically thin, now her cheekbones stood out and made her face look almost hollow. Colorless lips and cheeks rounded out the sad picture.

"Son of a bitch," she murmured. She dropped the book and pinched her cheeks so Claire wouldn't think Lexy's days were numbered. "I am soooo calling in late to work tomorrow. This body needs some serious sleep." While she futzed with her appearance, the buzzer sounded, heralding the arrival of Claire and food.

Lexy flung the door wide and smothered Claire in a bear hug, almost dislodging the bags emitting tantalizing, spicy scents. They moved in, locked the door and settled the bags on the living room coffee table before Claire got her first real look at her friend.

"Damn, girl, you look like death warmed over. You need to sit yourself down, let me fix you a plate and start spilling about your crazy weekend." She held Lexy's shoulders and gave her a small shake. "Really, you're okay, right? Worn out but okay?"

"I promise, Claire. It's a *major* case of wipeout, nothing more."

"Hmmm … I've got a feeling this is going to require some imbibing," Claire said. "You have anything here?"

"Jeez, woman, ask a silly question."

Lexy selected a chilled bottle of her favorite white Rioja, a good match to the tangy flavors of the food Claire unpacked. Fortified with wine and Lexy's chopsticks from Hong Kong *(Okay, so it's Thai food; the sticks are still the same.)*, the two friends plopped onto the floor and flipped open the plastic takeout containers.

Steam wafted upward and teased their noses with the piquant aromas of green curry and chili pepper. The girls dove in. Brown rice, curry and coconut milk in all its creamy spiciness, chicken done to tenderness landed in Lexy's stomach. Her favorite spring rolls followed, hot and sweet with dipping sauce, then pad kee mao, wide noodles steeped in chili sauce and garlic.

Lexy mumbled something incoherent as she devoured the food, a mix of fire and sweetness. *Mmm … heaven.* She sighed, content and relaxed for the first time in what felt like eons.

Before either woman realized, the containers stood empty, the wine bottle not far behind. Little had been said, and the quiet time had brought a sense of calm. Lexy knew her short reprieve had ended and the time had come to share her story.

"Claire, thanks for coming over and bringing me food." Lexy gave her friend a reenergized smile. "This is the first I've felt human since before I left. And that's saying a lot, considering how beautiful Eleuthera was. When I first got there." She shook her head, dislodging the knot she'd pulled her hair into to avoid interfering with her feast.

"So, Lex, now that you've got some sustenance in you, it's time to scoop me on your weekend of mayhem. Details, please."

The ladies moved from the floor to comfy positions on the couch and armchair. Claire snugged a pale blue pillow to her lap, and Lexy tucked her feet under her as she began her story.

"You already know how it began … practically flying into a hurricane on a moment's notice, with nothing but the vaguest info about a buy I've ever had in my entire professional life." Her fingers tapped a rapid beat on the back of the couch. "That was more or less fine, and I met up with Matt—be still my heart, he's as sexy as *ever*!—and he brought me to Eleuthera himself. All that was good. And God, Eleuthera is stunning! I'd love to go back sometime, when there's no bullshit going on."

She started to smile, but a tiny head shake refocused her. "Anywho, that's just the start of everything …."

Lexy spewed the details of her weekend, punctuating the tale with flying hands, pointed looks and occasional pacing around the room.

She began with meeting Jack Hughes, then the adrenaline rush of spending scads of Mrs. Stellery's money on the most beguiling gems she'd ever seen. She sped on to the sketchy details of Romel's slash-and-gut murder, followed by her questioning and the runaround to get the jewels released. The quick, down-and-dirty visit to the pirate museum after hearing Matt's tall tales came next, and finally—after opening a second bottle of wine—she finished with the possibility that the helicopter and guard hired last-minute to transport the jewels may've crashed into the Hudson River that evening.

"Good Lord, woman," Claire said, and exhaled audibly. "I think I need another drink."

"That's what I keep saying." Lexy topped off her friend's wineglass. "I mean, seriously, come freakin' on. Talk about a crazy-ass weekend." She moved around her tiny living room, tired but still keyed up, and stopped in front of the fireplace. She fingered the seashell on her mantel.

"I still don't know if I'm being paranoid about the crash tonight. Maybe all the talk this weekend about curses and thieves has messed with my brain." She replaced the shell and faced her friend. "I had the news on before you got here, but they didn't give any new details. How awful would it be if that crash was somehow connected to the cursed jewels Romel and Matt told me about?"

Claire scoffed.

"I'm serious, Claire; you had to hear those two. I'm sure Caribbean locals thrive on those stories, but they must have some basis in truth. You should've seen that museum." She trailed off at Claire's skeptical look. "Okay, come on, I'm not *that* gullible. I know most of that crap is for the tourists. But for Matt to say something too? He's not trying to put one over on me, and he isn't exactly a native, despite how much he tries to be."

She strode the length of the room, her feet finding the squeaky floorboards. "Their stories give credence to the possibility. Maybe there really *is* something off about the jewels." She stared at her friend. "Even Mrs. S. would barely give me the time of day about the background and provenance, and that's sooo not like her. Why else would she be so closed-mouthed? I think she knows more than she's telling."

Claire crossed her legs, the top one bouncing as she digested Lexy's story before weighing in. She saw her friend pick up the shell and start fiddling again, and she paused to find the right words.

"Lex, you know I don't like to jump to conclusions, so the first thing I'll say is that the whole cursed-pirate-jewelry idea is pretty thin. Not that it doesn't have some validity," she hurried to add. "I'm not rejecting the idea outright, but if you put aside your crazy-exhausting weekend and look at the individual events on their own, I think you'll find there's a sound explanation for everything."

Claire stood and stretched, tired of sitting. She grabbed the takeout remnants and cleared the coffee table. "Take this, for example: hello, it's hurricane season, so naturally you could encounter horrible weather flying to the Caribbean this time of year."

She carried the trash into the kitchen, calling over her shoulder, "And the murder? Well, having an entire estate full of high-end merchandise left after an auction that probably angered the losing bidders certainly speaks to motive, but not to cursed jewels. The gems weren't even stolen, and now Mrs. S. has them."

Lexy heard running water patter over the plates as Claire washed. *Good friend for washing, slightly less-than-desirable friend for not falling precisely into line with my theory.* Still, Claire's comments made sense and soothed Lexy's tattered nerves.

"Don't get me wrong." Claire poked her head through the kitchen doorway to make her point to Lexy. "I'm super-keen on the idea of you having your hands on pirate treasure, 'cursed' or not. But, and this is awful to say, the bigger likelihood about tonight's crash is that a couple of those helicopters we always see zipping over the river might have gotten their flight paths crossed and not been able to recover in time."

She ducked back, and Lexy heard the clatter of plates landing none-too-gently on the drying rack. "Most likely, you'll get a call tomorrow morning from Mrs. Stellery thanking you for all your hard work."

She clicked off the kitchen light and rejoined Lexy, settling onto the sofa beside her. "Or knowing her, no phone call but a nice chunk of change will show up in your next paycheck." She laughed and her friend managed a chuckle.

"I know you're right, Claire." The words floated out, half a sigh, half a release of accumulated tension. "Still, that's a damn lot of weird-ass shit going on in succession there, you gotta admit." Lexy turned her head, slanting a half-grin at Claire. "Seriously, thanks so much for coming over and letting me spew. I can't tell you how much better I feel. Maybe I'll even get a decent night's sleep, God willing." She smiled. "Imagine that."

The two girls sank deeper into the cushions, content after the wine and flavorful dishes to do nothing but vegetate and enjoy their company for a few minutes.

Lexy started to ask for the low-down on Claire's weekend when the chime of her cell phone echoed in the quiet room. She glanced at her clock and sent a quizzical look Claire's way. "It's almost eleven. Who'd call me at this hour?" She got up to find her phone. Looking back, she threw a smirk over her shoulder. "Surely not the parents, right? Checking in on their dear daughter?" She added a raspberry.

She snatched the device and saw the caller. Troubled eyes found Claire. "It's Mrs. S."

Chapter 13

"Why the hell is she calling me at this hour?"

"I don't know, Lex. Just answer the phone." Claire grabbed the pillow again, squeezing and watching her friend.

"Mrs. Stellery, hello." Lexy felt the need to be more formal than familiar. "Is everything alright?"

She stiffened as she listened to her client confirm the helicopter crash had been the one transporting her newly-bought jewels. The ones she'd paid a million-and-a-half dollars to obtain. Lexy felt the blow more so because she'd allowed Claire's logic to sway her. She'd begun to believe the events weren't linked to the gems. To her. *Boy, was I wrong about that.*

She stuttered a vague reply to Mrs. Stellery's barrage of information and instructions that the police would contact her in the morning for her statement. Not able to get a scant second word in, Lexy soon found herself on the receiving end of dead air and plopped into the chair.

"Seriously? Is it possible to have this much go wrong in the same weekend?"

Clearly a rhetorical question. Claire kept silent, waiting for the onslaught.

"You obviously won't be surprised to hear it was Mrs. S.'s charter that went down. With her jewels."

Lexy trembled as she filled in Claire. "And how do you like this … Mrs. S. reaching me even before the police?" She shook her head in awe at the socialite's broad and powerful reach. "She told me the police would call me in the morning, that I should get a good night's sleep."

She jumped up as worry escalated into fury in a heartbeat. She paced. "A good night's sleep? What the fuck?" she yelled. "Come freakin' on! Who's she kidding, pretending to be helpful now?" She whirled to face Claire. "You realize what this means, don't you?"

Claire nodded, and Lexy plowed on. "It means she knew exactly what sort of danger I could run into on this trip. She didn't sound the least bit surprised. She'd hired an *armed guard*, for Pete's sake! Who's now swimming with the fishies at the bottom of the Hudson. If there even are any fish in the Hudson."

Lexy paused for a breath. "She knew all along the risks and the potential problems I might encounter on the trip, and she sent me down there anyway. Completely blind. That's unbelievable." *And unforgivable.*

She smarted, bowed down by what felt more like a friend's betrayal of trust than a client's lack of divulgence. "Should I be grateful she hired a guard to carry the jewels on the final leg, instead of me? Is that terrible of me to think?"

She sat down and hung her head. "She never said a word. Not through all of our conversations this morning about the murder and getting me and the gems back today. Not when I landed and she told me the new plan for transporting the stones. Not a single damn word."

A few minutes passed before Claire broke the heavy silence. "So, what exactly did she say about the gems? Where are they? And how did she find out the crash involved the helicopter and guard she'd hired?" Claire fiddled with the pillow. "All this happened only a couple hours ago. Sounds like she got her hands on a hell of a lot of information very quickly."

"Yeah, don't I know it," Lexy replied, exhaustion replacing her dissipating anger. "But that's Mrs. S. … she knows all the right people.

Plus, she's so damn rich she can buy information at the drop of a hat if she has a mind to. The only thing that actually surprises me about her call is that it took her so long to make it. Then again, clearly I'm not on her priority list."

She leaned back, and her head fell against the couch. "She told me she'd been in touch with the charter company as soon as the helicopter was five minutes overdue. She knew something was wrong almost before the copter hit the river." Lexy turned her head to Claire. "And I should've known better. I should've suspected she knew more than she was telling."

"Damn." Claire couldn't think of anything else to say. "So what's next?"

"Ahh, next. Next." Lexy sat up, gave her head a little toss and looked at her friend. "Next, my dear, is me saying I love you for being here, but then kicking you out so that *I* can crash … in my bed." She smiled. "Tomorrow's 'next' will be a long, in-person convo with the woman of the hour. I want some answers. And I guess that will be followed by a chat with the police. Beyond that? I can't think of a 'beyond that' at the mo', so that'll have to wait until my brain regroups. Sound like a plan?"

The women stood and hugged each other, and Claire gathered her bag to leave.

She turned at the door and said, "You know, Lex, you and Mrs. S. have been working together for years. Maybe she really didn't anticipate any danger until after you guys spoke this morning about the fellow in the Bahamas. She might've decided on the armed guard after she realized there could be trouble, don't you think?"

Lexy considered her friend. "I suppose you could be right. But that doesn't negate the fact that she clearly put thought into that today, while I was traveling, and still said nothing to me until she was forced to. Or that she neither gave me time to investigate the gems before I flew south, nor gave me any significant information about the assignment before the trip. And if tonight proves anything, it's that she can get her facts together pretty damn quick.

"You know her fairly well, too, Claire. She's not one to make such a massive investment without having all the details she can possibly find. God knows what other information she hasn't shared with me.

"For the moment, it is what it is," she added. "I'm going to try to get some sleep tonight, and tomorrow I'm going over there to give her a piece of my mind."

Claire sighed. "Okay, Lex. You know I'm behind you all the way. But please—for your sake—try not to burn any bridges, okay? I know you love your job, despite how bonkers it makes you."

With a hug, Claire left, and Lexy zipped up the locks. She tossed a final tired look around her living room, then pitched the lights and headed to bed.

Damn. I wonder what the hell tomorrow's gonna bring.

Chapter 14

The next morning Lexy rose at nine-ish. Heavy on the "–ish" as she struggled to get moving. She stared in the bathroom mirror and brushed her teeth. The gray curves still hung in a perfect color match below her eyes. *I should go for broke and put on gray eye shadow today, too.* She spit and stuck her tongue out, half-laughing at her sorry appearance.

In her bedroom she donned a pair of jeans and slipped a purple, fitted tank top over her head. *Thank God for an easy dress code.* As par for Lexy's course, she poked through her jewelry box and chose carefully. Tanzanite and white gold drop earrings, an abstract silver pendant and a plethora of silver stacking rings finished her off.

The clock glowed 10:15 a.m. as she slipped on a pair of comfy high-heeled sandals. She'd rung the shop to let William know she would pay a visit to Mrs. Stellery and not to expect her for a couple hours. As she tossed her makeup kit into her bag, her intercom buzzed, competing with the echoing refrain of a U2 song that emanated from her alarm clock.

Startled by the prospect of a visitor before her morning coffee, Lexy straightened and turned toward the door. She hesitated, not expecting anyone. Her typical response to unsolicited inquiries: ignore them until they go away. *A much safer option than inviting inside the next pseudo-deliveryman killer, I always say.*

But since midmorning felt early enough to be killer free, she reconsidered and hit the exchange button on the intercom, inquiring about her visitor.

"NYPD, ma'am. Detectives Sobel and Langston. Would you buzz us in?"

"What?" she replied. "The police?" *Here at my apartment? You've gotta be kidding me.*

"Are we speaking to Alexandria Nichols?"

"Yes, that's me."

"If you'd please let us in, ma'am. We have some questions for you regarding yesterday's helicopter crash."

Holy shit. That was friggin' fast. I can't believe they showed up here. I figured they'd find me at work later.

As she pressed the entry button to disengage the downstairs locks, she sent a quick, guilty glance around her apartment. She'd expected to hear from the police given Mrs. Stellery's forewarning, but she hadn't anticipated them turning up on her doorstep at the crack of daylight. *What amounts to my crack of daylight.* She took another look around.

There's nothing to worry about, Lex. The apartment's fine, I'm fine, and it's nothing more than a little chat. Nothing to freak out about, nothing to be afraid of. Except, maybe, for the pseudo-deliveryman killer turning into the pseudo-fake-cop killer. Grrr, my brain. If only it'd shut up once in a while. Maybe I should take up deep-breathing exercises ....

In the time it took her random thoughts to spiral out of control, the police arrived at her door. A sharp rap sounded. She started, then called, "Who is it?" keeping clear of the door. *In case they decide to shoot first, then ask questions.*

"NYPD, ma'am. Detective Sobel," came a husky feminine voice. "We're here to talk about your involvement in yesterday's crash."

"My involvement?" Lexy opened the door as far as the security chain allowed. "Please show me your IDs before I let you in."

The two officers held up their identification.

As if I have any clue what a real NYPD ID looks like. Taking them at their word, she closed the door, slid back the chain and offered them entrance. They exchanged pleasantries and sat down. Detective Langston, a wheat-haired man with dimples and chocolate eyes, asked her to describe the events prior to handing off the gems to the guard, including her engagement by Mrs. Stellery.

Lexy complied, taking both officers through the details as best she remembered them. She left out nothing and paid particular attention to Romel's murder, along with her swift and complete release from the Bahamas—in possession of the jewels. When she got to the part where she landed at Newark Airport and received new orders to transfer the gems to a security guard, she paused for a bolstering breath.

She gripped the arms of her chair and continued. She told them about the urgent voicemails, the conversation with Mrs. Stellery, the meeting with the guard and subsequent confirmation phone calls to ensure his identity. "So you know, Detectives, that last-minute request surprised me a bit, but though slightly unusual, it's still not the most bizarre thing Mrs. Stellery has ever done." *Just potentially the most dangerous ....*

The detectives took notes and peppered her with questions. She ended with how she'd relinquished Mrs. Stellery's property and left the airport.

Detective Sobel chimed in. "At any point in your interaction with the guard, did you see or hear anything out of the ordinary?"

"No, nothing at all."

"Did you see the guard interact with anyone? See anyone follow him as he left?"

"No, I didn't. But I'm afraid I can't help there," she replied. "I left first. I'd already set up a car service for last night, because I'd planned to bring the jewelry directly to the shop to store the pieces in our safe. The boutique has a sophisticated security system along with an oversized vault on the premises. I'd made those arrangements with Mrs. Stellery prior to leaving Friday. The car would take me there to deposit the gems in the safe, and I'd turn them over to her this morning after my final appraisal.

"When we spoke after I landed, she told me the new plans and that she'd have the guard meet me in the ground transportation area, since that's where my ride would be. My driver had met me by then, so I turned over the lockbox and left straight after. Actually, I don't even know which direction the guard went, where he needed to go for the helicopter. So it's definitely possible someone followed him, and I wouldn't have seen. Though there's still the question of how anyone could've found out, since Mrs. Stellery set this up so fast."

She blew out a whoosh of air as she wrapped up. "Truth is, I only dealt with him for ten minutes or so. Once I found him, and we made the calls to Mrs. Stellery, I handed over the safe and left."

She looked at Detective Langston, who had stopped scribbling and leveled his brown eyes at her. "It's crazy to think the helicopter and the guard and the jewels are all gone. Do you have any idea what happened?"

The detectives exchanged a look before Langston commented. "We're still investigating the crash. We'll know more after the black box is recovered and the data is analyzed, which we expect to happen later today. The good news for your client, however, is the lockbox she supplied you came outfitted with a GPS locator beacon." He sent a small grimace Sobel's way. "Apparently, your client has quite a bit of pull with the NYPD and the mayor's office; she'll have the gemstones in her possession this afternoon."

"What? Are you for real? The safe had a tracking device? Holy crap," she muttered, closing her eyes. "Sorry, Detectives. I'm a little surprised, though really, I shouldn't be. The GPS makes sense, given the amount of money she paid to get her hands on those stones. Of course she'd take extra precautions with them. But wow, this whole story keeps boggling my mind."

After a few minutes finishing up and exchanging business cards, the police left. Lexy, one hand on the knob, the other flat on the door holding her upright, shook her head and tried to sort out the latest information.

With a quick exhale she turned away, determined to continue with her original plan: find Mrs. Stellery and speak her mind in person.

Lexy picked up her pocketbook, peeked in the hall mirror to make sure her lipstick hadn't worried off and slammed out. She cringed and offered her neighbors a silent apology. *Hell, most of them are probably long gone on a late Monday morning.*

Lexy stomped down her front steps and splurged on a taxi to the Stellery residence, anxious to look her client in the eye for an explanation. She didn't have to compete for a cab, so within minutes she and Ahmed zoomed eastward along Houston, Algerian music intriguing but too loud. He deposited her on Mrs. Stellery's doorstep before she had time to fully develop her rant.

Charles answered her strident knock and led her, stalking, to the downstairs parlor where Claudine Stellery waited.

Apparently, my arrival is not unexpected.

The older woman nodded but did not rise when Lexy entered the sun-splashed room.

"Mrs. Stellery." Formality ruled. "I imagine you know why I'm here."

Lexy moved into the room, feet sinking into the antique Aubusson rug which shrouded her steps. A beat of silence reigned. Two. Her left hand trembled at her side while the other gripped the strap of her purse, squeezing it into submission. Considering their history and years of acquaintance, Lexy tried her utmost to contain her fiery emotions. She needed a clear answer as to Mrs. Stellery's knowledge of the recent events.

"I would very much appreciate a full explanation of exactly what the hell went down this weekend regarding those damn jewels I spent half your friggin' fortune on for you." *Damn, so much for staying cool.*

"Young lady," the unflappable Claudine Stellery quickly replied, "I will not tolerate such cheek from you. I understand you may be shaken by what transpired this weekend—"

"Are you kidding me, Mrs. S.?" Lexy burst in. All pretense of calm evaporated like steam off a sizzling frying pan. "Shaken is hardly the word for me right now. Try livid."

She strode closer to where the elderly matron sat in her high-backed chair, feet demurely crossed at the ankles, the picture of propriety, not an emotion flickering across that aloof, old face.

"Try scared out of my gourd. Try hugely, incredibly disappointed in you and your lack of trust. Disappointed that after years of working together you still felt the need to hide important information about this job. Information that very well could have affected my safety.

"And disappointed you didn't clue me in about how important this find really is and what it means to you." She paused, leaned down, stared into icy blue shards that melted a touch. "If you'd only shared what you knew, maybe I could've helped in some way." She moved away, putting distance between them physically and emotionally. "But you didn't, and now I still don't know what else you expected to find with the jewels. And the question is, are you going to tell me?"

Claudine Stellery gripped the arms of her Chippendale chair and levered herself to her full height of five feet four inches in her heels. She stood there, imposing in her regality, despite her diminishing stature. She leveled a cool gaze at Lexy and then spoke.

"No."

"Wh-what?"

"Not yet, Alexandria." She sliced neatly through Lexy's stuttering protests.

Claudine watched the younger woman pace, keeping eye contact with her as a hunter with prey. "There is simply too much at stake right now for me to divulge further details about the jewels." She added with a whisper of dismay slinking through her voice, "Including your safety, which I am truly sorry not to have taken into greater account before you set forth on this trip. For that, Alexandria, you do have my sincerest apologies."

Those words startled Lexy with their genuineness, yet she continued to stride around the room, anger and frustration slow to dissipate. "But you have the gems now, Mrs. S., or you should today at some point. The police told me about the GPS, so I'm sure you already have a crew of divers scoping out the crash site, right?"

Click, click, out to the parquet floor, then a turn and back she went. "What more are you looking for? When are you going to share your secrets?"

Lexy's eyes lanced Mrs. Stellery like steel daggers. The elder woman remained silent, hands clasped in front of her.

"By the way, I have a doozy of a secret for you. Turns out those jewels might well be part of a stolen cache of goodies from the pirate, Captain Calico Jack Rackham. Stolen jewels," she repeated, going for flare. "*Cursed* jewels." She let that sink a moment. "How do you like that for a secret?"

Her words brought Mrs. Stellery upright. "Nonsense. There is nothing stolen nor cursed about those jewels. I repeat, nothing. Wherever you got your information, Alexandria, must be suspect." She wagged a finger in Lexy's direction. "I will have no more such talk. Nor will I allow you to spread such absurd stories. And will you stop that infernal pounding across my floor, young lady!"

With that slip of composure, Lexy saw the first chink. She came to a halt in front of her client.

"Come on, Mrs. S.," she cajoled. "Clearly, something is going on here. If you tell me, I might even be able to help."

"I am sorry, Alexandria, but the fewer people who know about this, the better, so I must demand your complete silence for the time being." She studied Lexy a moment. Then, that crinkle having been exposed, she offered a branch. "Until I am ready to reveal the truth at the Jewelry Information Center's gala celebration. In two weeks' time."

"A gala?" Lexy took a moment to assimilate the information. "You mean the JIC's Gem Awards? You're unveiling some sort of … I don't know, what … a story? History? A tall tale? About the jewels we bought? At the JIC's Gem Awards Dinner?" Lexy crossed her arms as she faced her client.

One of the premier jewelry industry events to occur in New York City, the Annual Gem Awards Dinner honored the jewelers and media professionals who served their vocation with outstanding panache, creativity and communication skills. For Claudine Stellery to use that platform as her own personal display case showed moxie that surprised even Lexy.

"That's what you're talking about, isn't it? That's the only industry bash happening in the next few weeks. Everybody who's anybody will be there." She leaned in again to stare down Mrs. Stellery. "You're telling me you've got some grandiose plan to reveal something about the gems at the awards dinner?" Lexy shook her head in amazement. "You've got to be kidding me."

Claudine stiffened and inhaled deeply, increasing her presence threefold. Her pale periwinkle suit made her a study in muted strength. In her baldest voice she said, "I most certainly am not kidding whatsoever." She fixed a cold, misty blue gaze on Lexy. "Have you forgotten that I am this year's recipient of the Jewelry Style Award?"

If Claudine Lansing Stellery ever sniffed in disdain, Lexy would've heard it then. And with the dramatic events of the past few days, that information had flitted straight out of Lexy's crowded brain.

"It's the perfect stage from which to unveil my newest possessions."

The yearly award went to a personality who, by virtue of their jewelry sense, style and prominence in society and the media, embodied glamour and energized the jewelry industry.

"The securing of these particular gems, and their presentation into American gemological society on the grandest level, are the first steps in my ultimate goal of disclosing my family's long-hidden history." Claudine's nostrils flared as she delivered her speech, a sure sign of her imminent overheating.

Lexy cocked her head and frowned.

"Nothing will prevent me from revealing the truth to the world. My nephew and I have searched too long and worked too hard to do otherwise."

Lexy latched onto the words, surprise flashing in her eyes. "Your nephew? You have a nephew?" She could tell from Mrs. Stellery's expression that the comment had been made in error.

"I don't understand what you're saying, Mrs. Stellery." Lexy stared at Claudine's face, now carefully blank. "You've been working on some kind of massive jewel hunt for what, years? But I'm only finding out about it now? How long have you had me unwittingly involved in your crazy plans? How many other secret 'errands' have I run for you?

"And on top of all that, this search of yours is some kind of family quest? This is ridiculous. We've known each other for years. I thought all of your family was gone. Now you tell me you not only have family, but your nephew has been helping you all along? Or, hell, maybe you've duped him too?" Fire shot from Lexy's eyes. "Does he know he's been helping you, or am I the only one you kept in the dark?"

Lexy's shocked expression spoke clear as day. "Jeez, Mrs. S., this is too much!" Without pausing to let Claudine speak, she continued. "I can't believe this. I feel like I hardly know you, even after so many years." Running a hand through her hair, she turned her back on the older woman. "Damn. This … this on top of everything else this weekend, blows me away."

The two women stood there, silent and separate, for several minutes.

Lexy walked to the window overlooking the sunny, sparkling garden. *It looks so serene. So completely contrary to how I feel right now. How could Mrs. S. have kept this from me? How could I not have seen any of it?*

She breathed deeply as she turned around, composing herself. "I need time to digest all this, Mrs. Stellery." If Lexy's use of formality dismayed Claudine, not a flicker of it crossed her features. "This is a hell of a lot of information for me to process after everything that's happened. I'd better go."

She headed for the parlor door. As she passed through, she paused and murmured over her shoulder, "Goodbye, Mrs. Stellery."

"Alexandria …."

The familiar regal tone, laced with the barest hint of hesitancy, carried across the room. Lexy waited a beat, then turned back to her client. But Mrs. Stellery said nothing further. Lexy left in silence.

She didn't see Claudine Stellery slump into her chair, alone and smaller than before.

Chapter 15

This is gonna take some getting used to. God, I really wish my brother was around to talk to. Damn it! Life really bites sometimes.

Lexy wandered down the street, aiming for the subway that would shuttle her to the shop. Her sandals slapped the heated concrete. She paid scant attention to her surroundings as she dodged the foot traffic on Sixty-Third and headed east.

Sun slammed down. *Why the heck are there so many tourists in this part of town in the middle of summer?* She wended through the pedestrians. *Are they crazy?*

The heat of the city rose around Lexy and assaulted her with its tang of rotting garbage and overwatered sidewalk roses. The combination of too many people, too many scents and too much disjointed information from someone she'd considered trustworthy spun her head.

A buzzing sensation filled her ears. She felt bombarded and oddly scrutinized as she paused and looked around. A light shudder passed through her, though nothing appeared out of the ordinary. *Keep going. There's nothing wrong, just too many people crowding me.*

Her meanderings brought her to the subway, courtesy of memorization by rote, and she headed downtown on the F. She transferred at West Fourth Street, climbed upstairs for an arriving E train and rode until she landed at Canal Street. As she exited the station, she clicked her cell to check the time. Almost 1:45 p.m. Her stomach growled.

There's no point arguing with my stomach. Besides, I've had enough of people for the moment. Better to grab lunch before I head to the boutique and have to deal with everyone.

Lexy gave a modicum of thought to her destination, deciding on Walker's on North Moore Street. It met her requirements for the perfect retreat: location near enough to her shop that she could walk within minutes, restaurant enough that it could pass for a lunch venue and bar enough that it could serve her purposes.

She walked to the pub, tugged open the squeaky wood-and-glass door and entered. Her last visit had been months ago. With a half-smile, she ducked around the corners, feeling like she tiptoed through someone's charming old house. A two-top near a window overlooking the street made for a good spot to settle. A few tourists populated the tables, but the late lunch hour meant fewer crowds fighting for space. The side room offered a good blend of privacy and company at a distance.

A scruffy young waiter clad in jeans, a Rolling Stones T-shirt and a spattered apron swung by, order pad in hand. Lexy ordered the best thing on the menu: a quarter-pound burger, medium rare, with fixings on the side. Fried onion rings and a Dogfish Head 60 Minute IPA draft rounded out her meal. The fellow disappeared, and when he returned he set down her beer, then melted away.

Ah, salvation in a glass. She eyed the frosty pint dripping a ring of condensation on the scarred tabletop. *Well, it's only one. And it's with lunch, technically.*

Giving in to temptation, she let the citrusy, hoppy flavor of the ale burst to life on her tongue. It eased past the constriction in her throat that had plagued her since the visit with Mrs. Stellery. One sip, two sips. A third, and finally she could swallow without feeling her throat close.

This is ridiculous. Feeling betrayed by Mrs. S. is not right. She's not worth this. Get a grip already. So she chose to keep me in the dark about the jewels, about having family. So what? It's not like she's my best friend or owes me any explanation. If she wants to keep going on her crazy treasure hunt or family quest or whatever, then fine. Have at it, Mrs. S.

Lexy paused in her mental fistfight and took another deep swallow of beer. *Hmmm. Either my little chitchat worked, or the beer's high ABV is already mellowing me. Whichever, I don't suppose it matters. At least I feel a little better.*

The server returned and deposited her food with a clatter. Lexy snapped open the napkin and laid it across her lap. She dolloped ketchup over her hamburger and topped it with lettuce and tomato. Bun reseated, she lofted the burger in two hands and munched into the meat, squirting grease and inhaling the smoky, rich scent of grilled beef.

Heaven on a seeded roll. She eyeballed the trickle of blood and fat as it dripped from her juicy burger onto the plate. *Mmmmm.*

She sat there for a while, alternating swigs of beer, bites of burger and crunches of crispy fried onions. For twenty minutes she thought of nothing and no one, and she let herself be absorbed by her meal.

Her reprieve soon ended. She looked down at the dish, empty but for a chunk of pickle. The crinkled napkin lay scrunched on the table. The lace of the beer dipped low around the edge of the glass. The clinking, murmuring sounds of the other diners gradually filtered into her consciousness. She lingered, nursing the last drops of beer. Putting off going to the shop. Mulling over the morning's conversation.

Lexy stared out the window and rehashed the weekend. Everything from being ordered to the auction to the murder, the crash and Mrs. Stellery's reluctant admissions about the jewels and her nephew unsettled her. She felt twisted like a tangled electrical cord shoved out of sight.

And I really don't feel ready to face everybody's questions. No doubt they'll have tons. I'm sure shop gossip's left everyone with an opinion.

She rested her chin in her hand and regarded the passersby through the glass. Across the street a man in a baseball cap stood watching her. Before she could make out his features, he turned away and strode down the block. *Nice, buddy. Take a picture next time, why don't you? Nosy.*

She brought her thoughts back to her situation. *Time to get it together. I can hardly put off an appearance because I don't feel like going to work. Hell, if that's the case, I might never show face again.*

Stopping that thought, she air-tapped her index finger in the direction of the waiter, motioning for her check. Once she had it in hand, she laid money on the table and allowed herself to continue the thought.

Nah, I don't really mean that. Sure, the prima donna bullshit and excessive travel is exhausting, but I do love the essence of my job. Buying gems and designing jewelry for the hottest boutique in New York is incredible. Plus, if Mrs. S. stays true to past behavior, I'll make a huge commission on this last job.

And that could mean the difference between staying on with the shop or having enough capital to venture out on my own. I've got to stick with the plan and think long term.

Lexy sighed, planted her hands on the table and shoved herself up. Stealing glances at the other diners as she walked to the exit, she wondered if any of them were happy, if anyone ever experienced true contentment, true satisfaction with their lives. *I wonder ... but I doubt it.*

The patter of her shoes on the pavement accompanied the cycle of her thoughts. *Maybe I'm burnt out. In the city that never sleeps, maybe I need to stop hustling for a while. I haven't been home long enough to garner any third dates in almost a year. God, that's depressing. So maybe I need to slow down. Then again, maybe I think too damn much, and all this nonsense with Mrs. S. and the jewels is not helping.*

Maybe, maybe, maybe. The refrain felt like a never-ending tattoo pummeling her mind. Relentless and defeating.

I have to snap out of this somehow. Damn, I miss my brother so much. He could always put things into perspective and help sort me out.

Lexy's eyes misted as the random thought entered her head. *Nope, can't go there right now. Too much. Way too much to handle and too soon.*

A flashing orange hand caught her eye, and a voice yelled at her to pay attention. She stopped her physical and mental ramblings and focused on the nearby streets. Her distracted, post-lunch stroll had taken her five blocks out of the way. *Christmas! I can't believe I did that.*

Hitching her purse, she turned around. *And I can't believe my dogs didn't bark at me.* She eyed her not-exactly-walking shoes and snorted. Double-checking her direction, she headed toward the shop and shoved her wayward thoughts into the back cupboard of her brain.

Fifteen minutes later, Lexy stared past her somber image in the store's front window and watched her colleagues, smiling and head bobbing, deal with their customers. Caught in a vague sense of loneliness, of being the outsider, she sighed. Before anyone could see her hesitation, she keycarded herself inside.

Lost in thought, she didn't notice the tall, capped figure reflected in the glass behind her, glaring at her. She didn't feel the stranger's gaze on her, didn't feel his eyes follow her as she entered the shop.

With an encompassing but empty smile for the room, she dodged past the sparkling display cases and entered her office. Spared for the moment, she closed her door and set to work.

Chapter 16

Jack Hughes had problems. Problems leaving Eleuthera. Problems returning home to St. Thomas. Then problems flying to New York to regroup with his aunt.

The murder on the island had been a major hassle, but the Royal Bahamian Police had to let Jack go. They had found a partial fingerprint on the saber used to slay Romel, but the print didn't match Jack or anyone else lacking an alibi. With no clear motive or evidence to detain them, Jack and Pete had been allowed to leave, though the murder remained unsolved.

Pete had shifted one of his charters and flew them north at the end of the week. Thursday afternoon arrived before the men got to Manhattan. Jack expressed his appreciation with a bottle of his friend's favorite tequila. Over the years, having a buddy with a pilot's license had proven handy. Jack had requested Pete's last-minute assistance numerous times—most often to accommodate his aunt's treasure-hunting expeditions—and Pete had always come through. With the recent trouble, Jack didn't want to waste more time getting to his aunt and making sure she—and the gems—were alright.

Now the men entered Claudine's downstairs parlor where she sat in a high-backed armchair. She set aside her *Wall Street Journal*, stood and embraced Jack.

A bit startled at her show of warmth, especially in front of Pete, Jack nonetheless gave her a solid hug in return. His aunt felt bonier than she had the month before, when they'd last seen each other.

"How are you, Aunt Claudine?" He studied her face.

"I am well, thank you, Jackson. I am glad you extricated yourself from that nastiness on Eleuthera." She angled her head in his direction. "I trust you are no longer on the Bahamian Police's Ten Most Wanted List?"

Jack laughed. His aunt could deliver a snarky remark with the best of them. "No, ma'am, I think they're done with me. Best I can tell." He motioned his hand in the direction of Pete. "You remember my friend, Peter Lambert, don't you, Aunt Cee? He's been pretty helpful flying me all over the Eastern Seaboard these past few years. He wanted to say hello and see how you're doing after last weekend."

Pete moved into the room. He extended his hand to shake Claudine's and eyed the posh surroundings. "It's nice to see you again, Mrs. Stellery. Jack here told me a bit about the brouhaha this past weekend."

Claudine shot her nephew a questioning glance. Jack merely nodded at her, indicating not to worry.

Pete said, "I thought I'd stop by with him when we got here to check how you're doing. Sounds like you had quite the adventure yourself, what with that helicopter crash. Terrible news," he added, frowning.

"Yes, Peter, it was tragic. That poor guard …. The police are still investigating, of course, but they do believe the pilot lost control of the craft and that precipitated the crash into the river. The lockbox has been recovered and the jewels are safe." She folded her hands in front of her, having said as much on that topic as she would in front of Peter.

Jack continued, though, missing the flicker of dismay that crossed his aunt's face. "I can't believe how much mayhem seems to follow those gems." He directed a half-joking headshake Peter's way. "We heard some rumors about them while we cooled our heels in the Bahamas, didn't we, Pete? Aunt Cee, if you'd heard those stories … hell, I don't think you'd've been so anxious to get your hands on them."

Claudine slid an icy gaze toward her nephew and said, "Really, Jackson, it is beneath you to go passing tales. You must have bored Mr. Lambert half to death. Let us not inundate him with idle gossip any further, shall we?"

Oblivious to her pique, Jack said, "Come on, Aunt Cee. You know Pete's heard scads of our family's escapades since we were kids … what makes this any different?" He glanced at his friend. "Besides, you get a kick outta listening to us ramble on about all these mystery jewels and misadventures, don't ya, Pete?"

Pete's lips compressed before curving into a cheeky grin. "You bet I do, bro." His raspy voice rumbled into the quiet room. "They're what I live for." Sarcasm trickled through, but he smiled politely at Claudine.

With tact bred from years of experience, she directed the conversation away from all things gem-related. Jack picked up on her cue and let the subject drop. The three chatted a few minutes longer, and Pete prepared to leave.

"Well, Mrs. Stellery, I'm sure you're wanting to catch up with Jack here, so I'll head on out." He looked around the luxurious room, then focused on Claudine. "Take care of yourself," he said as he squeezed her hand goodbye.

"Jack, old man." Pete smirked. "I'll touch base with you later."

Another handshake and he left.

Claudine ushered Jack deeper into the room and had him sit in the matching armchair to her right. She heard Charles close the front door and called out, "Charles, come in, please, if you would." No request filled her voice, though, only unequivocal command.

When Charles entered, Jack rose and offered him his chair. "Charlie," he said with a slap on the butler's back that sent him staggering, "good to see you again. You doing alright, taking care of my aunt? You know, she's still ringing me at all hours of the night. Come on, Charlie, you've gotta keep her in line, now." Jack winked at the older fellow, who flushed and ducked his head with a glance to Claudine.

"Jackson, do not embarrass the man," she said. "Come along. Sit down and tell us everything that happened on Eleuthera."

Jack swung a nearby chair closer to the two and sat himself down. "Sure thing, Aunt Cee. The short version or the long?"

"The relevant details, please. Long or short as those may prove."

Jack began his tales with meeting Lexy—though not introducing himself as Claudine's nephew, per her instructions—and ended with his release from the Royal Bahamian Police. "They found a partial print on the sword, but it didn't match me, Reginald Edwards or anyone else they'd detained. That, coupled with Lexy's inadvertent alibi, and they let me go."

"She alibied you? How so?" asked Charles.

"After everyone returned from the auction, the ladies stayed up with the resort owner for some drinks. The rest of us said good-night, but I decided to keep an eye on Lexy from a distance. The bidding had gotten pretty ferocious before all was said and done—"

"Yes." Claudine interrupted him with a withering glance. "I could tell as much from the price I paid for the jewels."

"Hey now, Aunt Cee." Jack held up his hands, all innocence. "You wanted me there to deflect attention from her, to keep a lookout and make sure she wasn't the sole object of focus down there. I was doing my job," he replied with a grin. "As I was saying, I wanted to make sure she made it back to her condo okay, so I hung out and watched from the shadows."

His aunt shot him a probing look.

"And I gotta tell you, that girl can drink," he commented with a disbelieving headshake. "Anyway, long story short, after the party broke up, I followed her back to her townhouse, waited for her to go to bed, and I dropped the glass of water I had with me. Kind of stupid to have it, I guess, but as it turns out, she heard the noise and told the police, thinking it could've been something suspicious."

His aunt and Charles eyed him with reproof.

"Hey, guys. Me? Not suspicious," he said. "When I told the police what happened, though, all I said was that I'd been out for a walk.

Her testimony corroborated my story." He leaned back and crossed his arms, looking from one to the other.

His aunt questioned him. "Did you notice anyone who gave you cause for concern? That night or at the auction?"

"Not especially. A few heavy hitters were bidding, but only one seemed put out by Lexy's winning. And even he didn't have his nose too badly out of joint. Guy by the name of Evan Maxwell. Ring any bells?"

Claudine shook her head. "No, but we will thoroughly investigate him regardless. Charles." The butler produced pen and paper from his jacket and took down the name. "Anything else, Jackson?"

Jack hesitated. Saying more could speak volumes, if he started looking too closely at his motives. "There *is* one other person you may want to look at." He tilted his head at them. "How well do you know that guy who was her ride to and from Eleuthera?"

Jack felt Claudine weigh her answer before speaking. "I do not know him personally, but I know Alexandria has used his services"— Jack smothered a snicker—"several times in the past, and she has been acquainted with him for many years. Why? Do you think he bears looking into?"

Jack watched his aunt watching him. He wondered if she suspected his motives went deeper than simple regard for the safety of the jewels. He thought about how to answer.

"It's just that they seemed pretty …."

What do I say here? Tight? Friendly? Cozy? All those things are perfectly normal, especially under the circumstances. Still, whether it's my Johnson or my gut talking, something didn't set right. "I guess I'd say they looked pretty chatty when I saw them leaving Sunday morning. I'm worried that with so much craziness going on, Lexy may've let something slip that she shouldn't have, that's all. We were all shocked when we found out the security guard had been murdered."

Claudine gave her nephew the once-over.

Jack could only guess how much she saw.

Still, she agreed. "You know, Jackson, as much as I trust Alexandria and her instincts, it would be prudent to delve into her contact's background. I recall his name is Matthew Aldridge. British fellow. Charles."

Another name went onto the list.

Jack spoke up again. "And how about you, Aunt Cee? Are you really doing okay with all this? I'm sure even you hadn't anticipated all these crazy circumstances. Pretty wild stuff."

He leaned forward, hands crossed between his knees. "Won't you now, at least, tell me what else you know about these jewels? I know you believe they mean something important to our family, but please, Aunt Cee, tell me what's behind all your searching. You've been at this too long without a solid explanation. Besides, with all this nonsense going on, I'm starting to worry." He gave her a half-smile, but his eyes sought answers.

Hers remained steadfast. "I am sorry, Jackson, truly I am." Sincerity seeped through the soft words. "But I will not reveal anything more until I am ready with as much information as I can amass before the JIC dinner. It could only put you in harm's way. I will not do that. I have already risked Alexandria." She shook her head. "And I am disturbed I had not foreseen such a possibility."

She gathered herself. "Once I reveal the truth to everyone at the gala, the danger will be negated. Please believe I am doing this for your own good."

"The danger? To us? What're you talking about, Aunt Cee?" A frown crinkled Jack's forehead. "Wait a sec." He held a hand up. "Do you mean to tell me you think there's something dangerous about those jewels?"

Disbelief clouded Jack's face. He peered closely at his aunt, then sent a look over to Charles, who shifted in his seat. "Seriously? I thought you wanted me down there to keep an eye on Lexy, divert attention and scope out the competition. Since when have you thought getting the jewels could be dangerous?"

After a pause, Claudine said, "Jackson, I simply could not take chances. I needed your presence on Eleuthera to ensure a smooth transaction. It turns out I was right to be cautious."

The synapses began to fire and, piece by piece, Jack made the connections. "You mean …? Come on, you think the murder had something to do with those gems? Even though they weren't stolen?" He shook his head, letting the idea simmer. "And what about this helicopter crash? You think that's connected too? Not an accident?"

Claudine and Charles exchanged a look. She crossed her hands and laid them in her lap, as if preparing to lecture. "All I can disclose is that I am taking every precaution to keep you and Alexandria and the jewels safe. You are here, Alexandria is home, and the jewels are guarded by my personal security company. I will say no more for the present, but please believe me, I have only your safety in mind."

Jack surged to his feet and paced. "But what about you, Claudine? And what about Charlie, here? Going about on your treasure hunts. What about *your* safety?" He propped his hands on his hips as he paused to stare at his aunt. "Do you expect me to sit by and not do anything while you flat-out tell me the two of you are deliberately putting yourselves in danger?"

"Yes, Jackson," came the quiet, steely reply. "I do. You must do nothing further for the time being, lest unwanted attention be drawn to us."

She stood and walked to him, reaching out her hands to clutch his own. "Please, Jackson, you must not do anything more until I say. Please."

Jack stood there, poleaxed by the plea from his aunt, perhaps the first time in his life he'd heard her say the word. That more than anything swayed him. Shaking his head, his words became a counterpoint. "Alright, Aunt Cee. I'll wait to hear from you before I do anything else. Though I can't believe I'm actually agreeing to this."

She squeezed his hands, then let go. "Very good, Jackson. Thank you."

Practically another first for Jack. Even Charles wore a surprised expression as his gaze ping-ponged between the two.

"Well then," Claudine continued in a light voice, "I believe Charles and I have some work to do."

Jack knew a Claudine Lansing Stellery dismissal when he heard it.

He hugged his aunt, then shook Charles's hand. "Alright, Aunt Cee, I'm going. But I'll check in, frequently, and I'm staying in town until this gala shindig of yours, of course. Call me if you need anything at all."

"Yes, dear, I will."

Jack didn't believe her for a second.

Charles rose to escort him to the door.

"Stay, Charlie, I'll see myself out. I'm sure my aunt has an elbow-long list of things she's dying to get started on. Just be careful, please. Love you guys. So long."

As Jack left the parlor, he overheard his aunt say, "Come now, Charles, let us get to work."

Chapter 17

"Okay, Stace, be subtle. When I say so, turn around and look at the guy behind us. He's half a block back, in the navy baseball cap and white T-shirt. I swear he's been following us. Every time I look around, he's there. He's giving me the creeps."

Lexy angled her head at Stacey, who strolled beside her the following Monday on their lunch break. They stopped at the corner, waiting for the light to change before crossing.

"Okay, now."

Stacey obliged and glanced around as if taking in the scenery on the pretty August afternoon. She noted the man gazing into a storefront several yards away. He looked like Joe Anybody, meandering down the street on his lunch hour.

"I see him, Lex, but what do you want me to say? He looks harmless enough. Especially from a distance." She laughed. "He also looks like the rest of Manhattan, roaming around for lunch." Stacey turned back to Lexy. "Are you sure it's the same guy you saw earlier? Half the sidewalk is wearing Yankees hats."

When traffic cleared, the friends started forward, jostling with the crowd as they headed back to work.

"Why on earth do you think you're being followed? You don't think it has something to do with the buy in the Bahamas, do you?

Because that would be silly." Surprise laced Stacey's voice, and she took a sideways step to keep her eyes on her friend.

"Ugh, I don't know, Stace. But now you're making me think I'm paranoid," Lexy replied. "And yes, of course it has to do with all that nonsense from my trip. You don't really think I'm this bonkers all the friggin' time, do you?"

She glanced over her shoulder again. *No baseball cap guy now. Not that I can see through the scads of walkers, though.* "Okay, yes, I'm a bit out there sometimes."

Stacey snorted at her friend's comment.

"But generally I'm not known for full-on walking delusions." Lexy stuck out her tongue and gave a Bronx cheer. "Besides, it wasn't only today," she added. "I'm serious, Stace. Ever since I've been back I've had the oddest sense that someone's watching me. On my way to and from work, running errands."

A shiver rolled over Lexy, as if someone had blown cold air down her neck. "Paranoia or not, it's freaking me out. I feel … spooked. And uncomfortable. It's hard to explain. I can't think of any reason for these weird sensations other than that job. It's like every time I turn around, some guy has his eyes on me. Blegh." Another ripple of unease slid up her spine.

Stacey laughed off her friend's worries. "Girl, don't even think you'll wrangle a compliment out of me. You know you're gorgeous, and if you're feeling men's eyes on you, then damn, it's probably for the obvious reason that they see a beautiful woman walking down the street. Oh, to be so lucky," she added with mock wistfulness, the back of her hand pressed to her forehead.

Lexy flicked her eyes up and down her friend, taking in the wavy auburn hair, friendly smile and short, curvaceous body. "Hell, Stace, you're one to talk about getting attention." But Lexy refused to let Stacey's words placate her. "Besides, you know there's a huge difference between being scoped by some dude and being stalked." She sighed. "This feels different. And I'd swear it's the same guy every time I look."

They reached the shop's entrance and paused under the sage green awning, watching the staff cater to the customers on the other side of the window. As they stood there, Lexy's focus shifted and she caught another glimpse of the dark cap and white tee reflected in the pane.

She pointed. "There he is again!"

The two women spun and spotted his jean-clad legs turning the far corner. They dashed along the sidewalk, scooting past the pedestrians. By the time they reached the corner, though, the man had blended into the cocktail of sidewalk surfers.

"Damn it!" cried Lexy. Turning back to Stacey, she asked, "Now do you believe me? It had to be the same guy." Frustrated, she sighed and swiped her hair out of her face.

"I'm sorry, Lex, there's not much I can say." Her friend gave her a quick squeeze. "It could've been the same guy from a few minutes ago, but that's no shocker."

The two backtracked to the boutique. "We didn't go far for lunch," Stacey reminded her. "God knows New Yorkers walk everywhere, so it wouldn't surprise me if it was the same man."

"But if he was all Mr. Innocent Guy out for lunch like us, why did he run away?"

They reached the shop's door, and Stacey paused before swiping her card to let them in. "I don't know. But it is good that you're aware of your surroundings. Not to freak you out or anything," she hurried to add, "I just mean that—without getting crazy about it—you're smart to keep your eyes open. Know what I'm sayin'?"

Stacey gave her friend's arm a quick pat. "I wouldn't worry if I were you."

Lexy shot her a "Who, me, worry?" look.

"Your head's on straight, but you've had a lot on your plate lately. How about we go out for drinks this week? Let's say Wednesday? It'll be fun and a good way for you to chill a bit. How does that sound?"

"Sure, Stace. Chillin' sounds like a great idea. This past week's been a blur here at the shop. Every five minutes, something new pops up. It'll be good to relax and hang out."

And to keep occupied.

Lexy's gaze roamed the work floor before she directed her feet toward her office. "I'll also ring Claire to see if she's free to grab dinner tomorrow. Two whole nights of post-work fun and enjoyment in one week … holy smokes, why don't I go crazy while I'm at it, huh?"

She threw a cheeky smile to her friend as she ambled toward her workbench. "Thanks for the head-check, Stace. I appreciate it."

"Anytime, girl." Stacey winked. "Chat at ya lay-tah."

*****

The following evening, Lexy and Claire snuggled into a corner table at Las Ramblas, a miniscule tapas restaurant in the West Village and one of their favorites. With a smile and a flourish, the waiter displayed the wine bottle and proceeded to pour a small amount for tasting. Lexy did the honors.

"Hmm, damp cork, pretty color, totally inoffensive smell." Her eyes twinkled at the waiter as she took a sip. "And delightful on the palate." She laughed, and he poured the bright, flavorful Tempranillo into both glasses. "Thanks, Raul, very delicious recommendation, as usual."

He smiled at Lexy, used to her antics.

Raul whisked away and moments later served their first dish, a steaming, garlicky platter of shrimp, *Gambas San Martin*, with a too-tiny basket of fresh, toasted bread. Silence reigned as the two dove with crusty bread bits into the sizzling sauce. The shrimp, flavorful and tender, melted on the tongue, but the sauce descended from heaven.

"God, I love the Spanish," Lexy declared.

Claire added, "And I love that someone opened this wonderful Spanish restaurant in my backyard. How very considerate of them." She smiled over another bite of shrimp. "So, Lex, how goes things? Really."

Lexy's eyes followed Raul's progress, weaving around the tables as he moved toward them with another addition. He deposited a triangular plate with three golden, hot *croquetas de jamon*, along with a *cazuela de chorizo con alubias*. The combined scents of ham, sausage and spicy peppers and onions tantalized her nose. She inhaled, savoring the aroma as much as the flavors.

"Ah, Claire." She let out a long breath. "Better, now that you're here. And so is the food." She grinned and wrinkled her nose at her friend. Leaning in, she grabbed her fork and dished a portion of the food onto her plate. "But it feels like eons since we last caught up. This week has flown by. It's been crazy."

She shoved a bite of *chorizo* in her mouth and blissfully closed her eyes as the spices zinged her tongue. Lifting her fork again, she used it to gesture at Claire.

"Crazy-bad, I mean." She rolled her eyes. "Not bad-bad. Nothing else has happened like the Bahamas madness. I mean, besides those stalker-ish feelings I've had. Not bad like that, but crazy, work-wise."

She gave Claire the evil eye as her friend reached for the last nugget of bread, then waved Raul over to replenish the basket.

"Though I did get the heebie-jeebies again yesterday when me and Stacey went for lunch. We saw this guy behind us outside the restaurant, then later taking off around the corner when we got back to the shop. Well, I think it may've been the same guy. But Stacey did make me realize I've been a little tightly wound these days, you know?" She took another a sip of wine. "Hence, the reason I invited you to dinner tonight—besides the usual and customary grounds, of course. I need to chill a bit. Apparently," she said with a smirk.

"I couldn't agree with Stacey more." Claire laughed. "And I'm glad you managed to leave work at a reasonable hour so we could do this." As soon as Raul dropped off a full bread basket, Claire perched herself on the edge of the *cazuela*, the flat dish which held the last savory drips of the *gambas* sauce. "God, this stuff is like crack," she mumbled around a dripping bite overflowing with chopped peppers and garlic.

"Hey, paws off, and let me get some before you scarf it all." Lexy dug in. "Anyway, look who's talking 'reasonable,' Miss High-Class Super-Novelist who works until all hours."

Claire started to protest, but Lexy went on. "You know, Claire, I'm going to make some changes." Lexy held up her hand to ward off an interruption. "Yeah, before you chime in, I realize I've said that before, *a lot*, and you're right." She paused and stared at her friend, dead serious. "But things are different this time. It feels like now is the right point in my life to get off my ass and do what I've talked about for so long." She shook her head slowly, feeling for the right words. "I'm not sure if it's all the weirdness since Eleuthera, or that I finally accept I'll never be 100 percent ready, or what, but something has to give. Now. I can't do this any longer. I can't stay unhappy, not when it's within my power to change my situation."

A smile inched her lips upward. "If Mrs. S. holds true to form, I'll get my commission check this week, and it'll be a doozy. But even without any more last-minute trips around the world for her this week, work's been utter madness since I got back. I finally finished that white gold and sapphire ring yesterday; remember that design I showed you? I've got three more jobs in the works, a new one starting tomorrow, and on top of that I have another estate sale in Scarsdale on Friday. Unreal," she said, and huffed. "Anyway, my point is I've got a plan this time."

Claire looked up, distracted from the dripping beans and onions in red sauce she was about to fork into her mouth. "Hmm? A plan? That sounds promising. What kind of plan?"

"First, I'm meeting with my boss tomorrow. I'm going to request shifting one or two of my clients to other designers and decreasing the number of overseas trips." Lexy's eyes gleamed as she scooped up a toasty, melty bite of *croqueta*. "Mmmm. And I've started looking into the free business courses the public library offers through SIBL. They've got a ton of resources online and in-person, so I've made an appointment with a counselor there for Friday evening."

"SIBL? You mean the business library, right?"

"Yep, the Science, Industry & Business branch of the NYPL. They've got so much to offer. For free, too," she added. "Of course, when I meet with the counselor I'm going to see what they recommend in the way of small-business ownership classes or training. You know, my boss, Christian, has always been open about how he runs the shop, but there's so much I need to learn about running a business by myself."

Lexy smiled at Raul as he swung by their table to top off their glasses.

Leaning in, she said, "My goal is to reduce my work at the shop and cut down on travel, so I'll have a wee bit of time to start learning how to build my own business." She smiled, and the grin livened her face and glowed from her eyes.

Claire, seeing her friend animated about her work for the first time in too long, said, "That's fantastic, Lex! I'm so excited for you." She reached across the table and gave Lexy's arm a squeeze. "Good for you for making your decision. Taking that first step is so hard, but it's so worth it. I know you've wanted to do something, make a change, for a long time. It's scary when your life feels all gray and unhappy and hollow. You know I've been there, too … feeling lost and incapable of deciding, worried you're making the wrong choice. It can paralyze a person. I'm really glad you seem so certain now. I'm very proud of you." She smiled and gave another squeeze. "Good luck tomorrow with your boss. How do you think this'll go over?"

Lexy thought a moment. "To be honest, I think he's going to be okay with it. You know he's a pretty cool guy, and he definitely knows how hard I work. And how much money I bring in." She smirked. "I hope I'm not totally off the mark, but once he hears me out, I really think he'll be okay with my decision." She took another taste of the wine. "Which doesn't mean I'm not prepared for him going ballistic." She rolled her eyes again. "Anything is possible, but at this point I feel rather prepared to deal with whatever happens."

"Yeah, you go, girl." Admiration rang through Claire's voice. After a moment she said, "This is a huge step. And it's only the beginning of big challenges. But I know you'll succeed. Please remember I'm here 100 percent to support you. 'Cause I sure as hell understand what it's like being in your shoes …."

Two years earlier, Claire had been strapped to a seventy-hour-a-week job, but persistence, talent and luck had recently ranked her on *The New York Times* Bestseller List with her debut novel.

"Here's to you and your new endeavors." She lifted her glass and clinked with Lexy's, the tinkle floating through the air. "May success be yours."

"Thanks, Claire. I know I can always count on you." Lexy's eyes sparked with anticipation. "I'll keep you posted on how things go after I talk with Christian tomorrow.

"Oh, and regardless of what happens, Stacey and I are going out for drinks after work." She chuckled, then added, "Either way—if I get the okay, or if I get canned—I've decided I definitely need to let loose a little more. Life's too short, as we know." With a quick slug, she emptied her wineglass. "You should join us if you're free. We'll stay in Tribeca and probably hit anotheroom. Have some beers, see if we can pull some guys." She smiled slyly.

Claire snorted. "You're sure welcome to go trolling. However, I think my fiancé might have a problem if I did, so I'll play wingman." She drummed her fingers on the table, then added, "Hey, Lex, I was wondering if you've talked to Mrs. Stellery again? Not to segue back to that and bring you down, but I have to ask."

Lexy looked around for Raul before answering. She caught his eye, waved him over and ordered a single glass of the Tempranillo, knowing Claire wouldn't mind her indulgence. He brought the wine, and Lexy fiddled with the glass stem before replying.

"No, I haven't spoken to her since last Monday when we argued." Her hand went up to forestall her friend. "Now, don't give me any grief, okay? I'm not ready to deal with her yet. And apparently neither is she, since my phone hasn't exactly been ringing off the hook."

"Hey, I'm not taking her side or anything. I'm just curious if you've heard more about the jewels or the crash or her crazy search." She reached across again and laid her hand on her friend's. "You know I'm behind whatever you decide about her."

"Sorry, Claire. I didn't mean to jump down your throat. Damn, I'm still so frustrated and upset that she didn't trust me with her secrets. I mean, come on. I can travel all over God's green earth for her, spend her fortune on precious gems, and she can't tell me one little secret?" Her throat began to tighten. "Shit." She tilted her glass and drank a hefty swallow.

"At any rate, the awards dinner is Saturday night, so I'll see her there, at least. Maybe she really will enlighten us with her story. I guess I'll have to wait and see."

She tried to lighten the mood. "Hey, maybe I'll be able to scare up a date tomorrow night for the dinner. Wouldn't that be cool?"

Claire humored Lexy's switch in topics and agreed. "Yeah, girl. With your face, I'm sure you could scare something … ha-ha-ha."

Lexy sneered and gave her friend the finger. Claire tossed back her head, laughing. Not long after, they finished the last morsel of food and settled the bill.

They stood outside the quaint establishment, and Lexy bear-hugged her friend. "Thanks again for coming out tonight, Claire. It means a lot. Be careful getting home. I'll touch base tomorrow. 'Night."

"Sounds good, Lex. Home safe."

The two parted company. Claire walked back to her apartment on West Eleventh Street, and Lexy, flinging the occasional, not-too-paranoid look over her shoulder, aimed for the subway. Nothing appeared out of the ordinary. This time.

Still, let's mix things up a bit, Stalker Boy. She changed her usual route and took the 1 train from Christopher Street down to Franklin.

I'm sure as hell not ready to let my guard down. Not for a while.

Chapter 18

"It's about damn time!" Stacey chuckled, raised her glass and called to the group of friends gathered around. "Here's to the first of many successful steps our dear Lexy has finally taken. Cheers!"

Glasses clinked, and in Lexy's case, sort of smashed, accompanied by shouts of "Wooo-hooo" and "Congrats on getting off your butt and doing something" and "Took you long enough, girl."

"Jeez, guys, it's not like I climbed Mount Everest or anything," Lexy said, her words blurring together a bit. "But I really, really, *really* appreciate your support. You guys are the best! And so is Christian, for giving me the go-ahead to lighten my workload. Woo-hoo."

When she had sat down with her boss earlier in the day and aired her feelings, she suffered a few tense moments. But the discussion had been fair, and he treated her concerns with respect and honesty. And Lexy had gotten what she wanted. Still, the encouragement of her colleagues and friends spoke volumes. Several co-workers had joined her, Stacey and Claire for drinks; their support reaffirmed that she had made the right choice.

Now she celebrated with her friends and attempted to pick up the cute guy at the end of the bar. She ogled him and sent telepathic "come hither" vibes. So far, the vibes hadn't worked.

She swallowed another sip of her tart IPA and blearily eyed the crowd around her. For the first time in ages, she hung out at a pub, laughing and having fun with a group of friends.

But I still need a date for Saturday night.

She decided she'd ply her charms on the guy at the far side of the room. "Claire, I'm gonna go over there and hit on him," she slurred to her friend. "Whaddya think of that?"

She peered into Claire's face, who backed away at the onslaught of Lexy's beer breath.

"Whoa, girl," she replied, waving her hand to dissipate the fumes. "Um, if you really want to chat up that guy, then here, have a breath mint first." She dug into her purse and offered an Altoid. "But maybe you want to rethink that decision and save your skills for another night? You're not exactly operating on all thrusters at the moment." Claire laid a hand on Lexy's shoulder, holding her in place for the time being. Holding her upright, too.

Lexy would have none of that. "C'mon, Claire. You know I need a date for the shindig-do-da thingy." She blew upward to float a wisp of hair out of her eye. When that didn't work, she batted it with a wobbly hand. "He could be the one." She leaned toward her friend. "You know." She winked. "The *one*." Then she burst into drunken laughter.

That did it for Claire. "Alright, girl, you need to go home. And I mean now." She said the words with love and definitiveness. "Come on, Lex, it's time for you to say good night and for me to pour you into a cab."

Lexy scrunched her face. "Aw, don't ya see, Claire, my girl? This is me having a life! A fun, normal life." She bestowed a drunk-happy grin on her friend. "Pretty cool, huh? And I don't want to leave yet." The grin reversed itself into a sloppy sad face.

Claire laughed at her. "Oh, yes, it's pretty cool, this fun life of yours. But still, you are *sooo* going home now."

Lexy tried to summon one more protest, but her effort proved shoddy as she bungled her words.

"Yes, ma'am, off you go, and if you don't text me when you get in, I will ring your phone off the hook until your drunk ass answers and tells me to stop." Claire smiled at Lexy and held her friend's face between her hands. "You got me?"

"Where'za love, Claire?" Lexy mumbled. "Jeez, mon." She giggled, entertaining herself.

"The love's all in my getting your drunk butt into a taxi, that's where. So you don't stagger all the way home." She laughed. "Now say your goodbyes before you fall over."

Lexy huffed but did as told, stumbling through her farewells. Though she drank often, and solo too many times, the culmination of the scary weekend, a frenetic week-and-a-half at the office and her life-altering decision had walloped her.

No wonder I'm blitzed off my ass.

She snickered and sashayed out of the bar with Claire's help. They hailed a cab. With Lexy safely stowed, Claire bent and spoke through the open window. "Text me when you get home, woman, or I'll have your head."

Lexy snorted and promised she would.

The cab sailed down the street, into the night. Claire turned toward the subway.

Neither woman had noticed the tall man looming in the shadows outside the bar.

Watching them.

Nor did Lexy see him flag a taxi behind her. He followed her home. He stood across the street and tracked her movements up to her apartment.

He stayed there until Lexy turned out the lights.

Chapter 19

The rest of the week raced by without word from Mrs. Stellery. Friday afternoon, Lexy's cell pinged when her banking app signaled a deposit had been made into her online account. Though she appreciated the money, she still felt subdued by Mrs. Stellery's actions. She logged into her account and saw the substantial commission, glad it would make a sizable contribution to her new-business fund. Glad it would take her a step closer to the life she wanted to build.

Saturday morning poked its head up with a jolt of sunshine. Lexy, usually one to sleep in whenever possible, rose early and dressed. Last evening's session at SIBL with her small business counselor left her too keyed up to waste the day. A boatload of work awaited her.

After a quick run to Dunkin', she settled on the couch with her laptop and books, a lemon poppy seed muffin and a steaming cup of java. The coffee's scent invigorated her and helped her focus. She packed in several hours of reading and online research before her growling stomach got her attention. As she piled together a turkey and provolone sandwich, she glanced at the clock on her microwave.

"Holy shit. Where the hell has the day gone? I better get a move on."

With the sandwich in her left hand, she went into her closet and started sorting through her accessories with her right. "Thank God I already have my dress picked out. Whoops," she said as a bit of sandwich blew out of her mouth. *I better not spill on my outfit.*

After she finished, she popped into a hot shower, then proceeded to doll herself up for the awards dinner. A quick chat with Claire helped ease her worry about seeing Mrs. Stellery. Even though the call reminded Lexy she hadn't found an escort for the event.

"You know, someday I think it would be friggin' cool to attend one of these bashes with a date. And I don't mean you, Claire," she said in a rush, reminded of the occasions Claire had substituted for a real date. "I mean a damn man. Grumble."

She twirled in front of the full-length mirror hanging on the back of the bedroom door. "But who knows … maybe I'll meet a guy tonight. I gotta say, Claire, I look al-*right.*"

Lexy wore a simply styled dress in a dark teal hue. It had a deep neckline, narrow shoulder straps and a low back. The dress fit snugly through the hips and hung straight down in an elegant drape to hit a perfect one inch off the floor. The dress created the ideal backdrop for the knockout punch: her jewelry.

Two wide, white gold cuffs cut with intricate swirled patterns adorned her wrists. An emerald-cut aquamarine solitaire shimmered with a pure, light blue-green sheen in a simple white gold bezel-set ring perched on her right hand. Around her neck hung her favorite piece of jewelry, one of her own designs. Twin woven white gold chains suspended the top corners of a matching rectangular, aquamarine pendant, twenty-five carats large and firing flares and sparks from its etched bezel setting. A discreet pair of diamond studs—*After all, why go overboard?*—completed Lexy's look.

Tendrils of dark hair cascaded from her updo and made her feel like a Grecian goddess. Delicate silver heels and a clutch rounded out her attire. Lexy gave herself a low wolf whistle in appreciation.

Claire chuckled. "Be sure to take some pictures, will you. I'd love to see how you turned out."

"Sure thing, Claire. And, whoops, I've got to run. That's Jimmy beeping in. He must be downstairs with the car." Her eyes swept the room before she doused the lights and grabbed her purse and wrap. "Off

I go to the Plaza Hotel. Lah-di-dah for me." She laughed. "I'll give you a shout tomorrow, let you know how it all went down. Chowda."

She sailed down the stairs like royalty meeting her carriage for the ball.

Outside, Jimmy handed her into the Town Car with an appreciative bow. "Aren't ya lookin' like a princess there, Miss Alexandria."

Lexy beamed and gathered her skirt to step in. She turned toward the car and froze. The smile vanished from her face, and she clenched the top of the open door. Down the block, she caught a tall, darkly-clad man ducking behind a tree at the corner. She strained to see him in the fading light, but his back faced her, then he turned down the side street. A quick shiver slid up her spine.

That could be anybody. She gave herself a mental headshake. *Just because he dodged behind the tree when I looked up, doesn't mean he was watching me.* She tried to boost her ego. *Hell, he was probably strolling along, saw me and wanted to check out the hot chick in the gorgeous dress. Yeah, that's probably it.* With a bolstering breath, she turned and settled herself into the backseat.

But as soon as Jimmy closed the door, she reached for the Bushmills. *One little fortifying drink should do it. Between seeing Mrs. S. again, the creep-out with the dude a moment ago and the fact that I'm going dateless, yet again, to one of these galas, well, hell, I could use a little liquid courage. God, I really hate going solo to these things. I hope the rest of the guys from the shop are on time.*

With that thought lingering, Lexy forced a smile and said, "To the Plaza, Jimmy, if you would."

A short time later, he eased the car up to the grand front entrance on Fifth Avenue and assisted Lexy out, a fashionable fifteen minutes late. She said farewell and climbed the red-carpeted steps. *Forget the princess, I'll go straight for Queen Bee.*

She walked through the stunning hallways, drinking in the ornate architectural details, and followed the discreet signs past the magnificent Palm Court to the Terrace Room. She stood back from the crowd for a long moment and surveyed the scene. Before her, groups of glamorously dressed attendees mingled about the terrace foyer, chatting as they awaited entrance to the main room. Awe stole over Lexy's face at being in such a gloriously restored, historical space.

She stepped forward, searching out her co-workers, and tossed waves and smiles to her industry colleagues. She stopped for a quick chat with one of the female buyers she recognized from Eleuthera. Overhead, elaborately decorated arches led the way to the main room below, giving her a view of the tables set for dinner. Classic navy tablecloths and crisp white linen napkins set the stage for large bouquets of billowy white roses. Crystal chandeliers flung out sparks of brilliant light and highlighted the ceiling's paintings. At one end, on a raised dais, the head table reigned, the place of honor for the award recipients.

As the designer and boutique of choice for Claudine Stellery, Lexy and her associates would draw a great deal of attention from this point forward. As she glanced around the crowd, that thought sent a tinge of nerves through her. She sought out a glass of champagne, finally saw her boss and headed Christian's way to chat.

Before the call for dinner, Lexy wended through the crowd to use the powder room. *Funny they don't call it a toilet.* On her return, she registered a familiar face. Jack Hughes. Startled, she took a step back before he could see her. *Wow, he really looks hot in a tux. I guess he made it out of the Bahamas.* While trying to discreetly back away, she trod on someone behind her. *Good job, Lex. Why not try a little harder to draw attention to yourself. Shit.*

Jack looked up and strolled over, giving her a slow up-and-down stare. His eyes turned a shade darker than the liquid amber she remembered. She shivered a touch, as if he'd caressed her.

"Well, hello there, Lexy."

He smiled at her, and his dimples did something weird to her stomach. *Then again, maybe it was those two glasses of champagne.*

"Nice running into you here. Small world."

Seeing Jack threw her. Both his presence after his detainment on Eleuthera and her immediate reaction to him. "Hi again, Jack Hughes. I see the police let you off the island." The comment slipped out, straightforward and snarky, before she could temper her thoughts. *Oops.*

Jack barked out a laugh. "Right you are, girlie. I'm a free man. Turns out their evidence, along with some corroborating testimony, put me in the clear." He winked at her, but she remained wary. "I had business in the city this past week, and now, here I am."

Lexy studied him. *Hmm. On the one hand, I'm not totally surprised he's here. This dinner's a prestigious industry celebration. Lots of people attend, professionals and collectors. And considering how he bid at the auction, I'd imagine he's quite a collector.*

She kept her thoughts to herself even as the other hand reached up and smacked her in the face. Metaphorically. *So Jack Hughes is here. The guy questioned in Romel's murder is in New York City around the time of that awful crash, and at the same time I'm feeling stalked.* She shivered and goose bumps rose. *Too freaky for comfort.*

"So, Jack, I don't recall seeing you at this dinner before." *And believe me, I'd've remembered.* "What brings you here tonight?"

"Actually, I haven't been here in years. I spend the majority of my time on St. Thomas, so I'm not usually in town for the dinner. But this year, I know one of the recipients and thought I'd come along for support."

A soft chime struck three times. At the signal, the guests began to move into the main hall for the dinner ceremony.

"Excuse me," Lexy said. "Did you say you know one of the award winners? Which one?"

The triple tones rang out again. Instead of answering her, Jack laid a firm hand on Lexy's elbow. Anticipation zinged up her arm. Her eyes flicked to his to see whether he felt something, too. He stared straight at her. "I think we'd better go in now." His tone sounded huskier than it had a moment ago.

"Um, yeah, right. Dinner's a good idea." She managed a smile.

Jack escorted her into the main hall, and Lexy took a seat with her colleagues. While scoping out the glitterati sitting all around, Lexy's eyes found another Eleutheran guest. Situated at a table a few yards from hers, Evan Maxwell looked trim and handsome in his tuxedo. Their gazes connected, and she threw him a tiny wave and a smile. He stared hard at her, straight-faced.

Lexy frowned. *Maybe he doesn't recognize me.*

Then she saw his face clear, and he grinned, stood and sidled around the tables to cross the floor. The lights reflected in his blue eyes. *Hmm, another good-looking guy. But my insides sure don't do the happy dance with him like they do with Jack.*

"Lexy, hello. Don't you look ravishing this evening?" His gaze scanned her face and lighted on her unique jewelry.

"Why, thank you, Evan. Ever the charmer, I see." She laughed. "Nice to see you again. I didn't realize you'd be among the guests tonight."

"I hadn't planned to attend. However, I got called into town for a meeting on Monday and decided to join the soiree this evening." He scrutinized the full room, taking in the shimmer and flash of the expensive decorations. "This is quite the bash the JIC is throwing. Who knew?" he mused softly.

"Yes, they do it up right, that's for sure." Lexy tried to gauge his interest. "If you're enjoying yourself, maybe you'll attend next year, too."

Evan shifted his focus to her. "Maybe I will."

The tinkling sound of silverware on crystal ended their conversation. The president of the JIC stood at the podium on the dais. As she began her introduction for the awards portion of the evening, Evan returned to his seat.

Lexy glanced around the room, and her gaze collided with Jack's. He wore a slight frown, but it dissipated as she watched. She turned toward the speaker for a few moments, then glanced back to Jack. He still stared at her. She felt the weight of his study, sharp and scorching. Unnerved, she did the only thing she could think of. Lifting her flute, she offered him a silent toast and a wink. He acknowledged with a grin and inclined his head. They both returned their attention to the stage.

The presentations droned on. *Of course, I'm only here for one reason, and that's to see Mrs. S. collect her award. More to the point, I'm here to bask in her reflected glow and to hear whatever story she has to tell about those gems.* Lexy's fingers tapped lightly on the table.

The rest of the speeches had been delivered before the president announced the final honor of the evening, the Style Award. Polite clapping trickled through the crowd. Murmurs of "Thank God" and "I'm so hungry I could eat a horse" whispered around the tables. The waitstaff had served the first course an hour earlier.

"I hope Mrs. S. is quick about this," Lexy whispered to Christian. "That salad plate wouldn't tide over a flea." He smothered a laugh.

The president concluded her remarks, and Claudine Lansing Stellery strode across the platform to accept her prize. Applause rang through the hall. She stood there a moment, savoring the accolades.

A regal air surrounded her. She had dressed simply in a black, cap-sleeved silk sheath that dipped to a vee at the bodice and fell straight to the floor. She wore no jewelry. The clapping died down, and silence seeped into the room. A burly man with a leather case stood in the wings. Claudine beckoned him.

"Thank you, Madame President, for that laudatory and gracious introduction. Thank you, as well, to all of you who support the JIC in its endeavors, and who have encouraged my selection as this year's Style Award Recipient." A smattering of applause rippled through the audience.

"Perhaps you are surprised at my obvious lack of jewelry for this evening's event. Especially since you are well familiar with the outstanding work that Ms. Alexandria Nichols of CJS Design continues to do for me year after year." Lexy exchanged a pleased smile with Christian as murmurs tittered around the vast space.

"Tonight, I have brought along something I would like to share with you. Thomson, if you would," she said to the man with the case.

He set it at the podium, extracted a key from his pocket and unlocked the heavy box. Claudine lifted the lid. The gathering heard a soft collective intake of breath as those closest to the stage glimpsed the container's contents.

People edged forward in their seats to get a better view. Those sitting in the far reaches had to make do with the projection screens placed around the room.

Anticipation shone on the faces of the audience.

Leave it to Mrs. S. She has them gripped.

First, Claudine removed the tear-shaped emerald drop earrings and fixed them to her lobes. She waited a heartbeat, then lifted her head high to give the first viewing. A rumbling swept through the crowd, exclamations of delight and envy. Next came the emerald-and-diamond matching cuffs. She slid them onto her arms and held them upward as if she were the Queen of England, addressing the masses. The whispering grew.

"Thomson, once again."

The guard withdrew the massive teardrop emerald necklace and fastened the gold chain around her neck. The pendant sat perfect against her pale skin, nestled above the vee of her neckline, and sparked brilliant green fire out to the room.

"Ladies and gentlemen." She paused for dramatic flair. "I give you the Rackham Jewels."

Chapter 20

The gathering erupted into thunderous ovation. Claudine Stellery basked in the extended celebration, modeling the jewelry to its brilliant, best advantage.

Holding court, she raised her arms to the crowd and motioned for quiet.

"Now that I have your undivided attention," she began with a coy smile, "I would like to tell you a story."

The remaining rumbles died away, and silence ruled as she began her chronicle in sharp, clear tones.

"A story of greed and piracy, of lies and lost fortunes and of one family's attempts to reclaim their rightful property. My family's tale." Crystal blue eyes scanned the assembly, held in rapt attention. Precisely as she expected and desired.

"I was born and raised on the Caribbean island of St. Thomas. My childhood abounded with accounts of my ancestors' explorations and occasional misdeeds." Her lips curved in a slight smile. "The tales ran the gamut: sometimes fanciful, sometimes bloody ... always entertaining.

"But one story captivated us with every telling, whenever the family came together. The tale of our lost fortune.

"Ladies and gentlemen, I am the direct descendant of the pirate, Captain John Rackham. Better known as Calico Jack Rackham."

An echoing gasp escaped the audience.

"The jewels you see before you this evening"—she gestured to encompass herself—"are but a small portion of my family's lost treasure, recovered at last."

*****

As amazement swelled through the audience, Lexy remained silent and stared at her client holding sway in the spotlight. *I was right. I can hardly believe it, but I was right. Those jewels really are pirate bounty.*

Cursed pirate bounty.

She thought of the troubles that seemed to follow the gems, and worry iced her spine. *Son of bitch!* She shook her head. *This is crazy. How on earth can Mrs. S. be descended from pirates? From an infamous pirate?* Then she remembered her conversation with Matt on their return to Nassau. According to him, there could "easily be plenty of pirate descendants floating about."

This is too much. I didn't even know she was born in the Caribbean. The realization struck her. *My God, Mrs. S., who the hell are you, really?* She looked to the stage. *Well, you'd better have a good explanation, that's for sure. What other surprises do you have for us?*

*****

Claudine Stellery quieted the audience and continued, moving from behind the podium with the microphone in hand. Her gems winked in the bright lights, and all eyes fixed on her.

"The saga of these particular jewels began long ago, in the early eighteenth century." She sent a hard stare over the group. "I would expect the majority of you know Jack Rackham as a pirate. If you know of him at all. A colorful pirate, wearing outrageously expressive clothes. I think it is clear from whom I inherited my interest in fashion."

Claudine raised an eyebrow, and snickers trickled through the crowd. She felt their curiosity, wondering where her story would take them. "Some of you might even know he created a version of the Jolly

Roger flag which is one of the more accepted designs in current history."
She paused and let the quiet engulf the room.

"I challenge that notion and tell you this: Jack Rackham was not
only my ancestor, but a privateer by legal right, unjustly hung for piracy
in 1720."

Claudine Lansing Stellery surveyed the crowd, not expecting
naysayers, but looking for believers. She wanted to engage them in her
story, to make them feel the heart of her tale. To know the truth as she
did.

She stepped forward. Her shoe snagged the hem of her dress. She
tripped and heard a quick intake of breath from those seated on the dais,
but she caught herself. A touch wobbly, she proceeded.

"I have uncovered the truth, after years of research into my
family's history. Calico Jack did not die a pirate in the true sense of the
word. Rather, he died an employee of the English Crown." She walked
along the edge of the stage. Her jeweled cuff glinted as she gestured,
straining to impress her point. "He was not a pirate, but a man trapped in
the mayhem of unruly times, and the treasure lost upon his death
rightfully belongs to me and my heirs."

Claudine held the crowd enthralled. "The jewels I wear tonight
are but a small portion of the cache awarded to my ancestor as payment
for services rendered to the Crown. A cache that has long since eluded
my family's discovery. Until now. I am proud to wear these tonight, and
to say that my quest is only beginning."

She approached the platform steps. Urgency coursed through her
and seemed to hum off her body. She was determined to reach her
audience, to make them understand. "Let me tell you about my ancestor.
He was a fool. At times, a great fool. But he did one thing right in his
life. Before he died, he aligned himself with the right side of the law."

Her knowing glance skimmed over the audience. "Rather like the
prodigal son learning the error of his ways and seeking shelter in his
father's house. The short of Jack's story is that he did indeed start out a
pirate. He commandeered the ship, the *Treasure*, from Captain Charles
Vane and thus began his career. He plundered unsuspecting Spanish
galleons that passed through the Straits of Florida en route from the

Spanish Main to the Old World. He began as a terrible sort, but at the behest of the English Crown, he changed his ways."

Claudine descended the three short steps to the main floor. She stumbled at the bottom and lurched forward, a wave of dizziness creeping over her. Across the room, Jack started to rise, concern at her unsteady behavior clear on his face, but a man from a near table jumped to assist. She thanked him under her breath, took a steadying pause and looked aghast at her lack of coordination.

Lexy watched, surprise widening her eyes.

Claudine regained her composure and scratched idly at her wrist while recalling her train of thought. More even-keeled, she continued. "Jack Rackham spent the first part of his Caribbean career pillaging ships, slaughtering sailors and raiding their coffers. He excelled to such an extent that he drew the notice of the king of England himself, George I."

As she moved among the tables, making eye contact with her audience, Claudine fiddled with the large pendant at her neck. It began to weigh heavy on her chest. Heavy and almost painfully hot against her skin. She ignored the sensation, eager to continue.

"England and Spain had long been embattled. In late 1718, the English officially declared war against Spain and King Philip V, who had been attempting to reunite the Spanish and French thrones under his leadership.

"The war continued, both in Europe and in the New World. In 1720, Spanish interests attacked the English settlement of New Providence. Its location in the Bahamas, along the Straits of Florida, made it a crucial outpost. King George, knowing of Jack's prowess in the Straits, enlisted his services as a privateer for the English navy. He offered Jack a vast share in what spoils he might capture, along with freedom from prosecution for piracy. For the first time in his life, Jack Rackham did the right thing. He accepted the King's letter of marque and began sacking Spanish ships with renewed ferocity, no longer killing and torturing, simply intent on disrupting their commerce and keeping the riches out of Spanish hands."

A beat passed as her breath wavered. She rubbed at the increasingly weighty pendant. It burned at her touch. That made her notice the strange, tingling sensations in her wrists, along her arms, as if the bracelets cut off her blood circulation. She made fists, then rotated her forearms. A blotchy red cast appeared on her skin around the cuffs.

Uneasy, she gripped a chair back. "A moment, please."

A table away, Claudine saw Jack shift in his seat. He hesitated, a question in his eyes. *Good man, Jackson. Hold still. We are almost there.* She had made him promise not to reveal his identity until she completed her speech tonight. She would be very put out if he interfered now.

He eased back into his chair and waited.

A coughing spasm wracked her body. Her fingers flexed on the chair to steady herself. Those at the nearest tables sat with uncertainty etched on their faces. A strange sensation settled over the crowd. People fidgeted and leaned in to hear what Claudine Stellery would say next.

She refocused and struggled to draw a deep breath, needing to tell the rest of her story. *I must finish this. For Jackson's sake as well as my own.*

"But there was a problem. The English-appointed Bahamian governor, Woodes Rogers, never knew of Rackham's letter of marque." She rubbed at her wrist, redder than before and raw around the edge of the cuff. *I will not stop now.* "After Rackham's ship, the *Revenge*, was captured by Rogers's bounty hunters while searching for pirates, Jack and his crew were tossed in jail. Rackham's document went missing. He was tried and hung before he could prove his innocence."

Again, she stopped. Someone at a nearby table offered her a glass of water. Impatient, she waved it away. Her nephew balanced on the edge of his seat. She felt her throat tightening, and she fought to inhale deeply. *I must go on. Our story must be told.* She coughed. "But at last, I have uncovered the proof of my ancestor's innocence. I found the letter of marque from King George. And now, I have found this stu-stupendous collection of jewels you see before you. Part of Rackham's compensation from … from the king."

Claudine's breath wheezed out. She clung to the chair for support. Looking up, she saw her nephew, alarm imprinted on his face. He stood and started forward, but she shook her head at him. "But there's more …. So mu-much more. This is only the beginning of my search …."

Her voice faded. Her gaze darted around the room, eyes glassy and feverish. "There is still so much to di-discover!" she cried suddenly. Then her voice trailed off again, whispery and ghost-like. "To be found …." Her face beseeching, she reached out her arm and rasped, "Jack—"

She crumpled to the floor.

Jack raced around the tables and joined the mob that surrounded his aunt.

"Claudine!" he shouted. "Someone call 911!"

*****

Lexy stood rooted, horrified. *Oh God, what's happening? Mrs. S.!*

She tried to get closer, but the crowd pressed her back. Too many people swarmed around. She stood on tiptoes and saw Jack Hughes hovering near Claudine. *Jack? What the hell is he doing with Mrs. S.?* Suspicion skimmed through her. *God, please let her be okay ….*

Lexy's knees shook as she watched with her colleagues while the paramedics rushed through the melee. They cleared a space around the motionless woman and began to work. *God, this is awful.* Lexy paced, gnawed on her fingernails. To her boss, she said, "Someone's got to call Charles. He has to know. He's all she has …."

But as her words hit the air, she remembered Mrs. Stellery's slip during their last conversation, her mention of a nephew. Christian dialed the Stellery residence.

"Wait! I remember something she said. She made a comment about having a nephew, so be sure to ask Charles." He nodded and turned away to give the butler the news.

At a loss, she stood there, mind reeling. She waited to hear whether the EMTs would give word of Claudine's condition. The throng around Mrs. Stellery had lessened, but Lexy had no idea what had happened.

She felt a presence and glanced around, surprised to see Evan Maxwell standing at her side. She wondered how long he'd been floating nearby. "Evan, what are you doing here?"

"I came over to see how you were doing. Claudine Stellery looks like more than simply your client; I gather she's your friend as well." He paused. "I recognized the jewels from the auction on Eleuthera. What an incredible story." Evan touched her arm and peered at her. "Are you alright?"

She stared at him, mute. Though her brain registered his hand on her, the nerves couldn't feel the contact. She had gone numb. "Um, I don't know, Evan. Honestly, I just don't know."

She turned toward the paramedics and saw them lift Claudine's inert body onto a stretcher. They seemed to move with ease, as if she were light, insubstantial. That thought knocked against Lexy's heart. *Please, God .... Please. Let her be okay.*

Evan nudged her gently. She tore her stare from the medics' exit, but not before noting that Jack Hughes followed them. *What the hell is going on? Who is this guy?* She shook her head and faced Evan, trying to focus on him.

"Is there anything I can do? Should I get you something? Food, something to drink?"

Part of Lexy remained disconnected. She stared at Evan, not hearing him. *Damn, I have no clue if Mrs. S. is okay or not. And it looks like I won't hear anything tonight. I want to go home. Now.*

Her brain finally kicked in, and she morphed into self-preservation mode. *Which means I need to get rid of Evan.*

"Thank you, Evan, for your concern." Lexy straightened and eased out of his hold. She put on her best "no-worries" pose and dredged up a smile. "That's kind of you, but I'm fine. At this point, all I want to do is head home and wait for word on Mrs. Stellery."

He looked ready to protest, but Lexy forestalled him. "Really, I appreciate your offer, but it's been quite a day and I'd like to get home."

She gave him a sincere look and laid her hand on his arm, all earnestness. "Thank you, though. I'm truly grateful for your thoughtfulness." *God, I sound like a simpering fool. I wonder if he noticed. Not that I care right now.* As far as she could tell, though, he seemed fine with her blow off.

"Very well, then, Lexy," he acknowledged. "But if you would allow me to check in with you to see how Mrs. Stellery is doing?"

"Sure, Evan, that would be alright."

Lexy gave him the number to the boutique, indicating he should find her there on Monday and not before. Some habits died hard for a single, New York City woman, despite the circumstances.

Evan left. With no reason to stay, Lexy said goodbye to her co-workers and did the same, after securing a promise from Christian to be kept informed of any news.

She meandered through the green and glittery Palm Court and marveled at how excited she'd been to attend the gala such a short time earlier.

Feels like a lifetime ago. She offered up another prayer for Claudine.

Outside, Lexy signaled the doorman to hail her a cab. She waited there, never feeling the piercing eyes that bored into her.

Chapter 21

The townhouse on East Sixty-Third Street stood empty, the owner gone. The apartment's other tenant had left an hour earlier. A man watched from an outdoor café halfway down the block. He sat for hours, dining slowly, blending in, becoming part of the background.

I can't take unnecessary chances. Not in this ritzy neighborhood. Not when I'm supposed to be out of town. I only get one pass in front of the apartment. Gotta make it worthwhile. Otherwise the neighbors could get suspicious.

Many, if not all, of the buildings had surveillance cameras. He pulled the brim of his baseball cap low. Sunglasses hid his eyes. He'd dressed to look natural on the summer afternoon, and he wore khaki shorts and a plain, dark green T-shirt. *No one should look twice at me, but if they do, all they'll see is a guy strolling down the street.*

They'll never suspect I'm casing the place.

He started down the block, keeping an easy gait. From the safety of the dark glasses, his eyes darted in every direction. He noted small details on the nearby buildings as he pretended interest in their architecture: alarm system notices, security cameras and their ranges of field, a random Doberman eyeing him from a perch in a bay window.

And as he neared the Stellery home, alarm system sensors on the lower-level windows.

No surprise there.

He walked on, nonchalant, head turning in a casual fashion. He checked the distance between the buildings on one side, their attachment to the next apartment on the other. He counted the number of windows facing the street. Everything he saw, he took mental snapshots of. *Something I can use later.*

When I'm ready to strike.

Experience kept him calm, unconcerned. He whistled as he meandered down the block, enjoying his stroll in the sun.

*****

The call came late Sunday afternoon following the gala. Lexy grabbed her cell, saw her boss's phone number and answered with tremors of dread quivering her body.

"No!" she cried into the phone. "You're wrong, Christian. She can't be dead!"

Her eyes welled, and she blinked, trying to keep the tears at bay. "That's not possible ...." One hand fisted tight and painful as she listened to Christian's somber voice, telling her the news.

The once-indefatigable Claudine Lansing Stellery was no longer.

"What happened?" Lexy asked. "Do you have any idea? Do the doctors know? Or Charles?" She paced her tiny living room as her brain raced. Without letting her boss answer, she continued, "Oh, God, poor Charles! He must be a wreck. I have to call him."

She paused for air, and her boss spoke. "I couldn't get many details. Charles was beside himself, in complete disbelief. This is ... a hell of a shock."

Christian inhaled and took a moment to steady himself. Claudine had been a big part of life at the boutique. Though sometimes prickly, her spunky manner had endeared her to the entire staff.

"All he could say is she suffered heart failure. Which tells us nothing, because the doctors haven't been able to determine what caused the failure. Basically, they're saying she died because her heart stopped beating. Well, duh." The uncommon snide remark that slipped out of Christian eased Lexy's tension in a small way.

"They'll do an autopsy, though," he added. "The doctors and the police are calling this a 'suspicious death' because she was otherwise in exceptionally good health for her age." She heard Christian sniffle. "I think that's what's got Charles … and me. She was always such a powerhouse. I never saw this coming."

Silence filled the line for several heartbeats.

"Oh, Christian, I'm just …. I feel so awful."

Lexy thought back to her last conversation—or rather, argument—with Claudine and felt even worse. New tears threatened, smarting her eyes. Knowing Claudine's last memory of her had been of their argument stung to her core.

But she wouldn't weep now. Not with her boss on the phone. Instead, a huge breath sustained her long enough to ask, "Is it okay if I show up late tomorrow, Christian? I'll definitely come in, but I could use a little time to adjust, if that's alright."

"Of course, Lexy. That's fine. I know what Claudine meant to you." He heard Lexy stifle a sob. "Take whatever time you need. And by all means, call if you need anything. If I hear more from Charles, I'll let you know."

Christian signed off, and Lexy curled up on her couch and let the tears go. *Life is a shit-show sometimes. I swear, first my brother, now Mrs. S.?* Her body shook as she clung to a tear-soaked pillow. *I don't have many people in my life I can rely on, and now there are even fewer. I can't believe she's gone, too. I don't know how to handle this, with everything else.*

After a time, she uncurled and stared at the ceiling, breathing slowly to calm herself. Once she recovered enough, she rang Charles at the Stellery residence, but voicemail picked up. Sighing, she left a brief, heartfelt condolence and impressed upon him to call if he needed anything or wanted to talk.

At loose ends, she knew only one thing would help. She called her friend. In the taxi home the night before, Lexy had briefed Claire on the salient points of Mrs. Stellery's speech. She also told her of the horrible turn the evening had taken.

Near seven o'clock, Claire pushed into Lexy's apartment with a bottle of wine in one hand and a sack of takeout in the other. Prior to her arrival, Lexy would've said she couldn't eat a bite. Then the tantalizing smell of Italian food whisked past her nose, and her stomach rumbled loud enough for the neighbors to hear.

Ah, comfort food.

Claire chuckled. "Girl, what are you feeding that thing? Or rather, not feeding it." She shook her head at her friend and engulfed her in a long hug. "I'm so sorry to hear about Mrs. S. Can I do anything?"

And comfort.

"You're already doing it, Claire. Thanks for coming over to keep me company." She pushed a stray hair back into her ponytail. "But Lord, that is getting to be a mighty repetitive refrain." She half-smiled. "I'm sure you've had quite enough of hearing it. Even I have, and you know how much I love to hear myself talk." A shade of the original Lexy peeked through her sadness.

"Nonsense. We do whatever we can for our friends, whenever we can. That's the way it goes."

The women set out the dishes Claire had brought. They settled into a cozy meal of garlicky focaccia bread, zesty meat lasagna and pappardelle in a spicy, fragrant, lamb ragout. They topped that off with a light Barbera d'Alba, a quaffable Italian red, and a fresh baby spinach salad. Though neither considered herself a gourmet, both happily claimed the title of "foodie." Well-fed foodie at that.

They said little while they ate, content with silent companionship. As they cleared the dishes, Claire asked what would happen with the Stellery estate, especially since Claudine had no family.

Lexy snapped her fingers, her memory sparked. "I honestly haven't the foggiest idea," she replied. "But I can tell you this much … there *is* somebody else."

"What? What do you mean, 'somebody else'?" Claire looked as surprised as Lexy had when Mrs. Stellery had let that fact slip. "Do you mean she had family?" Claire cocked her head. "I thought you said she and Jonathan never had any kids?"

"As far as I know, that's still true. Though God knows who might come out of the woodwork now …." Dismay colored her words. "I found out by mistake and was totally blown away. I could tell Mrs. S. hadn't intended to drop that particular bombshell. Anyway, there are obviously other ways to have relatives."

Lexy flopped onto the couch. "Apparently, there's a nephew floating around somewhere. And get this … he's been 'helping' her"— she air quoted—"with this family treasure hunt all along. I didn't get ahold of Charles, but I wonder if he knows anything about this nephew and where he came from. I never knew Mrs. S. had a brother or sister somewhere."

The women sat and digested the news while finishing their last sips of wine. Lexy stared into her glass. Her fingernails tapped a clinking beat along its edge. Realization spread across her face.

"You know what I have to do now, Claire? I have to find out what the hell Mrs. Stellery got herself into." Fire lit her eyes, matching the heat in her voice.

"Why on earth do you need to do that, Lex?" Claire frowned at her. "That treasure hunt has nothing to do with you and everything to do with whoever this family of hers is. You should let it go."

"You know I can't do that. I owe it to Mrs. S." Lexy picked up a pillow and began squeezing. "When I think about the last time we talked, argued, whatever …. I have to do something. I only now found out this treasure hunt had become the most important thing in her life. The least I can do is honor her memory by trying to find out what she'd gotten involved in. Besides, who knows whether this 'family' of hers can be trusted? Popping up out of nowhere looks pretty damn suspicious to me."

Lexy's eyes implored Claire to understand. "When I remember how we left things … this is the least I can do. Mrs. S. was so adamant about continuing her search, to her last breath. What harm can some digging on her behalf do?"

Claire paused and sighed. She shook her head, but, belying her action, said, "You know I've always got your back, Lex. Promise me you'll be careful, whatever you do. And that you won't do anything crazy."

Soon after, the two said their good-nights, and Lexy bolted the door behind her friend. Not tired enough to sleep, she uncorked another bottle of wine and proceeded to toast her dead client.

Midway through her third glass, she boozily thought up one more. Her sad, drunk voice whispered, "To you, Mrs. S. You crazy, conceited, rich, classy old lady." She sniffed. "I'll miss you. And I'll do whatever it takes to help finish your quest."

She chugged the glass and stood, then slumped down when her equilibrium didn't catch up with her body. "Whoops. Hey, sitting here isn't so bad, actually."

She closed her eyes. Barely coherent thoughts flitted in and out. *Don't you worry, Mrs. S. I'll keep an eye on that nephew of yours. Once I find him. Him and any other surprise relatives you might have. You can't necessarily trust those.*

Especially when they stand next in line to inherit a fortune.

Lexy faded away into drunken oblivion.

*****

He sat at the pitted table and swirled the pale gold liquid in the glass he held, thoughts spinning to match. The smell of cheap alcohol and day-old sweat permeated the room.

He allowed himself a small grin. *The old bat is finally dead. One less person to taunt me, to remind me of all I've lost, all my family's suffered.*

One less person stood in his way to the jewels.

My jewels.

His fist tightened on the glass as his anger rose. He still didn't have the jewels. *Killing Claudine was for spite. Retribution. But the delay is worth it.* He forcibly eased his grip on the glass and smiled again.

So worth it.

Now the time had come to finalize his plans to retrieve the stones.

They're mine. He seethed and pounded his fist on the tabletop. *They're mine, and soon I'll have them, no matter who gets in my way.*

Chapter 22

The next day greeted Lexy with a slap in the face. Despite that, she bore her hangover in determined Lexy fashion. She shuffled into the kitchen, rummaged around and mixed up a special hair-of-the-dog, spicy Bloody Mary. *Look, Ma, I'm getting my veggies.* She almost smiled, but being amused hurt.

She squinted at the clock on her microwave and paid homage with a toast to an old family friend: "Here's to us. It's cocktail hour somewhere."

After that, her day improved substantially, and she did her best not to dwell on Mrs. Stellery's death. She went to the shop and commiserated with her friends briefly before closing herself in her office. Not ready to tackle the mystery of the Rackham Jewels, and not sure where to start, regardless, Lexy put her mind to work on the CAD drawings for her current job.

The hours zipped along, and the clock had crept past seven when Christian tapped on her door.

"I thought you'd want to know I heard from Charles a few minutes ago. There's no official word on the autopsy results, but he expects to know something in the morning. He also sent his thanks for yours and everyone's condolences. I tell you, those two were much closer than we knew. He sounded completely lost."

"That's terrible. And it doesn't surprise me. Those two have been companions for so long." She tapped her stylus on her workbench. "Damn. I'm torn between not wanting to bother him and wanting to bother him. I wonder if I should call again."

After a pause, she said, "Hey, did Charles say anything about this nephew of hers? I forgot to ask you yesterday. Who is this guy?" Her raised eyebrow conveyed her cynicism. "I can't help but be majorly skeptical about him. Popping up out of the blue. Right when Mrs. S. finally discovers part of her lost family fortune."

Christian replied, "You're not the only one worried about that. And I said something to Charles, though he was so distracted I got very little information from him. He did say that Claudine and her nephew had been in close contact over the years. And he's a welcome member of the family. That's about it."

Lexy sighed. "Great, even the butler's been keeping secrets."

Her boss looked over her workspace then. "Say, isn't it time you got out of here? Especially after our big talk about you cutting back your hours. Go on now, go home and get something substantial to eat. You look about ready to keel over."

"Gee, thanks, Christian."

But Lexy took the remark as the kind reminder he'd intended. Though her hangover had long since evaporated, she still felt the effects of the last few days and knew she wasn't doing herself any favors by sticking around.

"You're right, I'm outta here. Thanks for everything, though, especially the update. I guess we'll have to wait to find out what joyousness tomorrow will bring, won't we?" She packed up her work materials and grabbed her purse. "'Night, Christian. See you tomorrow."

She was walking through the boutique when Christian's voice called her back. "Lexy, wait a moment, please." He moved toward her with a small slip of blue paper. "I'm sorry. This message came in for you earlier this morning. Will left it with me until you arrived, and I completely forgot about it. I hope it wasn't anything urgent?"

She skimmed the paper. Evan Maxwell had rung, inquiring about Mrs. Stellery. Lexy sighed again. "No, nothing urgent now. He's an acquaintance from the buy on Eleuthera and happened to attend the dinner the other night. He called about Mrs. S." Her hand shook as she crumpled the paper; she would have to call him back. "I guess I'll give him the news tomorrow. I can't deal with telling anyone else right now. Thanks for the message." She gave her boss a tiny smile. "Now I'm really off. See you tomorrow."

She stepped into the warm late-August evening and breathed deeply, glad to be free of the shop's air-conditioned confines. Her mind dragged with exhaustion, but she didn't feel like going home to roam about her empty rooms. She aimed westward after deciding to stroll along Hudson River Park, a short walk from her Tribeca shop. Twenty minutes later, she crossed the West Side Highway and left the hordes of after-work pedestrians behind.

Once in the park, she turned right, then left and back again, too drained to decide on a direction. As she circled, she caught sight of a tall man in a dark baseball cap. She flinched, heart racing, breath coming fast.

Come on, Lex. Get ahold of yourself. Chill the heck out.

She blew out a deep breath while she scanned the crowd milling nearby. She saw several men in caps, strolling through the park. Innocently.

Shocking. Men wearing ball caps on a summer evening. Get a friggin' grip already.

Pep talk done, she opted to walk south. The city had done a massive overhaul of the park, revamping and revitalizing the coastline along the west side. The park had been renovated in phases up and down the Hudson River, from Battery Park to beyond the George Washington Bridge. Sprinkled with sweet-smelling flower gardens, new amenities for all ages and wide-open green spaces, the improvements created a beautiful, peaceful environment with plenty of room to get lost in. Lexy headed for Battery Park City, trying to put distance between her and her latest freak-out.

She moved deeper into the park and found a pickup basketball game on one of the courts. She watched for a while, until a niggle of disquiet crept over her. Fingers of dread prickled her nape. Shivering, she gazed around, hair tossing in the evening breeze, but she saw nothing unusual.

No bizarro men in baseball hats. Her lips twisted wryly. Still, she decided to move on. Though scores of people meandered around, she felt uneasy. Darkness seeped under the cover of the trees where she stood. She looked for open space.

Wandering into the softening sunlight, Lexy found a park bench angled toward the sunset and pulled out the latest thriller she was devouring. Something full of murder and mischief. She laughed at herself. *Jeez, Lex, no wonder you're on edge ... look at what the hell you're reading.*

She dove into the story, engrossed and happy to escape. But before long, the same creepy sensation slithered over her. Unnerved, she looked around. Again she saw nothing out of the ordinary, no one near enough to account for the feeling. The last rays began to die, so she tucked her book into her bag. For a short time she sat and watched the sun slip behind the Jersey City skyline. It painted a stunning picture, blinding reds and oranges slashing the clouds, shredding the blue sky. Muted colors reflected in the shifting waters of the river.

But the eerie feelings returned and marred her enjoyment of the evening. They tiptoed in and wrapped themselves around her like a dank wool cloak. It struck her then that she sat alone, practically in the dark. As usual, she had gotten lost in the gorgeous sunset. When she poked her head around, she saw the rest of the park shrouded in the deepening twilight. A line from the novel popped into her head: "The gloaming crept closer."

That thought, innocuous as it had slunk in, inched along her spine and gave her chills. *I feel something creeping in, alright. Exactly what, I can't say, but I feel it.* A shudder coursed through her. Her mood darkened like the sunset. *Time to go. Before I get weirded out even more.*

She patted herself down to ensure she had all her bits and pieces. Craning her neck to confirm no one lingered near enough to snatch her, she took off toward the esplanade that led home.

A short pathway would take her to the north side of the waterfront park and bring her to a well-lit walkway. The route cut through a now-dark section of the park, where shadows stretched in wide patches and the security lights didn't reach.

She channeled her inner Dorothy, another female who had pondered a similar problematic choice of which path to take. *Okay, Lex, you've got two options: short and scary or long and lit.* She hesitated for a beat. *Don't be such a damn baby! Scary, possibly; short, most definitely.*

Off she went.

Strange how the park feels deserted. Lexy strode along, head up, swiveling to check her surroundings. She tried to inject a light tone into her musings to stem her worries. *I wonder where everybody else is. Maybe they decided to go home for dinner. Or to an early movie. Or ... bowling.* She engaged in a ludicrous monologue to keep from jumping to other, more frightening conclusions as she made her way along the desolate lane.

Conclusions like, There's a madman stalker out there, and he's killing off all the people nearby before coming for me, so no one will hear me scream.

Or, The park closed eons ago, and the Rangers didn't see me watching the sunset, so no one else is around, and when the madman stalker comes, no one will hear me scream.

Or, Those basketball players were in cahoots with the madman stalker and gave him the signal I was here alone, so no one will hear me scream.

Aghhhh! Damn it, just stop these stupid-ass thoughts!

She hastened her steps and approached the main walkway. It beckoned with its bright halogen lights, which cast a weird yellow-green glow on everything. A few joggers passed in the distance, the odd lights distorting them into amorphous blobs.

Almost there. She breathed the damp green air, striding forward. *Almost out of the dark. Close enough that every crunch and rustle shouldn't totally freak me.*

But she heard sounds. And they worried her. She turned to make sure no one had sneaked up behind her.

Bushes snapped. She squinted in the meager light, looking back the way she had come. She saw something on the path, sneaking out of the dark shrubs.

Oh my God ....

She came face-to-face with ....

A giant, man-eating squirrel.

"Agh!"

She jumped backward. The squirrel ran into the underbrush. Lexy burst into hysterical laughter. As she caught her breath, she mocked herself for being a wuss. "Oh my God, that was so incredibly stupid." A shaky hand rested over her pounding heart, willing it to slow.

After a few more sustaining breaths, inhaling slowly, she turned toward the lit-up walkway. A flicker of movement caught the corner of her eye. She froze as she looked over her shoulder. The hair on her neck rose. Chills chased down her spine. A tall man in a baseball cap appeared behind her on the path. He advanced soundlessly toward her, face indistinguishable.

"Holy shit," she whispered. "I am outta here."

Lexy hurried into the light. *Wuss or not, I'm not taking any chances.* Once she hit the main walkway, she threw another glance backward.

Gone.

Son of a bitch! Where'd he go?

Relief and worry vied for top honors as she headed north on the esplanade toward home. A brisk walk brought her to Harrison Street. She waited for the traffic lights to change, not-so-idly scanning the area around her. Lights flooded this section of the park. Strollers and joggers made for decent company. But the trip along Harrison to her apartment would be a different story—sporadic street lights and much less populated.

She didn't see anyone who seemed to focus on her. *No one running up to me, knife drawn and making stabbing motions. Not yet, anyway.* She inhaled again. *God, girl, control yourself.*

The lights changed, and with one last look behind her, Lexy crossed into the comparative darkness of her street. "At least it's only a couple blocks more," she mumbled, picking up her pace. "Almost home."

She continued to check and saw no one following her, no one on the street at all. *Which is also weird. I don't remember the street ever feeling this empty. Even when I've staggered home drunk at 4:00 a.m.* Despite her attempt at levity, another shudder ran through her.

A streetlight flickered, and shadows shifted. *Great.*

Still nothing behind her, though.

At last, she neared her door. One last peek backward, and she pulled out her keys. Sighing with relief, she started forward to climb the steps.

Ahead, a tall man wearing a dark baseball hat stalked down the street toward her.

Lexy trembled, almost dropped her keys.

This can't be happening. I have to get inside.

She ran up the steps, gasping. She shoved once, twice, until her key found the lock. She flung open the door, then slammed it shut. Afraid to look, she closed her eyes and leaned against the door a moment, trying to catch her breath, heart galloping. A minute passed. She pushed aside the window curtains and slowly scanned the street.

Empty.

Christmas, Lex! Now you're imagining people?

She watched a few minutes longer, but nothing moved on the dark street. With a deep breath, she shook her head. *Let's get upstairs and forget this whole evening ever happened.*

She pushed away from the door, rechecked the locks and climbed the hall steps. She didn't look back again, so she didn't see the man standing across the street in the shadow of a building.

He watched her from the darkness as she headed inside to her apartment.

Chapter 23

The next morning Lexy trudged to the boutique far earlier than usual. She'd tried to convince herself she overreacted the previous night, that the stress of the last two weeks had taken its toll, nothing more. But a nightcap and a pep talk didn't prevent a fitful night; she'd tossed and turned for hours. Bad dreams beset her when she managed to doze off, but every creak and hum had jostled her awake. When 7:00 a.m. rolled around and still she lay there, eyes popped open, she had to give up.

Dressing for comfort, she left by seven forty-five and made her way to a nearby Dunkin' Donuts. Extra-large coffee topped the list, followed by a sausage-and-egg Wake-Up Wrap. She couldn't resist the comforting, breakfast-y scent and dug in.

"Mmm," she mumbled to the clerk around a bite. "Definitely hits the spot."

Thus fortified, she shuffled to the shop. She needed to get her head back into her job. Forget everything that'd happened last night.

Her cell read 8:00 a.m. *Wow, something must be seriously wrong with me to get here this early.*

Lexy used her set of keys and pass card to let herself in. She disengaged the alarm, flicked on the lights and went straight to her office to boot up her computer. First order of the day: power through her standing load of paperwork, consisting of the usual nightmare of purchase orders, invoices and follow-up origination details for her current acquisitions. After finishing that, she began refining her initial renderings for her newest client.

The bustle of the other employees as they entered and started their days filtered back to her. She glanced at her computer's clock a while later, shocked to find it was after twelve. She'd made a solid dent in her workload and had kept thoughts of Mrs. Stellery and the stalker at bay. After a quick break for lunch, she'd have free time to dive into the search for information on Claudine's jewels.

She was gathering her belongings to run out for a sandwich, maybe to grab Stacey for company too, when Christian tapped on her doorjamb.

"Lexy, may I speak with you a moment?"

Though he kept his expression blank, Lexy read the concern in his eyes. Concern and something worse. *Oh, God. What new, awful news is he about to tell me?*

"Yeah, sure, Christian. What's up? You look like the world just ended. Or like you lost out on your Sotheby's bid for those Elizabethan pearls."

Her attempted flippancy sailed over her boss's head. He moved into her office and closed the door. Sitting in her guest chair, he rested his hands on his thighs and flexed his fingers.

Crap, this is bad. This is very bad. This is worse than Mrs. S. dying. Oh my God, Claire is dead! No, no ... control yourself ....

"Christian, before you freak me to high hell ... what is going on?"

"I'm sorry, Lexy," he said. "I heard from Charles a few minutes ago. The autopsy results are in, and he thought we should know ... Claudine was poisoned."

Lexy started to rise, but her legs gave out. She crashed down into her chair and sent it rocking. "What?" she cried. "You've got to be kidding me!" She shook her head, eyes wide. "Poisoned? How is that possible? How could they say such a thing?" *This is insane. This is totally beyond acceptable.*

"It's true, Lexy. I'm so sorry, but it's true. Charles got the call from the ME's office this morning."

Christian left and returned with a bottle of water. He handed it to her and closed the door again. She sat unmoving, bottle gripped tight, for a long minute. She took a huge gulp, then another.

"So, how do they know she was poisoned? And how the hell did it happen?" She pointed at her boss. "You do realize how completely out of whack this sounds, don't you? Mrs. S. … poisoned?" Again, she shook her head.

Christian gave her the meager details. "I know this is a shock, Lexy, but death by poisoning is the official verdict from the ME's office. The doctors ruled out natural causes and couldn't account for her collapse Saturday night, so they did the autopsy and ran a full toxicology screen. The ME rushed the results through, in deference to Claudine's social status. The results showed a rare heat-sensitive poison had impregnated her skin. At multiple points." He fidgeted in his chair, unwilling to continue.

Lexy waved him on. "And?" she asked. "Clearly there's more, or you wouldn't be pussyfooting around it. You'd better tell me everything you know, before I come over there and strangle the truth out of you."

He swallowed. "Charles told me that from the condition of her body—specific areas on her body, to be exact—it appears the poison had seeped into her skin …" he paused, shifted again, "… through the jewelry she wore."

Lexy's fingers clenched the armrests of her chair. Flex, release. She tried to breathe. In, out. No words would come. She sat there, shaking her head rapidly.

"I'm sorry, Lexy," he added. "Charles said the ME is absolutely certain. The damage to her skin at the points of contact with the jewelry leaves no doubt."

Christian's words floated through her fog, and she began to process them. "How is that even possible? How on earth could her *jewelry* have poisoned her? Hell, I handled those stones myself!" Disbelief coursed through her.

"That, unfortunately, I can't answer. I'm not sure if Charles knows exactly how it happened yet. We only spoke a few minutes. The poor man was in shock. On top of Claudine's death, he and the nephew now have to deal with the police investigation."

Lexy's head whipped up. "That's right. What about this nephew of hers. Did you find out anything about him?" She wagged a finger at her boss. "You know, that should be the first place the police look. We worked together for ten years, me and her, and never once did she mention a nephew. How do we know he's legit? And now Mrs. S. is dead, and gee, I wonder who might be next in line to inherit." She sneered. "I hope Charles is being very, very careful about whoever this guy says he is."

Before letting her boss reply, she pounded her fist on the desk. "I told her those damn gems were cursed."

"Cursed?" he asked, skeptical. "I know things have been more than a little off-kilter since you've returned, but don't you think that's taking a story too far?"

"No way. First Romel, then the guard and the pilot …. God, and now Mrs. S., too. All dead. All having something to do with those stones." She shook her head again. "This is awful."

She focused on her boss. "But I'm going to do something about it." Resolve hardened her gray eyes and her face set with determination. For the first time in weeks she felt more in control.

"What? What do you think you can do that the police and Charles can't? Lexy, please don't be rash." Concern edged his voice. "I realize how tough these past few weeks have been, but I don't think you should endanger yourself by getting further involved. Please. Let the police handle it."

Lexy rose, circled her desk and sat next to her boss. She grabbed his hand and said, "Christian, I have to. Mrs. Stellery may've been a persnickety ol' lady, but she was more than just a client; she trusted me and respected the work I did. We were partners, of a sort, for so many years. And I failed her, failed to trust her when she needed me." Tears brimmed, and she forced them back. "I feel as though I owe it to her, to our relationship. I have to continue her search, and now I have to do whatever I can to help find out who killed her and why."

Doubt settled over Christian's face.

She said, "And I have a place to start that even the police probably don't know about. Two places, actually."

"Lexy, be serious, please! If you know anything that could help the police, you have to tell them."

"Don't worry. I'll be careful. And if I find out anything worthwhile, I'll let them know. But all I have for now are a couple of contacts who would mean nothing to the police. I'll start there, see what information on the gems' provenance I can dig up. With a little luck, I'll find not only the other jewels she'd been searching for, but the person who'd kill her to get them."

Worry etched creases into Christian's face as he watched her for several moments. "Be careful, Lexy. That's an order." He stood to leave, then stopped. "And I can hardly believe I'm saying this, but if you need help—mine, or any of the company's resources—say the word."

"Thank you, Christian." Lexy's voice wavered, sounding huskier than usual. "That means a whole lot."

As Christian ducked through her doorway, she remembered to ask, "Oh, and what did Charles say about that nephew, anyway? Who is he?"

"Right, I almost forgot. He lives on St. Thomas and isn't often in New York. He's here now, though, seeing to his aunt's affairs. Apparently he'd been at the gala and witnessed everything first-hand. Poor guy. Charles told me his name. Damn, what was it? It reminded me of something funny …. Oh, yes." A small chuckle escaped. "It sounds like that tax firm with the crazy commercials. His name is Jackson Hughes."

*****

"I kid you not, Stace, with a fuckin' feather."

Lexy took a sip from her chocolate milkshake as they walked down the street. They were returning to the shop after Lexy had dragged her friend out for a powwow following Christian's latest bombshells.

"Seriously. All those years with Mrs. S. and nothing. Then down on Eleuthera with him … even at the dinner Saturday night. Neither of them said a damn word. What the hell were the two of them up to?"

Stacey slurped her strawberry shake. "Honestly, Lex, I have no clue. Sure, I can sort of understand her keeping secrets about the jewels and her pirate-family history. Maybe she thought she was protecting you or something. But why not tell you who Jack is, at least, especially when she knew she'd eventually introduce him as her nephew? If he's really her only living relative, why would she hide that from you? It doesn't make sense."

"You said it, girl. And how could keeping me ignorant of her exploits protect me? Besides, I still have serious doubts about him. Between being detained for murder *and* being here in New York while I've had all those creepy stalker feelings … I don't know what to think about him. And now this insanity about her being poisoned? Damn, what a mess!"

The two strode in silence. The day had melted into a humid, gray morass. Dark clouds whipped across the sky on winds that charged in from nowhere. If they didn't hurry, they'd get caught in a nasty downpour. They hustled down the last block and ducked under the light green awning as the rains came. A burst of lightning streaked above them, and they smelled the ozone in its wake.

"Whew, that was close."

"Yeah. Hopefully this'll blow through by the time we call it a day."

Stacey swiped her keycard and let them in. "So, what are you going to do now? I mean, are you serious about continuing with Mrs. Stellery's quest?" A frown wrinkled her brow. "Don't you think that's pretty dangerous, considering everything that's happened?"

"I realize that, but this is something I can't ignore." She gave her friend a quick hug. "Believe me, I'm not taking this lightly. Look at it this way: all I'm doing is some online research, making a few phone calls, stuff like that. I want to suss out more information on the jewels, figure out their true provenance, which I would've done even if this craziness hadn't happened. My goal is to uncover where they originated and if there really are any more out there.

"Pretty basic stuff," Lexy added with a quick pat on her friend's shoulder. "Nothing to worry about. And if learning the jewels' backstory sheds light on who else wants them, is willing to kill for them, then all the better. Mrs. S. would be avenged."

Stacey looked doubtful, but gave her friend a hug. "Don't do anything stupid, Lex." Then she smiled. "And keep me posted."

The women headed to their respective offices, and Lexy dove back into her work.

It was past closing time before she looked up from her workstation. "Son of a bitch," she muttered. "Where did the rest of the day get to?"

Her chats with Christian and Stacey had drained more of her time than she realized. She'd spent the afternoon clearing her plate of residual work for several clients in anticipation of their transition to new designers.

Strange timing. All this nonsense happening right after I get the boss's okay to lighten my load. At least I'll have time to research the gems now. She sighed. *But not today.*

After tidying up her space, she pulled out her purse and stowed her cell phone. As she did, her eye caught the light blue scrap of paper she had stuffed in there the night before. "Damn." The message slip from Evan, reminding her she hadn't rung him. She grumbled. "Another person to tell this madness to. Oh well," she murmured as she flicked off the lights. "He'll have to wait until tomorrow."

She arrived home without incident. After changing out of her work clothes, she reached for her phone. *First things first.* She tried a quick call to Claire to give her the latest news. Voicemail picked up, so Lexy left only a short, say-nothing message: "Okay, I'll catch up with you tomorrow."

Tomorrow, tomorrow. The refrain popped into her brain. *Oh great, who am I, Annie? Christmas! I must be ridiculously overtired. But there's still work to do.*

At her desk she rifled through the recent files to dig out the phone numbers of her Bahamian contacts.

Bam-bam!

She jumped and ran to the window. *God, I hope that was a car backfiring. I don't think I can handle any more excitement today.* She inhaled, held the breath for five seconds, then released it gently.

She scrutinized the block for several minutes, looking for anything unusual, anything out of place.

As normal as it ever is. She shook her head. *Well, hell. Maybe I'll hold those phone calls until tomorrow. That's soon enough.*

She glanced down again at the wavering shadows below her window. *And maybe,* maybe *my heart rate will return to normal by then.*

Chapter 24

The electronic bleeping of Lexy's desk phone startled her from her drawings the next day. Calls rarely came on her office line, as most of her clients contacted her by cell phone. *After eleven. Who's calling this number?*

"Lexy Nichols speaking."

"Lexy, good morning. It's Evan Maxwell." The silky tones oozed over the line. "How are you?"

"Oh. E-Evan," Lexy stuttered, off guard. "I'm okay, thanks. Hanging in. I'm afraid you've beaten me to the punch, though. I'd intended to call you today. It's been a whirlwind around here."

"I can imagine. And forgive me for intruding, but I did simply wish to check on you after everything that's happened. I heard the news about Claudine Stellery. Are you doing alright?" His polite inquiry drifted across the space, tinged with sympathy.

Lexy caught herself starting to sigh. "Actually, Evan, I've been less than brilliant." The words hitched in her throat.

"I'm so sorry. This must have been a terrible experience for you. To have her die like that, so suddenly and so violently. And in front of so many people," he added awkwardly. "Do you know what happened?"

She hesitated, uncertain whether she should mention the poison. *I'm sure everyone will find out sooner or later, so what's the harm?* "I don't have many details, but apparently the doctors believe she'd been poisoned."

"Poisoned?"

Lexy thought she heard shock in his question, but it sounded odd, strained.

"Are they certain? That's quite the leap to make, considering she was by no accounts a young woman."

His blasé remark offended Lexy, but she held her tongue. She knew first-hand the surprise that overcame you when you learned you'd seen someone basically die in front of you. Moving on, she said, "Yes, they're certain. But that's all the information I have right now." She paused. "It's such a blow."

Evan collected himself. "Yes, of course you're right. Again, I'm awfully sorry to hear this. Is there anything I can do?"

Lexy pretended to mull over his offer. In reality, she'd spent part of the morning planning for this conversation, only at her instigation. Because Evan made the first move by calling again, she figured this put her in a good position; he offered help without her having to ask.

Unwilling to dwell on how easily she slipped into an alter persona, Lexy sent a theatrical sigh across the cable. "Thank you, Evan, that's very considerate of you, but I wouldn't want to impose. After all, we barely know each other."

"Don't be absurd. If I can help you in any way, by all means, let me know."

Something forceful carried through his voice, but Lexy took scant notice, intent on securing his assistance.

"Well, if you insist …." she simpered. *God, simpering is for weaklings. And manipulators like me, apparently. At least for the moment. Damn.* "Actually, I wonder if I could pick your brain a little bit. About the jewels."

Silence. Lexy held her breath, unsure whether Evan would retract his offer.

"The jewels? I gather you mean the ones you obtained on Eleuthera. The ones Claudine Stellery called the Rackham Jewels."

"Exactly." Now she hesitated. "You see, I've given some thought to Mrs. Stellery's speech that night. You remember, the story of the pirate treasure and Calico Jack and her quest." She fiddled with a pen on her worktable. "I've decided to see what I can find out. About the rest of her story. That's where I think you might be able to help."

She drew a deep breath and plunged in. "What can you tell me about the jewels and their provenance? Where did they originally come from?"

"I'm sorry, Lexy. That's one area in which I can't offer you much information. I learned of the auction through an acquaintance who knows of my interest in these things. He didn't give much more than the time and location of the sale and a colorful description of the gems. I decided on impulse to attend, but of course, once I saw the stones I was quite hooked. After the sale went to you, though, there was no point in learning more about them."

Disappointment rolled over Lexy in a huge wave. After she had thought of asking Evan for his particulars about the jewels, she'd been certain he would have something of value to share. *Damn. He's as clueless about them as I am.* Fleetingly, she wondered about asking Jack Hughes the same questions, but so many doubts lingered. *Though, if he really is Mrs. Stellery's nephew, he might know a hell of a lot more than I suspect.*

Evan's voice pulled Lexy from her thoughts. "Sorry, what did you say?"

"I said I take it your interest means you're going to actively search for other jewels or treasure or whatever else might be out there. Are you sure that's wise, Lexy?" His voice was somber, dark. "It strikes me as rather dangerous, given what you've told me about Mrs. Stellery's death. It seems quite possible that it's related to this quest of hers."

Lexy chose not to divulge much. "I appreciate your concern, Evan, but I still have to do something for her; she was more than my client. But don't worry." She half-laughed. "I promise I'll be careful, no matter what I do. And I'm very grateful for your offer. If you remember anything that could help, please keep in touch. Who knows what might prove useful."

Evan tried once more. "You're certain? Then be sure to remain on guard. At all times." A beat passed. "I'll reach out to my contact to see if he has additional information about those gems. I'll let you know what he says. In the meantime, please keep me posted. I'd really like to know how things go. You can reach me at that same number for the next week, so call if I can help in any other way."

Lexy, mollified by his repeated offer of assistance, said, "Thanks, Evan, that's really nice of you. And I guess I'll be in touch, then. So long."

The conversation with Evan had taken longer than expected. Lexy finished her drawings, grabbed a takeaway lunch, then ate in her office while she made her non-work phone calls. First up, an old friend.

"'Ello, luv, how's things stateside?"

Matt Aldridge's cheery greeting settled over her like a soft breeze. She absorbed its warmth for a moment, letting it seep in and sweep away the dregs of the ugly week.

"Hey there, Matt." Her throat caught. *Lord, it's good to hear a friendly voice, especially from someone who knows nothing about this madness.* "How goes things in the southern half of this continent?"

"Oy, you know, luv. Things are always good on the sunny side of the world." He laughed. "What can I do for ya? Not that I don't appreciate the random, friendly-chat phone call, but knowing you as I do, there's likely something else behind this jingle." He chuckled again, his amusement sounding deep and true across the miles. "Do you need me to set up transport? Tell me it's not yourself heading this way again so soon. Not that I'd mind, of course, but it feels like you've only just gone back, luv."

The buzz of a boat engine rumbled in the background, and she wondered where she'd found him. "Well, Matt, it may seem that way to you, but let me tell ya, it feels like a lifetime's passed since I saw you."

Lexy pictured the *Kelsi* when she last had eyes on her, as she left the marina in Nassau. Even with Romel's murder fresh on her mind, that had been a better time. *I could never have guessed how much worse it was about to become.* "The reason I'm calling, Matt, is to ask you a favor."

Lexy gave her friend a synopsis of the events of the past few weeks. His random sputtering told her the tale caught him off guard. When she finished, she asked, "So, can you help me? Can you use your contacts down there in the Bahamas—or anywhere around the Caribbean, for that matter—to find out about those jewels and where they came from? I figure you have your finger on the pulse down there, yeah?"

Stillness crept across the line. One beat. Another.

She no longer heard the boat's hum. She tried again. "So … will you help me, Matt?"

Quiet, nothing but static slagged over the line for several seconds. "Matt?" Lexy didn't know what to make of his silence.

Fifteen seconds passed.

"Are you still there?"

What's going on? Why the hell isn't he answering me? Shit! Is he pissed at me for asking him for help? God, I hope not. I really need him. "Damn it, Matt, where are you?"

"I'm here, luv." Finally she heard Matt's distinctive accent. "'Course I'll help. Sorry 'bout that. Had a bit of a problem with the cell. Must've hit a dead spot. All's working now, and you've got my full attention, luv. So, go on … what exactly can I do for you?"

Relieved her friend sounded on board, Lexy reiterated her request. "I'm thinking you can use your island network connections to do some digging into the history of those gems. Not much in the way of provenance existed when I bought them. I'll research what I can here, but I hope you'll have better luck down there, being closer to the action, so to speak. Is that cool with you?" She gave a small laugh. "As I recall, you said something about 'where there's a rumor.' Maybe there *is* something to those stories you've heard, after all."

"Sure thing, luv," Matt replied. "I've got just the person to start with." He paused. "But I may need a few days to beat the bushes. Some of the characters I've a mind to chat with may not be easy for me to locate." He chuckled. "Not that that'll stop me. No worries, luv. I'll see what we can do for ya."

"Thanks, Matt. I really appreciate you helping me out with this. And, hey, please be careful. Things've been crazy here. You never know what might jump up and bite you in the ass."

Hmmm, there's an appealing image. Her mind unexpectedly segued for a moment. *Ugh, brain, get out of the gutter!*

"By the way, I'm also going to reach out to Sabine Rothcoate. Remember her? She's the owner of the resort. I'm hoping she can help too, or at least put me in contact with the estate executors. I turned over all the documentation I had to Mrs. S. when I got home, and I don't want to bother Charles for that. But I'm hoping one of them will be able to shed some light on where those jewels actually came from."

Their conversation ended with Matt promising to reach out as soon as he located his sources. Fingers crossed, Lexy then dialed the resort on Eleuthera. She reached Sabine's voicemail. Keeping the message brief, she inquired about the estate, Reginald Edwards and the executor's contact details.

"If you'd please call back at your earliest convenience, I'd greatly appreciate it, Sabine. And I hope things are … happier now than when I left. Take care."

With a click, Lexy hung up and sat back in her chair. *I really hope these guys can help. I have a feeling I'm gonna need it.*

As she let her thoughts run rampant, she twirled in her chair and hoped for the best. Hoped to find answers to the questions that spun around her. Hoped to figure out who'd want to poison Mrs. Stellery and why. And hoped to solve her friend and client's final mystery. She gave herself another few moments of respite.

Feeling a bit more centered, she turned back to her bench and her remaining tasks. *Jeez, I feel like I've already worked a full day, but it's only two thirty. Grrr.* She laughed at herself. *This is par for the course, though. And hell, work-wise, this is so much better than even three weeks ago. Now, at least there's a fighting chance I'll leave by six o'clock. Woo-hoo!*

She settled in, not quite content to wait for her friends to get back to her, but satisfied enough to give them time and give herself a breather.

All in all, it's been a pretty decent day. Though it's not over yet.

Chapter 25

Charles closed the oak doors behind the attorneys. He and Jack wandered through the downstairs foyer into the front parlor. The butler slumped into a seat near the unlit fireplace, new lines aging his face.

The week had passed in a maelstrom.

Since Claudine's death, traffic through the townhome had not stopped. Close friends offered their sympathies. The steady flow of police investigators began after the autopsy had been completed. The lawyers and accountants vied for attention. In the midst of the chaos, Jack had conducted his business from afar, not having planned for an extended stay in New York. He juggled his workload and turned over the most pressing items to his partner until he could return to St. Thomas.

Thursday evening arrived, and the two men finally, blessedly, had an empty house. Once the coroner's office released the body and the police had given the all-clear, Jack and Charles said their farewells to Claudine. With so much speculation swirling around her death, the two opted for a private service held earlier that morning. Both had surmised she would've preferred that, along with a memorial service for her friends after the investigation had been resolved.

Now the two old friends kept each other company. The only other occupant of the big mansion, Claudine Lansing Stellery's ghost.

Jack headed for the decanters and poured a full three fingers of his preferred Bushmills. He lifted the glass, swirled and inhaled the hint of nutty sweetness mixed with the heady scent of Northern Ireland. A small smile crossed his face as he recalled how Aunt Cee kept it on hand … for him.

"Charlie, can I pour you a drink? You sure as hell deserve it."

For once, Charles acquiesced. "Please, Jackson. That would be … cathartic."

Jack half-laughed and poured. Only his aunt and Charles ever called him by his full name. Unless Pete wanted to bust his chops. Still, "Jackson" suited far better than "sir," an ugly habit Jack had divested Charles of years earlier. He handed the sparkling tumbler of whiskey to the butler before planting himself in the chair next to him.

What a fuck-all week this's been. He raised his glass, clinked Charles's and said, "To Aunt Cee. I'm gonna miss the ol' gal." The words pushed past the lump in his throat. A quick pull of the fiery liquid went a small way toward easing the constriction. "I promise I'm going to find out who did this to you—with your help, of course, Charlie."

Jack studied the older man, trying to get a sense of his resilience. He hoped not to add too much stress to his already overburdened friend, but knew he would do so regardless. Charles could well hold the key to Claudine's death, and Jack meant to uncover it.

"Understood, Jackson. We cannot let whoever did this get away with it. There is certainly too much still at stake. More than even the police know."

Charles stared into his glass, then sipped at the amber liquid. The heat warmed weary old bones. The hand that grasped the tumbler shook, and he rested it on the arm of the chair, lest he spill. "There is a great deal that you do not know about your aunt and about what we have undertaken these last several years. I can only say I am truly sorry Claudine had not taken you into her confidence sooner."

Jack started to speak, but Charles interrupted him. "I know for a fact she sought only to keep you from harm's way. She did not want to burden you until she had learned everything she could. But now I wonder if your knowing might have prevented this horrible, horrible act." Charles's voice caught, his throat clogged with unshed tears.

Jack's heart went out to the older man, and he laid a comforting hand on his arm. "Charlie, you know as well as I do—perhaps better, since you lived with her—how obstinate Claudine could be. While I wish she'd confided in me, we both know that once she made up her mind, there was no way you or I or anyone but Claudine would change it." He took a deep breath. "There's no way to know if my involvement would've altered anything, so don't think that way. What we have to do is go on from here." He tossed back another swallow of the Bushmills, savoring the burn, the distraction.

"So, Charlie. It's time to tell me what you know."

The doorbell chimed, so inopportune Jack could've laughed. The butler started to rise, but Jack waved him off. "I'll see who it is. Stay and rest."

He strode across the foyer, peered through the peephole. His eyes widened, and he opened the door.

"Pete. Hey, man, what're you doing here?" He enveloped his friend in a back-slapping man-hug, then gestured him inside.

Peter came into the main entryway and took a look around. "Hey there, Jack. I had a job bring me back here this afternoon, so I wanted to come by in person and give my condolences." He shook his head and said, "Damn, I can't believe that feisty son of a gun is gone."

Jack nodded and tried pulling his friend in, but he stayed near the doorway. "Yeah, me too. Why don't you come in for a drink? It's just me and Charlie here, finally."

Pete clapped his friend on the shoulder, but declined. "No, man, I don't want to intrude. I've got some business to take care of tonight." He winked at his buddy. "But I wanted to stop by, let you know I was in town." He stepped back. "Why don't we catch up tomorrow? Give me a ring, let me know if you wanna hang. Maybe catch a game or something." He stared at Jack's worn-looking face. "And if you don't mind me saying, you look like shit, so you should probably hit the hay soon, anyway."

That teased a mirthless chuckle out of Jack. "Thanks, buddy. You're all heart. *So* glad you stopped by. How 'bout a kick in the balls while you're at it?" Jack punched him in the shoulder, and Pete laughed. Then launched into his smoker's hack.

After he got himself under control, Peter let his gaze roam around the foyer, his eyes pulling in the details. "You know, this place sure won't be the same without the old bird knocking around. What're you guys going to do with all her stuff?"

Jack looked askance at him, a bit startled at the callous remark.

Peter shook his head sharply, shrugged and said sheepishly, "You know what I mean .... Sorry, man, none of my business."

Jack shook his head, half-laughing at his friend's tactlessness. He stuck out his hand, and they man-hugged again.

"'Night, old man."

"'Night, Pete. And thanks for coming by. Appreciate that."

After Peter left, Jack locked up and found Charles in the parlor contemplating his now-empty glass.

"Who was that, Jackson?"

"It was Pete. He had a charter that brought him back to Manhattan, so he stopped to pay his respects. To us both. I'll catch him tomorrow. He told me I look like shit and to get my ass to bed." A smirk accompanied his words, the grooves creasing his face.

"Ah, a good friend indeed." Charles eyed his glass a moment longer, before deciding he'd had enough. "Sadly, Jackson, there is much we need to do tonight before we rest."

"I know, I know. We'd better get going before we lose the rest of the evening. Another drink for the road?"

"No, thank you. I believe I will need a clear head for the night's proceedings. Shall we begin?" Charles stood and moved into the hall. "The best place to start is your aunt's study. Though it pains me to go in there without her; it feels like an invasion of her inner sanctum." He squared his shoulders. "However, it is where she kept almost the entirety of her research and files. Let me show you what she has found."

They climbed the curving staircase toward the upper reaches of the townhome. Outside Claudine's study, they paused, a silent sign of respect for the woman they knew and loved. Charles led the way, opening the door to her private world. A palpable hush settled over them as they entered. Charles strode to the antique writing desk on the far side of the room, footsteps alternately pattering on the hardwood and sinking with soft thuds into the rug. The subtle floral-spicy scent of Claudine's Clive Christian No. 1 perfume lingered in the air to haunt them.

"I have the security codes for the files, so we will begin there."

He extracted one key from the ring he'd taken from the desk drawer, then moved to a closed door set in an interior wall. It opened without a squeak. He entered and punched the code to the first of several industrial-grade filing cabinets.

Jack stared.

"Her research began in earnest when she married your uncle Jonathan and finally had ample funds with which to launch her endeavors …."

Chapter 26

Lexy entered her office with an extra-extra-large coffee, grateful she'd made it to Friday. *Every little bit helps. And these days I'll take what I can get.*

Tweaking the renderings for an afternoon client presentation topped her agenda. Her boss had been more than accommodating in recent weeks, and she wanted to express her appreciation with a stellar meeting.

After finishing the drawings, Lexy focused her attention on her own "quest." She searched the shop's databases, looking for any clue to the jewels' enigmatic provenance. She also wound her way through various websites, to no avail. Without having the gems to examine—or the mediocre documentation that had accompanied them—her options were limited.

She tunneled her fingers through her hair, then rested her head in her hands as her elbows bumped onto the desk. *Think, Lex. Damn it, just think. There's no use getting frustrated when you've barely begun. Relax.*

Clasping both hands behind her neck, she leaned back, expelled a long breath and gave a light rub. That helped. She noticed the clock. *Lunch would help, too. Right, then. Time to feed the troops. Troop. Whatever.*

She stopped by Stacey's office, but her friend had already eaten. Undeterred, Lexy headed to the Cosi sandwich shop around the corner, taking the long way while taking in the sun. The day sparkled. The humidity had broken.

And yay, the streets don't smell like garbage day after the union's been on strike. I almost feel like things'll be okay.

The rejuvenating walk helped restore her to pseudo-normalcy, so she decided on a to-go sandwich to eat while working. The sunny sojourn had also reminded her of another avenue she'd planned to explore, making her eager to get back. The line at Cosi moved quickly, and Lexy wafted forward on cartoon scent-waves of fresh-baked bread. A short wait for her spicy tandoori chicken sandwich made her salivate. She grabbed a drink, paid and returned to the shop.

Out of habit, she glanced over her shoulder as she approached the boutique. *Nothing out of whack. Whew, that's a relief.* An involuntary residual shudder ran through her. *I guess it was my imagination. I haven't seen any strange-looking men in ball caps for a few days now. Thank goodness.* She swung open the door, and a mellow chime sounded. As she passed through the showroom, the office manager hailed her.

"Lexy, I took a phone call for you. Someone named Sabine." He handed her their standard blue memo slip.

"Damn, I can't believe I missed her. It figures she'd call while I was out. Shoot. But thanks, Will."

She ducked into her office, reading the message along the way. Though brief, it proved helpful. Sabine left the executor's contact information, confirmed she knew nothing specific about the jewelry, but offered assistance should Lexy have other questions.

"Well, it's a start," she murmured.

Her mind wandered to Matt, and she hoped she'd hear from him soon. Days had passed since she requested his help down south. She'd expected to hear something by now, but didn't want to nudge him yet.

He's doing a pretty big favor, and he said it could take time. I'll give him until tomorrow. It would really suck if I interrupted him at a dicey point. And God only knows who his contacts are. She chuckled. *Some sort of Caribbean hooligan or something. I can only imagine.*

Her stomach grumbled as she inhaled the zesty scents emanating from her takeaway bag. *First things first. Lunch, then research.* As she laid out her sandwich and Coke and dug in, she drew up a mental to-do list.

First, eat. *Cool, I can cross that one off.* Crossing anything off a list always perked her up. Second, ring the executor—a man named Benjamin Albury, according to the message slip—and question him about the jewels. *I'll see if I can dig up any dirt on the estate owner while I'm at it.* Next, call Evan to check if his contact had discovered anything further about how the jewels came into Edwards's possession in the first place.

After all that—*and, hmmm, perhaps with my presentation squeezed in somewhere, say four o'clock*—she would tackle the other idea she'd remembered: investigating the mysterious pirate captain, Calico Jack.

Clearing her head earlier had helped. She'd almost overlooked perhaps the more logical route to pursue with her research, that of Mrs. Stellery's ancestry. She crossed her fingers, figuring it would be easier and faster to track down what she could about the infamous ancestor. *Surely there's a wealth of information on him. Surely.*

Lexy pondered the next step as she crunched through her bag of potato chips. After finishing, she reached for the slip with Benjamin Albury's phone number and rang his office in Governor's Harbour. A receptionist answered and gave her the aggravating news.

"Mr. Albury is offsite for the remainder of the day," she said. "I'll gladly take a message for him, but he won't be checking in until Monday. Is there anything else I may help you with?" she offered in an island lilt.

"I don't suppose so, unless you can share anything about one of Mr. Albury's recent clients, Mr. Reginald Edwards?" Lexy explained. "Mr. Albury is the executor for Mr. Edwards's estate, and I have a few questions I'd like to ask him. Concerning a purchase I made at the auction a few weeks ago. Might you know anything about Mr. Edwards or his properties?"

It's a stretch, but what the hell.

"I'm so sorry, miss," said the melodious voice. "I'm not free to give out information about the clients. But I'm certain Mr. Albury will be happy to help you. Especially if you were one of the auction attendees. I will give him the message to contact you straightaway Monday morning." She paused. "Is there anything else, then?"

Lexy thanked the secretary and bid her goodbye, then sighed at the temporary dead end. *Next.* She dialed a new set of numbers, cradling the phone against her shoulder, and waited.

Success came when Evan Maxwell answered.

"Hi, Evan, it's Lexy Nichols calling. How are you?" They exchanged pleasantries in a perfunctory manner, then Lexy jumped in. "I'm checking if you heard anything yet from your acquaintance. The one who told you about the auction on Eleuthera. Did he have any new details about the jewelry?" She held her breath, hoping for an affirmative.

"I'm sorry, Lexy. I'm afraid not. I heard back from him this morning, but no luck." Evan paused and in doing so, gave Lexy the impression that he weighed his words. "Apparently, he'd heard of the sale and the gems by accident. Only a few days before the auction, in fact. He knew nothing significant about the jewelry, had merely heard a descriptive rumor and that the gems were supposedly priceless. He knew I'd be interested." He stopped there. "So it seems I'm not of much use to you, am I?"

Lexy bit her tongue as she processed the dearth of information. While he spoke, she'd gotten the sense he was reciting from a script. That, or he'd planned what he would say when she inevitably followed up. She couldn't pinpoint why she felt that; something about his stilted voice raised the hairs on her nape. *I wonder if he really spoke to his contact.* She decided to test.

"Oh, I wouldn't say that, Evan. But perhaps I could speak with your associate." The smooth words sailed over the phone line. "What did you say his name is?" She waited.

"Uh … actually … I hadn't mentioned it." He regrouped quickly and said, "I'm afraid there's no use trying to reach him now. I barely caught him myself before he left for a business trip to China."

She heard a faint edginess lace his voice. *Annoyed with me for second-guessing him?* Tapping her fingers on her desk, she wondered again what it was about him that irked her.

Instead of questioning him further, she said, "That's too bad. It would've been helpful to know where he'd heard the rumors. You know what they say about rumors, right?" But she didn't finish, nor did she let him interrupt. "Anyway, thanks again for asking him. I have to get back to work now. If you think of anything else that could point me in the right direction, please give a ring."

Before she could add her goodbye, he spoke up. "Say, Lexy, before you go …." Something shuffled in the background. "Have you learned anything more yourself? About the jewels. And about how Mrs. Stellery died. Have you had any news?"

Lexy recalled their earlier conversation; his inquisitiveness about how Claudine died set her teeth on edge again. She knew some people had a morbid sense of curiosity. Still, something creepy sneaked through his words and crawled over the phone line to gnaw at her. She couldn't rid herself of the feeling, so she tried to rid herself of him.

"No, I haven't gotten any new details. About either subject," she added, not wanting to say "Mrs. Stellery's death" out loud. "And I'm very sorry, but I really have to go. I've got a client meeting shortly. Thanks again, Evan." *For nothing.* "So long."

"Goodbye, Lexy. I'm sorry I couldn't be of more help, but don't hesitate to call if you think of anything else. Be careful and … well, just be careful. With wherever your search leads you." A click and then silence.

Lexy threw off a quick shudder at his ominous statement and turned back to her computer. *Damn. After three thirty.* She had her presentation to finalize. The bulk of the work was complete. She'd made the last edits that morning and had only to upload the drawings to her tablet. Still, that left no time to tackle her investigation of Calico Jack beforehand. *The day's flying. I hope the meeting goes fast too, so I can get back to my research.* She gathered her materials and went to set up in Christian's office.

The meeting progressed with one detour, which had Lexy altering her design on the fly for the client to approve. Easy enough and a common occurrence, but when their discussion ended, the clock read five to five. After the client left, Lexy scooted into her office before she could be interrupted and sat down to Google Jack Rackham.

She found page after page of websites jam-packed with contradictory information about the colorful pirate. *Wow, this is a shit-ton of info to go through. It's gonna take eons.*

Not more than thirty minutes in, a knock sounded at her door, and Will poked his head around. "Lexy, someone's here to see you. Should I bring him back?"

"To see *me*? I don't have any more appointments today. And it's almost closing time. Who is it?"

"He wouldn't give his name, but he says he's an old friend of yours. Tall guy, dark hair. Looks normal enough." He grinned at her. "But why don't you meet him out front if you're not expecting anyone."

Old friend? It couldn't be Mike if this guy has dark hair; besides, Will knows Claire's fiancé. Could it be Matt? Nah, why the heck would he come all this way when he could easily call if he'd found out anything? Nonetheless, a happy thrill zipped through her as she followed Will to the front of the shop.

A lone man, casual in jeans, an old pair of Reef flip-flops and a dark brown T-shirt, occupied the room. She saw his back as he leaned over a display, examining its contents. *And a fine back it is.* She spent a moment observing the hard, lean muscles molded underneath the soft shirt. *Not to mention a class-A butt. Whew, Matt, you sure know how to make a woman sigh in appreciation.*

As if he'd heard her imaginary sigh, the man straightened and turned toward her.

Not Matt. Lexy started. *Jack Hughes. Here in my shop. With his very un-dark hair. What the hell is wrong with Will's eyesight? Is he colorblind? I ought to smack him for surprising me.*

Because it was Will's fault she felt off-kilter in this man's unexpected presence. Will's fault her heart hammered at the sight of the tall, handsome guy coming toward her.

Yeah, all Will's fault, damn him.

Jack stopped inches from her. "Hi, Lexy."

"Jack. Hi."

She angled her head to look up at him; with him standing so close, he overwhelmed her. She told herself the questions she still had about him were what kept her pulse pounding in her ears. Her gray eyes locked onto his amber ones, searched them. "What are you doing here?"

"I need to talk to you," he began, and then hesitated. His right hand ruffled his hair off his face, the left shoved deep into his front pocket. He looked haggard, worn down like he hadn't been three weeks ago. Before everything imploded. *Still ....*

"About what?"

She wasn't ready to accept without question that he was Mrs. Stellery's nephew, despite Charles's secondhand affirmation. And she wasn't ready to give him an inch. There had been too many lies, too much covered up for her to be comfortable in his presence. "Why're you here?"

"I called a little while ago, and they said you were in a meeting. I knew I was taking a chance; I figured you'd just as soon hang up on me. But when I found out you'd be tied up for a while, I decided to come down and try in person." He studied her, trying to gauge her feelings. He saw a closed-off, suspicious expression. "I hope I'm harder to say no to in person." He tried a half-smile. "Please," he asked, tired eyes directed at her. "Can we go somewhere and talk for a few minutes?"

Lexy felt herself soften at the sad weariness he wore, out in the open, for the world to see. She struggled to summon her anger and wariness, hard to do when he looked so beaten. She straightened her spine.

Don't be such a dumb-ass. So he's got a pretty face and friggin' puppy-dog eyes. That doesn't mean he isn't dangerous. Mrs. S. spent years lying to me, and I thought I knew her. I don't know jack about this guy. She snorted. *Jack about Jack ... that's almost comical.*

He frowned at her, the quizzical expression replacing the downtrodden-doggy look.

Still, he could be useful. Her mind flew over the questions she had about what Claudine had been up to. If he had answers, Lexy wanted to hear them, wanted to know whatever he could tell her about Claudine's search. *The search I'm going to finish. Whether he likes it or not.*

All she had to do was say yes to him now. But she wouldn't be totally stupid about it. She gave him a once-over.

"Alright, Jack. We can go for that talk. Somewhere nice and public, though, with plenty of company nearby," she added, in case he got any funny ideas. "Wait here while I get my things."

Lexy stepped back and headed for her office, throwing a glance behind her. Jack watched, eyes hooded, as she walked away. His look sent another shimmy up her spine. *Damn, he is potent. I'd better keep my distance.*

While packing up and deciding where to go, she speed-dialed Claire and told her of her plans. "You know, never hurts to have my guard dog know where I'm at."

"You got that right, Lex," Claire replied. "And for that matter, you'd better call me when you get home. I'll expect a full report."

Lexy clicked off and made her way to the front, where she enjoyed another view of Jack, this time standing tall and strong in profile and in deep conversation with Stacey. As Lexy edged nearer, trying to remain undetected—and unaffected—she overheard a snippet of their exchange.

"… made all the travel arrangements for Lexy's work with your aunt," Stacey said. "I'm so very sorry for your loss. Claudine was quite the fixture around here."

Stacey laid a gentle hand on Jack's forearm and leaned in, offering sympathy and, knowing her as Lexy did, anything else he might be willing to take. That thought sent a trickle of jealousy skimming through her. *What the f—?* She shook her head in consternation.

Jack noticed her movement.

So much for discreet observation. "I see you've met Stacey." She nodded her head toward her friend, who stood by looking as if she was calculating the odds on whether Lexy and Jack would become an item. "She's been a huge help with all the travel I did for Mrs. S.—your aunt, I mean. Stacey, Jack Hughes."

Stacey tore her eyes from Jack. She turned toward her friend and said, "Yes, I was offering my condolences." Her eyes, however, said, "OMG, he is such a babe!"

Lexy inclined her head ever so slightly in agreement, but her own eyes spoke volumes: "Down, girl, I know nothing about this guy."

Stacey smirked at her. Jack's curious gaze jumped between the two women.

Before he could comment on the undercurrents Lexy knew he'd picked up, she spoke. "We're heading out, Stace. We've got business to discuss." She cringed as her friend smirked again. Lexy wrinkled her nose. "Business about Mrs. Stellery's affairs," she added. "We're good here, right? You don't need me for anything?"

"No, we're good. Have fun." She winked at Lexy. "Give me a buzz if you're around tomorrow for a drink."

"Will do, Stace. Chat with you tomorrow."

She shouldered her purse and flipped her long hair out of her face. Glancing at Jack, she said, "Let's go. I've got a place in mind. Then you can tell me all about who you really are."

Chapter 27

They exited the shop and headed toward the Hudson River. Silence of the pseudo-sort one only experienced on a rush-hour sidewalk in Manhattan surrounded them. That didn't bother Lexy, who struggled with what to say. She let the wind and the rustle of passing people, the honk of cars accompany them.

The relative quiet didn't last. Jack ambled beside her, not batting an eye at her long and quick New York stride. He asked, "Where we going?"

As if with her acquiescence they had become buddies. *I don't think so, buster.*

She left the snarky voice in her head when she replied. "There's this decent bar over on Greenwich Street. Good beer, cocktails if you're into that." Her raised eyebrow mocked him as the cocktail type, but got no reaction. "It's quiet enough to hear yourself think. Or hold a private conversation."

She led him up Church Street until it angled into Sixth Avenue, then headed westward along Walker Street. Every once in a while she tossed him a glance; he seemed content to scan his surroundings and keep quiet until they reached their destination. A few moments later they veered onto Beach Street, and after three blocks, turned north onto Greenwich.

"Here we are, Greenwich Street Tavern."

Lexy held open the door, gesturing for Jack to enter first. He moved to allow her entrance, but she shooed him off. "Thanks, but you go ahead," she said. "That way, I can keep an eye on you." She let a small smile soften her face.

"Sure." One side of his mouth lifted in a grin. "I don't think I'll mind." He went past her and scoped the pub's interior.

A solid oak bar with brass footrails dominated one wall. After-work patrons dotted the stools, chatting with the pretty bartender and watching the soccer match showing on ESPN. Turning, he saw a group of tables and two-person booths. A low wall topped with colored lights, tall enough to give that privacy Lexy had mentioned, separated the seats from the bar area.

With a tilt of his head, Jack indicated they'd take a seat at the back booth near the window. Lexy followed him, and they sat, squishing into the soft, brown leather seats. Jack picked up the drink menu and offered it to her, but Lexy shook her head.

"I already know what I want, thanks."

The waitress meandered over. "I'll have a Stone Oaked Arrogant Bastard, please," Lexy ordered, as ever appreciative that this small bar offered the specialty beer on draft.

Jack's surprised gaze popped up. To the waitress, he said, "Sounds good. Make that two."

"Hmmm." Lexy scowled at him. "Don't think you can get in my good graces by ordering the same beer as me. Have you even heard of that one or are you trying to play nice?" To Jack's credit, her stare made him squirm not one bit.

"It so happens, girlie …"

She snickered as she recalled her Bahamian nickname. *Ahh, familiarity reigns supreme once more.*

"… I know that beer. It's one of my favorites. I'm impressed *you* know it, though. The way you downed those rum punches and champagne on the island, I didn't peg you for a beer snob."

"I am *not* a beer snob."

Jack smothered a laugh at her reaction.

"And what makes you think you have any idea about what I like to drink and when?" Sparks flared, turning her gray eyes molten. "I do not discriminate against any type of alcohol." She paused. "Much."

Jack watched the fire dissipate as it spent itself through her words.

"Just don't ever order me a sweet, pansy-ass drink—no, rum punch does *not* count when that's all they're serving—and I won't have to hurt you," she finished, outburst over.

Jack chuckled at her, and that started the fire rising again. Before she could go *en fuego* a second time, he changed topics, fingering aside the gauzy sheer at the window and nodding toward the passersby. "You know, I do love New York. Under normal circumstances." He faced her, amazement apparent. "But damn, there are so many people here. How do you stand it all the time?"

She cocked her head, studying him. "For the most part, I'm used to it. I am, as I've recently discovered, one of a dying breed: a native Manhattanite. You'd be surprised how rare we are," she said, half-laughing. "I was born here, have traveled all over the world, but I always come back to home base. It's crazy, that's for sure, but as long as you have the means to get away for a while, recoup your sanity, it's a pretty damn fine place to live."

The waitress deposited their drinks. With a clink and a nod, they sipped, enjoying the smooth, hoppy taste of the cold beer. The interruption gave them the opening to switch from personal talk to the original intent of the conversation. Lexy steered the way, her gaze boring into him.

"So, Jack, now that you have some privacy, and I have some nearby help should I need it, why don't you tell me exactly who the hell you are and what you want from me."

"Got it. No holds barred. I can appreciate that. Hell, I'm glad you're sitting here listening. Here goes." He took a deep breath. "I *am* Claudine Stellery's nephew," he said, unwavering under Lexy's weighty stare. "My name really is Jackson Hughes, and I live on St. Thomas in the Virgin Islands, though I often have business here in the city. My mom and Claudine were sisters. My parents died about fifteen years ago, and it's been no one but me and Aunt Cee ever since."

He took a quick swig. "And I swear to you, the only thing I lied about is that I am—I mean *was*—Claudine's nephew. She made me promise not to tell you. And if you knew her at all, you know how formidable she could be." He paused and flattened his palms against his thighs, rubbing. "Everything else I told you is true."

Maybe. But what a doozy of an omission that was.

They sat there a few moments, neither speaking.

Lexy took a gulp from her pint. She searched his face. "So why all the secrecy, especially over the years? What on earth was Claudine trying to hide? Did she think she couldn't trust me? Did she never feel close enough to me to tell me her secrets? After all this time?" She played with the silver rings adorning her hand, twirling them around and around.

Jack hung his head before speaking. "You must feel like Claudine betrayed your friendship." A grimace pulled at his mouth. "I can't say why she did what she did. Now she's gone, and we may never know. But if she could do things over, she'd do them differently. I'm sure of that. She'd tell you how important you were to her."

His direct gaze sought hers. "All I can do is tell you the truth about what I've learned. Which isn't much, yet. When I got to New York after I was allowed to leave the Bahamas, Claudine started to tell me what she'd been doing. She didn't get far, though."

His comment reminded Lexy that the man sitting opposite her had been the object of the police investigation on Eleuthera. The good-looking man with the husky voice and tousled waves in his hair. *Remember that, girl, before you get all horny again. Held for questioning. In a murder investigation, for Pete's sake!*

Not wanting to give an inch, or have him guess how much she cared, she said with a thrust of her chin, "So, have at it, then. What did she tell you?"

He glanced at the other tables, confirming no one was within earshot, and began. "She said the jewels you purchased at the auction were only the beginning. She believed they were the clue to a much bigger treasure, as well as a link to something of great importance to our family history. Beyond our connection to Calico Jack." He shook his head, then added, "You might not believe me, but Aunt Cee didn't even tell me that much."

Lexy frowned at him. Jack's fingers drummed a restless tattoo on the wood table, as he took several seconds to compose his thoughts.

"I knew some of what she was up to before she died," Jack said. "With Charlie's help, Claudine had been treasure hunting, searching for lost bounty she thought belonged to our family. I assumed it was as simple as that. A game of sorts: research and paperwork, something to occupy her time. Maybe I deluded myself, not realizing complications could come up. I don't know. But I've helped them out when I could over the years, since I still live in the Islands."

He drained his glass. Lexy did likewise, then flagged the waitress for another round. The momentary silence suited her as she tried to absorb that this nephew had been in the picture all along. *But not in my picture. Oh, Mrs. S., what have you gotten us into?*

The waitress delivered their drinks and asked if they wanted to order food. Lexy took the initiative and had her leave menus. She had no idea how long this would take, or if she'd continue to sit through Jack's explanation. She downed a good-sized swallow, at the same time cautioning herself to remain alert.

With a frown, Jack resumed his story. "But what I didn't know is how dangerous a journey those two were on. For years, even. It wasn't until I flew up with Pete that she hinted at trouble. Then she told me she wouldn't say any more until after her announcement at the gala. To me! Her own nephew." He pounded his fist on the table, rattling Lexy's glass. "She felt it would be safer that way." He choked on the words and tried to hide his emotion with a gulp of beer.

A deep breath eased the tension in his shoulders. "I have new info now because Charlie showed me her research, and I started to go through her files. If it means anything, you're not the only one she didn't share her secrets with."

Lexy picked up her glass and stared into it, digesting his words. Then she lifted her eyes to his and the first genuine expression of empathy passed between them.

She tried hard not to let the loss, the hurt, reflected in his eyes affect her. Knowing Claudine had not even told her nephew the entirety of her plans soothed the sting of Lexy's sense of rejection. *That is, if I can believe him.* Her fingers played with the condensation on her glass, leaving driplets along the tabletop. *How do I know if I can trust him? Who can I talk with to find out if he's legit? Charles? Christian?*

"So, Jack. Now that you're discovering some of what Claudine was into, what do you want from me?" She cocked her head and raised her glass. Before taking a long drink, she asked, "You've got Charles, you've got their research. What do you need me for?"

He settled his elbows on the table, chin resting on his overlapped hands. Leaning forward, he pierced her with his eyes. "I need you, Lexy-girl, to help me find out who killed my aunt."

Her eyes opened wide at his bald statement. "What? Jack, believe me, I totally understand your reaction." She reached out, laid a hand on his shoulder and felt his heat seep into her palm. "I felt the same way when Christian gave me the news about the poisoning. But once I thought about it, I realized there was nothing I could do that the police couldn't do a thousand times better and faster. Really, Jack, there's no point in endangering yourself, especially now that your aunt is gone."

"Sorry, Lex, maybe I shouldn't have led with that thought," he replied. "Because it's more than that."

He pushed back, and her hand slid down his bicep to his forearm. They both stared at the contact … until Lexy placed her hand in her lap.

"Anyway, you were at the dinner. You heard what she said about our ancestor being a privateer, unjustly hung. Well, there's more to our crazy family history than that. From what I've read so far, she was after more than Rackham's loot."

He stopped and drained the last of his beer, then eyed the glass, considering another. He tipped his head toward the waitress. When she came around he ordered another, then looked to Lexy. Almost finished with hers, she nodded and reminded herself this wasn't a drinking contest.

When they had the booth to themselves again, Jack went on. "That's where you come in. I've barely scratched the surface of Aunt Cee's material. I'm blown away by how long she'd been searching and what she accumulated. I'm talking, on and off for at least twenty years." He paused. "A lot of it seems like total crap."

"She trusted you … I know that for a fact. And despite her secrets, I have complete faith in my aunt. Which means you're the only one who can help me now. You're the only one I can trust."

Lexy started to fidget under his heavy stare. She grabbed her drink to break the connection. "What makes you think I can help you? Or that I will?" She threw the words at him. "Or that I even want to? And what about Charles? Surely he can help more than me; he already knows about everything." She tossed back the remainder of her beer. "So why bother with me?"

Jack waited as the server dropped off their drinks. Then he blew through her questions one by one. "First, you can help because you know how my aunt operated. I've got piles of documents to go through. She took Charlie only so far into her confidence. I doubt you're aware, but you've done more for her than anyone besides him. And I think you know more than you realize. I figure you reading her stuff could trigger something, get us to the truth faster." He took a swallow.

"As for your willingness, well, you're here, aren't you? Not to sound too cocky." His grin belied the words. "But you're sitting here because you want to know what I know, what Aunt Cee was into. And because I believe you cared for my aunt, you want to find out what happened to her as much as I do."

Lexy twirled her glass gently on the table, letting Jack's words sink in and trying her best not to let him sway her so quickly.

"Next, there's Charlie. He got me started with her papers and gave me his version of what she'd been doing, but for the time being I'm trying not to pressure him. He was devoted to my aunt, and her murder has completely thrown him …." Jack glanced out the window. "I'm worried about him. He looks as if he's been scooped out. A shell. I've never seen him so lost."

He caught himself, then took another drink. "So that brings me right back to you, Lexy-girl. I need your help, and you need access to Claudine's research. Together we can figure out what she was involved in. And if we do, we'll be a step closer to finding out who killed her."

Lexy stalled, toying with her rapidly diminishing pint of beer. *He looks honest enough. But if I start basing my judgment on his looks, I'm in serious trouble. Don't be a fool, Lex.*

She sat silent a few moments longer. Then, decision made, she tilted her head and gave him a thorough once-over. "I have to think about this, Jack."

He leaned forward, palm outstretched to further plead his case, but with a quick toss of her hand, she had him backing off.

"Hold it right there, buster. I want some time to think this over. I sat here and listened to everything you've said, but I'm not going to decide on the spot." *Not about Mrs. S.'s hunt and not about you.* Looking around, she signaled to their waitress and motioned for the check. "I appreciate everything you've told me … about your aunt, her 'quest' … everything. I'll let you know in the next day or so what I decide, and that will have to do."

Their server left the bill, and Lexy hunted for her wallet. Jack was quicker, plopping down a few crumply bills that would make the waitress very happy. "I've got this. My invite, my drinks." She started to protest. "Nope. You heard me out, and I appreciate that. I'll give you the time you need to think things over."

His dark gaze lingered on her face. "But next time, drinks are on you." He stood and offered his hand as she rose from the seat.

Lexy paused before accepting. *If there is a next time.*

Chapter 28

Outside, the balmy summer day clung to a hint of sunset glow. Mellowed by her three beers, Lexy turned to Jack solicitously. "So, what's next on your agenda tonight?"

He chuckled and flashed a smug grin. "You're interested in my plans for the evening, huh? I didn't figure you for the type to invite herself along for the ride." He winked. "Guess you must really like me."

The fading sun couldn't hide her deep blush. Refusing to acknowledge the flush and his statement, she said, "I was merely inquiring as to your direction from here, nothing more." If her words grew any loftier, they'd scale Mount Kilimanjaro. "If you're going back to Claudine's, it's easiest to catch a cab on North Moore Street to take you to the West Side Highway." She wrinkled her nose at him. "Don't go getting ahead of yourself, buck-o."

He tossed his head and laughed. "Yeah, back to Aunt Cee's first, then meeting up with my buddy Pete for the Yankees game. Been a while since I relaxed. What about you?" He wiggled his eyebrows. "Hot date tonight?"

Yeah, with a DVD. "Actually, I do have plans, but I'm stopping home first. That way." She cocked her thumb down Greenwich Street. "I live close by." She started off.

"Then I'll walk you home," Jack offered, falling into step behind her.

His words brought her up short and she turned, almost bumping into him. "Oh, um, no thanks. That's okay," she mumbled, annoyed at her slip. "We'll get you a cab on the next block."

The last thing I want is him knowing where I live. Or escorting me to my front door like this is some kind of date. No, thank you. The second half of her brain kicked in. *And yet, hey, that could be kind of cool .... Great, three beers, and I'm arguing with myself while the hot guy stands there staring at me. Agh.*

Putting some distance between them, Lexy thanked him again and backed away.

Jack saw where she headed—directly into a street sign—and pulled her toward him before she could make contact. "Whoa, there, girlie." His hands clasped her shoulders, pulling her face near his as the tug tumbled her into him. "Maybe you should turn around first, next time you try running away from me."

His slight grin hinted at amusement, but the desire that scorched from his gaze was anything but funny. Lexy stared, wondering if Jack could hear her heart pounding, wondering if he felt the energy arcing around them.

She pushed him away with a hand to his chest. "I wasn't running away, Jack. I was heading south is all." She eased back, this time with a pointed glance behind her, before adding, "North Moore is the next block. Are you coming or not?"

He held her look as he nodded his head at her question. "Oh, I'm coming, alright."

The innuendo caught her, but in her buzzed state she couldn't tell if his comment meant to tease, or if it had been intended as straightforwardly as it had been said. With a deep breath, she said, "Then, let's go."

They reached the corner, the pedestrian flow lighter now, the sky darker. Lexy eyed the cars sliding past the traffic lights and caught sight of an open cab. Before more could be said, she cocked a finger in the air and had the cab at their feet a moment later.

"Alright then, Jack. Here you go." She yanked open the door and grabbed hold of the top, waiting for him to scoot in. "I'll be in touch soon, and thanks again for the drinks."

She stood her ground as he brushed past her. The open door acted as her barricade while she recovered from the latest set of shivers he subjected her to. "Home safe."

She started to shove the door closed. He reached his hand out and covered hers where it rested on the doorframe, stopping her motion cold. "Are you sure you don't want me to walk with you, Lex? Given everything that's happened, I'd feel better if I could see you home."

Her spine danced at his words, at the heat of his fingers curled around hers, despite her brain's cautionary input. She knew she had to get out of there fast.

"Thank you, but really, I'm good from here." She pulled up a weak smile from somewhere and hoped it didn't reveal her conflicting emotions. "No worries. I'll talk with you in a day or two."

Reluctant, Jack let her have her way. "Sounds good, Lex." He stared another moment, then gave her a light squeeze. He slid his hand from hers, letting his fingers drift away in an achingly seductive caress. "Talk to you."

He ducked inside. The cab shot down the street, leaving Lexy staring at the gravel it spewed.

"Whew," she breathed.

With a tiny head toss and a reminder that she shouldn't pine after his vehicle, she moved to cross the street. A glance up the block sent another shiver up her spine. Not the good kind.

In the gathering dusk she couldn't tell for certain, but it looked as though a tall shadow lingered in the doorway of one of the closed shops. She convinced herself it was nothing, probably a homeless person looking for a place to rest. But with sidewalk traffic down to a trickle, she picked up her pace, looked around again and pulled out her cell to dial Claire.

Her call went into voicemail, and Lexy zipped through a quick but thorough recap of her meeting with Jack. She ended with, "I'm almost home now, but give me a buzz if you're up for grabbing a drink tonight. Mike too, if he wants. I'd really like your take on this whole thing. Okay then, let me know. Chowda."

She disengaged the phone as she turned onto her block. Sick of feeling paranoid but not opposed to her newfound vigilance concerning safety, Lexy cast a look in every direction as she approached her front door.

All clear. At least in the immediate vicinity.

Then a feather reached out from nowhere and tickled her spine, chasing chills up and down, raising goose bumps.

Another glance … no one there.

She jogged up her steps. At the top she turned and scanned the street before letting herself in. Near the end of the block, the shadows seemed deeper, sinister. They shifted, stretching and retreating … waiting, almost.

It's your imagination, Lex. Or the wind. It could be lots of things ….

She turned and went inside. Peering out the window, she shot the bolts into place.

Chapter 29

Late Saturday morning did a two-step on Lexy's skull as she tried to sleep off the remains of a nasty hangover. After she got home from her outing with Jack, Claire called from an event her publisher had thrown at Downen Lounge. She had put in her face time, then invited her best friend for a free beverage.

Downen Lounge, long past "It Bar" status, retained its chill vibe as a venue for laid-back drinks. After they'd found a quiet area in which to catch up, Lexy did the unthinkable. She ordered a Bushmills, forgetting one of the first things she'd learned in college, her old mantra: "Liquor before beer, you're in the clear; beer before liquor, never sicker."

At least this hangover is worth it. I really needed Claire's input on the Jack situation.

Lexy rolled over beneath her bedcovers and contemplated getting up for Advil. *Maybe in another minute.*

As she lay there she thought about Claire's comments: "Well, I am a bit leery of you two working together, but as long as you keep your head about things, you'll be okay. He probably should've said something to you about being Mrs. Stellery's nephew, but really, he was simply doing as she'd asked. You can't hold that against him. Not forever, at any rate."

"Yeah, I guess you're right, Claire. Maybe they're both a little slow on the concept of honesty. And sharing."

As filtered sunlight sneaked past the blinds she'd forgotten to close last night, Lexy pushed herself out of bed. Though she agreed with Claire, she wasn't in any particular rush to inform Jack. *First things first. Drugs, then a cuppa tea.*

Once she recouped enough brain power, she hauled her laptop onto the couch. She settled in and went back to the research she'd started at the office: finding out who Captain Calico Jack Rackham purported to be.

Like yesterday, her Internet meanderings produced a mass of contradictory information. *How the hell am I supposed to figure out which of this is true? There's so much nonsense here.*

After a couple hours of nonstop website pinging, Lexy felt somewhat comfortable cobbling together a rough overview of Calico Jack's life. She couldn't find many details about his early days, but a plethora existed on his life after he began pirating.

One topic in particular grabbed her attention. History recorded Captain Jack as one of the only pirates who allowed women aboard his ship at sea. And not only let them aboard, but had them as members of his pirate crew. At a time when people believed a woman on board in any capacity other than concubine would bring bad luck, Calico Jack sailed with not one, but two female pirates.

According to several of the accounts she read, the likelihood existed that the two women pirates, Anne Bonny and Mary Read, were actually both the brains and a good bit of the brawn behind Calico Jack's Caribbean operations. Consistent throughout the reports, both women had fierce reputations as stalwart and bloody fighters.

Beyond that, though, Lexy found the barest corresponding information about the three. She came across varying accounts of how both women joined Jack's crew. Differing tales told of the women's penchant for wearing men's clothes. Some stories claimed they were lesbians, others that they had a three-way with Calico Jack. *Shocker. Put two women on a boat and someone assumes something sexual happened. Nice imagination, people.*

Lexy at last uncovered several facts that appeared true by their repetition in what she read. Rackham and his crew had been jailed in 1720. Both women were pregnant when arrested, which stayed their executions. Each claimed Rackham as the father. *Apparently something sexual did happen. Randy bastard.* Lexy snickered as she shook her head. The two women escaped the gallows, but Rackham and the rest hung for their crimes.

Lexy pondered her finds as she set aside her laptop and eased back against the couch, rubbing her neck. She thought about calling Jack, then decided not to. *Tomorrow's soon enough. I wouldn't want to appear too eager and have him get the wrong idea about our working together.*

She noticed the time, 7:55 p.m. *Wow, it's past dinnertime. I can't believe I got so caught up.* She levered herself off the sofa, found her cell phone and speed-dialed Green Ginger Thai. *Gotta love delivery.* She sighed in appreciation.

Hours later, after a Thai feast and a movie marathon, Lexy readied for bed, a task made easier because she hadn't gotten out of her pj's. Staring in the mirror as she brushed her teeth, her mind wandered to what she'd learned earlier.

That's some crazy shit about Rackham and those women pirates. Hard to believe they escaped hanging because he'd gotten them both pregnant. So they said.

She rinsed and spat, then studied her reflection again.

I wonder if one of those kids is who Mrs. S.'s lineage draws from. Wouldn't that be a kick in the ass? I think that's exactly where I start looking tomorrow.

Chapter 30

Silence cloaked him as he crept through the window of the darkened home. He waited a beat to ensure the clipped wires and bypassed security system didn't sound an alarm. His assessment had been right. *Old woman, old-school security.* He breathed in the posh, stuffy scent of the Upper East Side mansion.

Time to get to work.

The floor plan came back to him as he skimmed through the downstairs parlor. The prize he sought lay on the second floor, in the master suite.

Adrenaline charged through his veins. He struggled to control his excitement.

Soon. He took a deep breath as he visualized his next step. *Soon I'll have it ....*

He climbed the stairs, freezing at a shrill squeak. His eyes flashed around him.

No movement.

Slinking down the hall he let his gaze roam the priceless artwork, but nothing diverted him. Outside the entrance to where his treasure lay, he paused and listened for any disturbance.

Nothing.

The door sighed as he opened it. Moving with assurance, he crossed the room. Anticipation tore through him, his fingers jittery with the hype.

He eased forward to examine a cabinet lock.

Tricky bitch. Old alarm system, but digital security for the files. His hand clenched into a fist. *That won't stop me.*

Minutes passed before the drawer slid open. He started to hunt through the first compartment. Not finding what he wanted, he moved to another.

It's gotta be here. Somewhere.

His sixth sense began whispering. He started to rush. One corner of his mind reviewed his escape route while he raced to find what he had come for.

In the minimal glow from his flashlight, he rummaged through the contents of the cabinet. Behind him, something creaked.

He shot a glance over his shoulder.

Nothing there … yet.

He seethed with frustration.

Gotta get what I can and get out. Now.

He grabbed and shoved folders into his bag. Then he ran to the door and peeked out. Something moved down the hall. He slithered through the opening and headed for the stairs.

Someone charged him from behind. "Stop, you son of a bitch!"

A hair's breadth in front, the thief skated through a grasp near the top of the steps.

Made it! He sprinted down.

Curses pealed through the air as the other man slipped and barely caught himself from tumbling down the stairs.

The thief dashed through the darkness of the parlor and out the window he had entered, staying clear of the well-lit front door.

Shit! What the fuck happened?

He didn't have time to dawdle. Glancing wildly left, right, he saw the flickering lights of an approaching police car. He knew his way around and slipped between the buildings, through the path in the shrubbery he'd created when he first had been there.

Dodging into the night, he let himself breathe as he neared the path's exit onto the next block.

Too fuckin' close. Damn that Stellery!

Expletives screamed through his brain as he melted into the night.

Retribution will come. I'll see to it.

Chapter 31

Damn subways. I can't believe how long that took. That was supposed to be a quick run, and now I've wasted most of the day.

Lexy arrived home near 4:00 p.m., after spending the day tackling neglected errands. She gulped down a turkey and avocado sandwich and settled onto the couch with her laptop and phone. She dialed the Stellery residence, expecting to hear Charles's voice. A busy signal buzzed in her ear. *Huh? Since when do people still have busy signals?* Positive she'd misdialed, she rang again and heard the *zzzz* of a busy tone. *How bizarre.*

Jack had given her his number the other night. She called his cell, only to be foiled again. *Grrr, voicemail.* She left a brief message, then returned to her computer. *Time for a little more digging into the two-timing Calico Jack.*

An hour passed before he returned her call. "Lexy, Jack here." His voice sounded brittle.

"Jack, hey. Thanks for getting back to me." She paused. "How is everything?"

He snorted. "Let's just say, pretty crappy. Again." She heard anger sizzling in his words. "We got robbed last night."

"What?" she cried as her hand tightened on the phone. "Are you serious? Are you and Charles okay? What the hell happened?"

"We're both fine, but Charlie is scared shitless. How much more does the poor guy have to endure? What a fuck-all thing to happen, after everything else."

He took a steadying breath. "It happened around three thirty this morning. The thief broke in through a parlor window. He cut the wires, disabled the sensors and disengaged the security system at the control panel. But he didn't know Claudine had upgraded the setup. She had a secondary system installed on a different platform. That system tripped a silent alarm, and the police arrived within minutes."

"Oh my God, Jack. Thank goodness they came quickly and you guys weren't hurt. Anything could have happened if you ran into the burglar before the police got there."

Her heart raced at the thought of him hurt. Catching herself, she held her breath to quell her reaction. *Or Charles, too. Either of them injured would be terrible.*

"Yeah, well, anything almost did happen," he bit out. "Something woke me up. Intuition, maybe? Or a noise? No clue. I listened at my door, then saw someone leave my aunt's rooms. I chased the bastard, but I tripped on the damn hall rug and almost pitched myself down the stairs. The son of a bitch got away."

The fury in his voice rang clear. *At himself, I'd imagine, almost as much as at the intruder.* She let out a whoosh of air and said, "Good Lord, Jack! You took a huge risk following him. Thank God nothing worse happened."

She shook her head to dislodge the instantaneous, gut-wrenching image of a crumpled, broken Jack lying on the floor of the front hall. Another breath. "But what about the police? You said they got there within minutes. They didn't catch the guy?"

"No dice. Seems our robber friend had been here before and done some groundwork. He left the same way he came in, because he'd cleared a path between the hedges that border our property. He sneaked away without the police noticing. Son of a bitch!" he yelled again, and Lexy heard the smack of a fist on some unlucky object. "That bastard's been here more than once, and I had no idea."

"Oh, Jack, come on now." She tried to reason. "I know you're pissed off, but how on earth could you have known? Give yourself a break, okay?" She paused as another thought reached her brain. "What was stolen? With you and the police there so fast, did he take anything?"

On the other end of the line, Lexy heard another indrawn breath, Jack trying to calm himself.

"The news is mixed. He didn't get any of her jewelry or artwork or antiques, which is fantastic, to say the least. The bad part? Looks like he went straight for her research about Rackham and started grabbing."

Lexy's quick inhalation conveyed her shock.

"He knew exactly where to find the cabinets with her records. Which is driving me crazy because who else besides me and Charlie could possibly know that?" Sounds of frustration and impatience flew across the connection. "Who the fuck could've been behind this? And what the hell did they expect to find in her papers?"

Lexy switched ears with the phone. "Do you know what he took? I mean, exactly. The other day it sounded like you hadn't gotten very far with the paperwork, so can you even tell what's missing?"

"No. And I don't know if I'll be able to, either. Most of Aunt Cee's things are ridiculously organized; that probably doesn't surprise you. But I swear she must've used some kind of made-up filing system or code to hide what she was doing with her research. I only got through a small portion of the material before the break-in. It was all over the place, nothing in chronological order. So that's something else I have to figure out.

"He ransacked the drawers. If I had to guess, I'd say he knew the files were important, but since he couldn't take it all, he tried to grab a little of everything. It doesn't seem like he knew her filing system, but at this point, who the hell knows."

Jack cursed under his breath. "It's a mess in there. I spent the day dealing with the police and the security company. I'm still waiting for their people to finish the on-site repairs, but I wanted to call you back."

"Well," Lexy said, "at least I can give you some good news. I've decided to help you. That's why I called earlier." Eagerness filled her voice. "With this quest of yours? I'm your girl." The words slid out before she could catch them, and she cringed at her Freudian slip.

Jack hesitated. The silence lasted long enough for Lexy to wonder if their connection had been cut off. "Jack? Are you still there? Did you hear what I said?"

"Yeah, yeah, I'm here, Lex." Another weighty pause. "But …." He sighed. "With the robbery now, maybe you shouldn't get involved in this mess. Things could get even more dangerous."

"Are you friggin' kidding me?" She jumped from the sofa and stormed at him. "I feel like I'm already up to my eyeballs in this bullshit. Don't forget, you're the one who came to me for help … despite lying to my face from the moment I met you. Don't think for one second that you can ditch me now. I'm going to help, and you're going to have to deal with it!" Ire poured out as Lexy paced her living room. "Of all the—"

"Okay, okay," he cut in before she could continue her rant. His light laugh sounded over the line. "You're in, woman, and damn, can you heat up fast. I guess it's good you're on my side."

He laughed again at her quick, insulted inhalation.

Then he sobered. "But I'm serious. Whoever's doing this isn't done yet. And now it's clear he's willing to risk himself to get whatever he's after. Which makes him one crazy, dangerous son of a bitch. We've got to be damn careful what we do from here on out. Got that?"

"Damn straight, I do. I have no desire for bodily injury, but I sure as hell want to get to the bottom of whatever Mrs. S. started. So, when do we begin?"

"Let's table this for today while the security guys finish up here. It's almost dinner anyway. I'd rather get a jump on things tomorrow. Any chance you can cut out of work early to come by and start reviewing stuff?"

Lexy chuckled. "That shouldn't be a problem. My boss is cool, and anyway, we're often off-site with our clients, so coming and going's no big deal."

She still paced around her apartment, thoughtful now and twirling a long strand of hair. "Hey, I have another question. Where are the jewels? I've been dying to get my hands on them—uh, shit! Very poor choice of words, Jack. Sorry …." She grimaced.

"So, umm, anyway … I've wanted to examine them at the shop since Eleuthera. Claudine changed the plans mid-flight, literally, and I haven't fully inspected them. We have two types of spectrometer, which would give a thorough analysis of the stones' makeup. I'd really like to have a close look at them to see what I can learn about their provenance. That should give us another clue to their origin and previous owners, or at least substantiate whatever documentation your aunt may've found."

"Yeah, wouldn't that be handy?" Sarcasm filled Jack's grumbling voice. "Too bad the jewelry is still in police custody. They confirmed the jewels were the vehicles for the poison that killed Aunt Cee, but of course, since the investigation's still open, there's no way they'll turn them over to me or Charlie. Sorry, Lex, no joy on that end."

"That's to be expected." She sighed. "Annoying, but not surprising. Right, then." She brought the conversation around and said, "I'll be there tomorrow by two thirty or three, latest. We'll start wherever you left off, see if we can determine how the hell she organized everything."

She paused, and her hand tensed slightly on the phone. "You should know, I've also started my own search into the jewels and their history. Nothing crazy. Some online research into Rackham, also a few inquiries to friends who live in the Caribbean." Her voice trailed as she waited for Jack's reaction.

"Excellent." He said it with a small laugh, and Lexy expelled the breath she'd held.

"I guess I'm not surprised you took the initiative. Aunt Cee always said you were feisty. Alright then, have at it and bring along whatever info you find."

"You're on, Jack. Until tomorrow."

She sat down to think. *Now, do I try checking in with Matt or wait for him to call with any leads? Damn it, I hate waiting.*

Not content to sit still, she went into the kitchen and poured a glass of Malbec. *Mmmm, a yummy, little pre-dinner drink.* She paced again and her mind wandered back to Matt. *It's already been a few days.*

Most likely I won't be interrupting much on a Sunday evening .... Aw, hell, I'll call.

She did, irritated when his voicemail answered instead of him. After leaving a short message, she hung up.

Lexy knew she wouldn't fare any better with her other contacts that night. Thinking about them brought Evan to mind, and an involuntary shudder slicked up her spine. *He certainly wasn't much help. Besides, I have no desire to talk to him anytime soon. Something about him creeps me out.*

"Damn it all."

One option remained. With the glass of wine at her elbow, Lexy dug into her research. Before long, she got lost in the gallivanting and grisly lives of the pirates of the Caribbean.

Chapter 32

"So, what gives? Why're you leaving early?" Stacey asked over sandwiches in Lexy's office the following lunchtime. "Not that you have to tell me, I'm just being nosy." She winked and took a bite of chicken salad. "Anything new and exciting going on?"

Lexy chuckled and choked simultaneously, then coughed up a bit of PB&J. She knew what her friend was angling for … information about a certain handsome nephew who had recently entered their lives. Lexy humored her.

"Actually, Stace, I'm seeing Jack Hughes this afternoon. Nothing crazy or exciting, but after we spoke Friday I agreed to collaborate with him, so to speak. We're going to figure out what Mrs. S. had been involved in all these years. We'll start to review her research files today. And I'm bringing printouts of anything relevant I found online, along with a couple books I picked up."

She bit into her sandwich, chewed, then added, "Really, pretty tame stuff, considering. A bunch of research into the jewels and the family's history." She wiped her mouth and took a swig of water to alleviate her peanut breath.

Stacey chuckled. "You mean to tell me you decided to help him out of the goodness of your heart? And that seeing him Friday did nothing to get your panties in a twist?" She snickered. "'Collaborate,' my ass! I'd like to 'collaborate' with him, alright." She gave a sly grin. "Talk about family jewels. I bet his are rock solid, Lex. You'd have to be dead not to notice."

Lexy, used to her friend's tacky, irreverent humor, pretended offense and replied, "Lord, Stace! He's Claudine's nephew, for Pete's sake. I'm helping him out." She chewed another bite and admitted in a mumble, "But I don't think I'd mind 'collaborating' with him either." And she suffered her friend's cackle.

Stacey sobered after a moment. "So does this mean you believe him now? That he really is her nephew?"

Lexy had clued in Stacey to her doubts about Jack's legitimacy early on. She tapped her fingers on her desk as she replied. "I think so, Stace. I guess I wanted to believe him from the start, but I was so shocked and hurt that Mrs. S. would keep something like that from me. Charles swears by him too, and he certainly has legal proof he's her nephew. Besides having a very convincing way about him." A corner of her mouth eased up in a wry smile.

"I hope I'm doing the right thing by trusting him, but I really don't see any other option." She ticked off the hurdles on her fingers. "The police still have the jewels, I'm running into all sorts of convoluted information online, I haven't heard back from either Matt or the executor from Eleuthera. I'm pretty much at a standstill. And he has access to all her files." She paused. "Almost all her files."

Her recounting of Sunday morning's burglary left Stacey shaking her head in disbelief.

"I'll head over there this afternoon, and we'll start going through her stuff. Jack said it looked like she had a strange system for filing, like she'd used some sort of code to make it difficult for anyone to discover what she'd been doing. All I can say is, it should be interesting to get my hands on that material."

She crumpled her napkin and shot a three-pointer into the wastebasket. "She shoots, she scores!"

"I'll say she scores." Stacey sniggered, again teasing her friend. "Maybe you should try getting your hands on something else while you're there. Or should I say some*one* else? Girl, you've been way too stressed lately, and there's a certain islander in that house who could be exactly what the doctor ordered." She laughed as Lexy made a face at her. "Just sayin'...." And she winked.

"Christmas, Stace, that's exactly what I *don't* need right now." But she laughed with her friend, and the idea lodged in her brain. "Go on now, get outta here. I've got things to finish before I can scoot. Catch you later."

*****

"Are you for real, Jack?" Bewilderment layered Lexy's voice an hour later. "I thought you were going to clean up the mess after we spoke. This looks like a paper shredder exploded." Hands on her hips, she swiveled and took in the piles of papers lying everywhere about Mrs. Stellery's study.

"Hey now, girlie, I put a lot of effort into this." He looked hurt until she raised an eyebrow at him. "Okay, not that much effort." His dimples flashed at her. "But there's a method to my madness. I pulled everything out of the cabinet and separated the files according to their dividers. I figure we get a better sense of how her system works with the first drawer's contents spread out in order. I put the labeled tabs on top of each pile. Not sure they'll be of much use, but they might give us a clue how she organized stuff. And we might see a pattern once we go through the other drawers. Sound alright?" He shoved both hands in his pockets, as if anxious for her approval.

She patted her bottom and chuckled. "I'm glad I wore jeans, since it looks like we're copping a squat on the floor. Yeah, that works. Not a bad idea, given how you described her system. We each take a pile, use the tab info for a quick idea of what's supposed to be there, then jump in." She took a deep breath, plopped down cross-legged and reached for the first batch. "Shall we?"

Twenty minutes in, Jack raised his head and asked, "Hey, what about that research you were gonna bring? Should we take a look before we get bogged down here? Going through your stuff's gotta be quicker than this."

"Oh, you're right. I totally forgot." She shook her head, surprised at how easily Mrs. Stellery's files had diverted her. "I have everything, and yeah, it'll be faster to flip through that than all this." She dug a sheaf of papers out of her tote and dropped the stack into Jack's waiting hand. "I'll give you the overview."

She proceeded with what she'd found online, along with her take on how true—or untrue—the majority of it had struck her. She finished with what she felt was the most pertinent find.

"Apparently, when the crew was arrested near Jamaica in November of 1720, the two women pirates living aboard the *Revenge* and marauding with Calico Jack escaped the gallows by 'pleading their bellies,' as several reports put it. That is, by claiming pregnancy. That's all well and good, until you learn they both claimed they were pregnant by Jack Rackham. Cheeky bastard," she added in an aside.

"So perhaps that's the start—or maybe the end?—of Mrs. S.'s ancestral search. Maybe she traced you guys back to one of those women pirates who figured so predominantly in Calico Jack's life. Though God knows, he could've been planting his thing everywhere." Lexy took the pile back and flipped through a few pages, pointing out various references. "Part of the problem I've found with all this online stuff is the huge disparity between the information on the different sites."

She handed the papers back to him, then retrieved a book from her bag. She turned to the page she'd marked. "This book, as far as I can tell, seems factual and is vetted to a degree by its publication. If we can rely on it at all, it says—despite how unlikely it sounds—that Rackham claimed to have only three loves in his entire life: Anne Bonny, Mary Read—those were the pirates, of course—and the sea." She looked up at Jack. "So that *could* make a case for him not siring a million kids throughout the Caribbean.

"And here," she said, and leafed again, "this is relevant, too. Even though they were arrested near the end of hurricane season, a massive storm struck the islands. The *Revenge* hadn't been unloaded by then, and supposedly the bulk of the treasure and the ship itself were lost at sea."

Her eyes sparked with anticipation. Jack grinned, his dimples flipping her insides. His excitement matched hers.

"Sounds like there's more treasure out there, Lex. Guess we'd best dive on into this pile of paper Aunt Cee left us, and see what we can uncover, yeah?"

"You got that right. But Jack, did any of this ring a bell with you? I know you've barely brushed the surface of this stuff, but do you recall seeing any references to the women pirates or this shipwreck? 'Cause if so, maybe that's where we should start our search. I hope it's not jumping the gun, but this is a massive amount of work. Without knowing how it's sorted, well, this could take a while."

"Hang on. I'm not sure, but I might've seen something about women pirates. I have an idea." He sat on his haunches, rubbing his hands on his thighs as his gaze roved the stacks.

The motion distracted her. *Down, girl.*

Without elaborating, Jack glommed onto a pile, leaving Lexy to her own devices. She sighed, crossed her fingers and began to read.

Chapter 33

Thirty minutes flew by, with Lexy no clearer on the organization of the files and with no "Aha!" moments from Jack. In the quiet the "friendly-call" calypso melody of her cell jangled above the paper shuffles, and both of them jumped. Lexy snatched the phone. She looked at the display, smiled and answered.

"Matt! How are you?"

"Ah, Lexy my luv, good to hear ya voice. I'm well, of course. How've you been getting on?" The blended English-Caribbean burr sounded smooth in her ear.

"I'm doing alright. Better now that you've called me back, finally. I had to straitjacket myself to keep from pestering you with a dozen check-in calls." She sent Jack a look and a thumbs-up. "So, what gives? You have news for me, yes? Tell me, Matt, and tell me now, sir, before I fly back to your lovely islands and wrangle it out of you." She laughed as she said it, but Matt recognized the underlying tone and knew not to delay.

Instead, he chuckled.

"Well, luv, I knew you were hot for information on your pirate there, but I didn't realize you'd jump down my throat for it. Oy, give a man some mind, would ya? It takes a fair bit of time in these parts to piece together viable info. You wouldn't want me telling you no lies, now would ya?" He laughed again, and Lexy knew he enjoyed tweaking her. When she held silent, he continued. "Right, then. I discovered something about your Cap'n Jack that you might find very intriguing. Care to hear?"

Shaking her head in mild frustration, she exhaled deeply through her nose and said pleasantly, "But of course, kind sir. Do tell what you've learned."

She heard her friend's deep, laughing rumble. "But wait a sec." Back to form, she said, "I'm with Claudine's nephew, Jack—and yes, before you interject, he's her real nephew, and we can discuss that later—and we're at her place, going through her research. I'm going to put you on speakerphone. Hang on a mo'." She balanced the phone on her knee, and Jack scooted closer to join the conversation. "Okay, go ahead. We're listening."

"Right, then. Well, 'ello, Jack, lovely to meet you over the wire like this."

Jack acknowledged, and Matt continued.

"I've been asking questions about Calico Jack around these southern parts, and also keeping an ear to the ground for bits on your man, Reginald Edwards. Turns out I've got quite a bit of news for you. Hang on to ya hats, boys and girls. It appears our dear ol' Reggie was indeed a thief."

Lexy and Jack eyed each other across the phone, neither one surprised.

"'Ello? Did you hear what I said?" Matt's tinny voice asked. "He was a thief. That jewelry from the auction? He stole it. Over thirty years ago. Anyone?"

Lexy spoke first. "Thanks, Matt, but that's not exactly shocking. You'd mentioned that possibility when I was down there, remember? And so much bullshit has happened since then that I'm not surprised. But that said, who, what, where, when, why and how? Well, scratch that, sort of. Tell us everything you learned."

"Right, then. It does get a tad more intriguing than simply that." Matt took a deep breath and began. "Thirty-odd years ago the not-soesteemed Reginald Edwards heard of a salvage attempt happening north of the Turks and Caicos Islands.

"Word was the salvor had uncovered an early-eighteenth-century wreck alleged to be the *Revenge*, Calico Jack Rackham's pirate ship. It sank in 1720 after a massive hurricane had blown it out of Jamaica, shortly after the pirates had been hauled off to jail. The story goes that the deserted ship had been lost at sea before the authorities could remove the treasure hidden aboard. The salvor claimed ownership of the wreck and everything aboard that he could find. So far, I haven't been able to uncover any records or information as to who that salvor was. But I am still looking.

"Anyhoo," Matt went on with relish, "it turns out Reggie was quite the little scavenger. He kept a low profile while the salvage attempts were under way, his eyes and ears open for word of any treasure that was brought up. Sure enough, though the wreckers tried to stay mum, word leaked out that they'd made an extraordinary find, a set of emerald-and-diamond jewelry: necklace, bracelets, earrings. The real McCoy. Pay dirt for ol' Reggie, if he could get his hands on it."

Matt paused as Lexy let out a low whistle. "Damn, Matt. Those have to be our jewels, of course."

She exchanged a glance with Jack, who nodded and added, "Yeah, there's no way there could be two finds that similar, both from Calico Jack's pirate ship. I mean, his *privateer* ship," he said, correcting himself.

"The details get sketchier from here out. The salvage attempts had gone on for quite some time, but apparently the wreck wasn't located until the start of hurricane season, which made continued diving extremely dangerous. Still, the team went out, and they brought up those first jewels. Somehow, Reggie found out where they were kept—wouldn't put it past him to've bribed someone—and he nicked off with them in the middle of the night.

"Of course the salvor was furious, but the authorities had no leads, and time was wasting. The team continued to dive the wreck for another week. They found nothing else. One night a severe hurricane struck, and by the time the team made their way to the site, the ship had disappeared. The spot where it had lain was completely wiped clean … as if it had never been.

"My sources couldn't tell me what happened to the salvor. There were stories of his turning to the bottle and never being heard from again, but I've no idea if that's the truth. And your man Reggie cottoned off to the Bahamas with his ill-gotten gains, and hid away the jewels on that plantation of his for the next three-plus decades.

"After he died the rumors started up again that he'd been the one who had stolen Calico Jack's gems all those years ago. Presumably, Lex luv, that's when your Mrs. Stellery heard the story and sent you down here to buy them."

Lexy shook her head, amazed by Matt's tale. "I guess that's possible. About Mrs. S. Though once we sort through more of her paperwork, I hope we'll know exactly how she found out about them." She inhaled and blew out loudly. "Unreal, Matt. Thanks for all this info. It's hard to believe those jewels really are part of Calico Jack's bounty. Of course, Mrs. S. believed that, but I guess it feels validated now, having your inquiries to back it up. And to that point, by the way, your sources … how credible are they, really?"

"Ah, Lexy, my luv." She saw Jack roll his eyes at the phone. "How could you even think to doubt them? They are the truest, shining-est sort of respectable sources that one could ask for," Matt replied, and she heard the grin in his voice.

"Now, truly, m'dear, I can appreciate the question. I'll simply say that I got the same details from a few different people so that I could be sure about what I'd been told." He grew serious. "That's why it took me a bit to get back to you. I triple-checked what I'd learned, to make sure all was as accurate as could be. My sources all swear by this tale: Jack Rackham's ship, the *Revenge*, with all its loot, was sunk by a hurricane in 1720, found and salvaged in the 1980s, had its sole recovered treasure—your jewels, there, Jack—stolen, got swept away again by a hurricane and has not been seen since."

Jack at last voiced his thoughts. "So, Matt, why couldn't you find out anything about that salvage team?"

"My thoughts exactly," Lexy interjected. "How come your sources knew so much about everything except who'd done the salvaging? That's a critical piece of the puzzle." She glanced at Jack and leaned in close to the phone. "Whoever found those jewels, well, they'd've been royally pissed off when the gems were stolen. And especially after the ship was lost again, without anything else recovered. Hell, I'd be apoplectic!"

Jack said, "Yeah, anyone would, and I'd sure as hell bet that salvor would've tried to recover the jewels, the ship or both. If he did, how on earth could he have kept that quiet?"

"Friends, I'm afraid I haven't got a good answer for you. At least not yet," Matt replied. "All I learned was that the losses damn near crushed the man, and nothing much seems to have been heard of him after that, outside the saloon."

Lexy sighed, stumped. Glad to have this news, but stymied by the lack of what could be a crucial part of the jigsaw.

She fiddled with the phone on her knee. "We can't thank you enough for all this, Matt. It's a huge help. If you can pass along our thanks to your friends, cool. And if you do uncover more about that salvor and his team, please call me. Anything might be useful." She gave Jack a pat on his leg. "Who knows, maybe thirty-five years later he also heard the rumors and decided to come back for another shot at the gems?"

"I agree," Jack added. "Finally, after years of silence, Reggie dies and word of the jewels spreads. It could've been exactly what he'd been waiting for. And if not the salvor—he'd have to have been kind of young back then—then maybe somebody else associated with the dive or the crew or something. Any other info on that, Matt, would be really appreciated. As was this. Thanks, man."

"Sure thing, mates. I promise, I'll keep me ears attuned and will keep you lot apprised of any new news." The grin returned to his voice. "In the meantime, try to stay out of trouble, would ya? Cheerio."

"So," Lexy said after disconnecting the call, "he gave us a lot of good info. But now I want more, especially about who that salvor was and what happened to him." She shifted and tilted her head at Jack. "I feel like my appetite's been whetted."

"Yeah, I'm with you on that." He eyed the stacks surrounding them. "We've barely made a dent here. Definitely have our work cut out. I wonder if Aunt Cee found out about the salvage attempt and discovered who was behind it. C'mon, let's get a move on." He toed a pile closer to Lexy. "Start digging."

She stuck her tongue out, and he chuckled, displaying his dimples again. She gave him a real smile and got down to business.

Four hours, a six-pack of Lagunitas and a large pepper-and-onion pizza later, and they'd made it only most of the way through the papers from the first cabinet. Neither could decipher Claudine's filing system, and the oddest bits of information were lumped together, making it necessary to review everything in each stack for any mention of Rackham and the jewels.

"I don't know about you," Jack said, glancing her way, "but I'm done. I'm going cross-eyed."

"Yeah, I think you're right. I could use a break." She rubbed at her bottom. "Plus, my butt is killing me."

Her glance moved over the scattered papers, lighting on the handful they'd put aside with meager references to Rackham and his treasures. The pickings were slim: a few mentions of his plundering and associations with Anne Bonny and Mary Read, a letter from an investigator in the Bahamas stating he would continue searching local church records. Thus far, nothing overly useful had arisen. Short work, which they agreed they'd review again with fresher eyes.

"Who knew Mrs. S. was such a freakin' paper hoarder? I mean, I found sales receipts from jewelry I designed for her almost nine years ago. Why the hell keep that? Or, at least file it in a safe deposit box for insurance purposes. Not here with your pirate info and your shopping lists and God knows what else." Exasperated, she turned to Jack. "When you said she had research files for everything she'd been investigating about Rackham, I thought you meant *all* these files were about him." She puffed out a breath. "Little did I realize …."

"You and me both, Lex. I had no idea there'd be so much useless crap mixed in." He shrugged, stood and offered her a hand up. "Still, we got through a good portion today. Let's call it a night and get back to it tomorrow, cool?"

"Yeah, Jack. The stuff has waited this long. What's another day?"

Chapter 34

Lexy's footsteps dragged after she parted ways with Jack. Tired from the tedious night sorting Mrs. Stellery's junk, she caught a cab home. As had become her habit, she looked around as she approached the front door and quickly keyed herself in. She zipped upstairs and into her apartment inside a minute, then locked up behind her. True to her routine, she tossed the keys on the sideboard. She started to walk away but turned back when she noticed the table looked slightly off-center against the wall.

"That's odd." She shoved it back into position. "Hmmm, maybe I knocked it on my way out."

She moved about, divesting herself of her accoutrements. In her bedroom she reached for her jewelry box and that, too, seemed a tad shifted from its usual spot. She poked inside, sifting around with a finger. *Yep, everything looks like it's here. Bizarro. Still, it's not that heavy. I guess I could've bumped my dresser and moved the box by accident.*

She glanced around the rest of her bedroom. *Did I leave the closet door cracked?* She nudged it open with her foot and carefully peeked in. *Is everything exactly as I left it?*

An eerie feeling stole over her as she walked slowly from room to room, eyeing her belongings. She didn't notice anything missing, but here and there other tiny things felt off. Chills crept up her spine at the thought that someone could've been in her home.

Uncertain what to do, she called Claire.

"Are you sure you're okay? And nothing was taken?"

"Yeah, I'm fine, other than being totally creeped out. And it doesn't look like anything's missing. Really, it's so bizarre. Any one of these things I could've moved or misplaced myself, but all of them? Or am I just noticing them now? It seems strange, you know?"

"That is weird. But I guess it's not exactly a case for the police. Are you sure you're alright staying there alone tonight? I could come over if you want."

"No, but thanks. I'm locked in and I've got the chain on. And really, if somebody had been inside, they probably only wanted to be here when I wasn't. Right?" A hint of uncertainty lingered in her voice. Then she sniffed the air. "It evens smells a little funny. Not sure how to describe it … but it smells a bit off."

"When was the last time you did laundry?"

"Oh, ha-ha, Claire. Real cool." She stuck out her tongue and blew a raspberry. Then she chuckled as her friend's comment lightened her mood.

"Come on, Lex. You walked right into that one." Claire laughed. "Anyway, knowing you, the likelihood is far greater that you moved all those bits and pieces yourself, and you never realized. You're probably only noticing now because you were looking to see if anything else was out of place." She paused, then chuckled again. "Besides, you're not exactly anal about keeping your belongings in order."

"You're right, I know. Me and my fanciful imagination at work. Again." She laughed once more, truer. "Thanks for talking me off the ledge, Claire. I've got some things to finish, then I'm going to crash. Say hi to Mike."

"Sure thing, girl. Sleep well. Ring if you need anything. 'Night."

Two hours later Lexy tossed in her bed while her fanciful imagination wreaked havoc with her sleep.

*****

"God damn it!"

The man pounded his fist on the table, the sound reverberating in the small room as papers scattered. "I can't believe there's nothing useful here. Why the fuck did I risk myself for this load of crap?" His rough voice filled the otherwise silent room.

He grabbed a handful of papers, stared at their mocking, worthless bits of black and white, then flung them across the room. Their teasing flippancy as they drifted to the floor taunted him.

"All that effort, wasted. There's not a damn thing here I can use. Son of a bitch! What I'm looking for must still be buried in those fucking files. I've got to get my hands on them. Before they find it. And God help them if they do."

Chapter 35

"Pay dirt!" Jack announced.

The next afternoon found them again sitting on the floor of Claudine's study. He grabbed Lexy's arm and yanked her across the carpet in his excitement, ignoring her protests.

"At last, we're getting somewhere. Here's tangible proof of Claudine's lineage." He held up several pages. "It's some kind of genealogical report. We'll have to go through it, of course, but looks like it goes from Aunt Cee all the way back to Rackham." He grinned. "Let's spread this out on the table and see exactly what we've got."

The two stood and stretched, knees creaking from their too-long squats.

"Ugh, sitting on the floor is fine and all, but this has been a bit too much in two days." She arched her back, then reached for the papers. "Okay, show me the goods."

Spreading out the sheaf in chronological order, they followed the timeline backward from Claudine Lansing Stellery's parents through the previous two centuries. The genealogist added notes about the marriages, births and deaths in the family. The report read like a rerun of *Dynasty*: who cheated on whom, who had mistresses set up in the guest house, who divorced, remarried and slept with their younger cousin/employer/neighbor.

Damn! Who knew Mrs. S.'s family was so colorful?

Lexy's eyes skimmed over the pages. As the timeline trekked backward, the story became more fascinating.

"Check this out." Lexy touched Jack's arm. "Here's where it starts to get really good. And hey, this other part looks like your aunt wrote it. Maybe it's a summary of the genealogist's work?"

Jack didn't answer. She pointed back to the historian's account and tapped her finger on the page. "Let's finish with the report first, before we get sidetracked by your aunt's write-up. Okay, we've gotten back to the pirates here, all three of them, it turns out: Jack, Anne, Mary. Have a look."

In the eighteenth century, given the high illiteracy level, much of the pirates' history had been oral, transcribed in later years by those who still remembered and who'd learned to write. The genealogist had relied on recorded oral histories, along with existing legal documents, to fill in the specifics of Mrs. Stellery's ties to Captain Rackham.

The two finished reading and stared at the papers, trying to absorb the words.

Lexy broke the silence. "Hang on. Am I missing something here, Jack? This report isn't done." Wide gray eyes probed his. "Let me rephrase that. Your side of the family diagram appears complete … but it looks like there's a whole other branch of Rackham's tree left unexplored. You could have other relatives still alive who're also direct descendants of Calico Jack."

"Yeah. Shit, yeah." Jack slowly nodded. "This is crazy! If I'm supposed to believe all this, Aunt Cee and I are directly descended from Jack and Anne Bonny … but Jack definitely had another kid with Mary Read. They were half-siblings." He shook his head, trying to focus. "But why doesn't this document go into any detail about Mary and Jack's kid? Why the hell does it stop here?"

"I don't know. But my guess is this was all relatively new information to Mrs. S. Going by the dates on these papers, this genealogist might not have finished the job …. And maybe that's what your aunt was really after."

Excitement glowed on Lexy's face. She wagged a finger at Jack. "Maybe Claudine was looking for more than the jewels, more than validation for your ancestor. Maybe she was searching for your long-lost family. Maybe that had become her real quest … to find out who else in your family might still be alive!"

Jack smiled at her enthusiasm. "Know what? That's as good a guess as any. I gotta admit, finding out I might have family somewhere kinda threw me for a sec there. But maybe it won't be such a bad thing, having a few more of us around." He smacked a hand to his forehead. "And hey, we have Aunt Cee's notes to read, too. Where'd you put those? Maybe she found out more than what's in the report. Her damn paperwork is so disorganized. She might've dug up other info."

They hunted around the table, then began to read the words of Claudine Stellery. For several minutes shocked silence pervaded the room.

Lexy speed-read, gasping occasionally—and drawing repeated frowns from Jack—then waited for him to finish.

Before long, he pushed away the pages and stared at her. He started to speak, stopped, then stood and paced the length of the room. Parting the window drapes, he leaned on the sill and stared at the darkened street.

He tried again. "It seems my family history just got more complicated. Again. Shit."

Chapter 36

"I'm descended from *Mary Read's* kid? Not Anne Bonny's? What the hell is going on?"

He turned to face Lexy, shoving his fingers through his hair. "This is ridiculous. I'm supposed to accept that Anne Bonny, a pirate, could read and write, *and* she kept a diary? Who on earth would believe that? A literate female pirate."

Lexy shrugged. "Apparently Anne kept one, and your aunt found it. That was one hell of a write-up."

"And if my aunt's interpretation of that journal is accurate, then a lot of what we read a few minutes ago in the genealogist's report is bullshit. Son of a bitch!"

He punched a fist into his palm. Lexy heard the slap and knew he'd hit hard enough to sting.

"Give me a sec, okay? Shit." He took a deep breath and let it out, staring at the ceiling. Then another. "Christ …. I guess it's better to learn all this at once. Now we've got to figure out what's the truth and what's a lie." He began pacing. "Let's start from the beginning and try to get the story straight."

"Alright. Let me grab my notebook and start a list, so we can put a sort of timeline together." Lexy felt in her purse for a notebook and pen, then sat at the table. "Okay, we know both women, Anne and Mary, were pregnant by Jack when they were imprisoned for piracy. The women's executions were stayed because of their pregnancies. According to what your aunt found in the diary, Anne Bonny's child was stillborn before she got out of jail."

Jack stood still a moment. "Mary Read contracts a fever in jail and dies in childbirth, but not before securing a pledge from Anne to raise Mary's child as her own. God, this is unbelievable."

He switched gears. "Based on the genealogist's notes, the prison records show two births and two deaths, with the deaths attributed to Mary and *her* child. But according to the diary, that's wrong." Distrust poured over his words. "What am I supposed to believe? Mary's child lived, raised by Anne. We're descended from Mary Read and Jack Rackham. Is that really the truth?"

With confusion evident, he continued. "So, Anne and the baby get released into her father's custody. But here's another kick in the ass: she didn't leave with only Mary's baby." He thrust a finger at the floor. "Mary had stolen Rackham's letter of marque."

Jack resumed pacing. His footfalls thudded when he reached the wood flooring. "I can't believe how crazy this all sounds. Mary had stolen the letter of marque from Rackham before they were jailed. I know the stuff we read online about their arrest sounds made up, but with the info from the journal to corroborate, maybe it's plausible. It sounds like Jack and the boys were so blind drunk when they were attacked, they couldn't fight off the bounty hunters."

The twenty-first-century Jack shook his head and snickered. "Anne and Mary had to fend for themselves. Mary lifted the letter from Rackham. It would've been a breeze. She must've stolen it and planned to use it to get out of jail and claim legal ownership of the cargo. Still … why didn't she do that in the first place? Why risk having the baby in jail and whatever other nightmares that must've entailed?"

"I'm not sure." Lexy drummed her fingers on the table, letting her mind sift through the latest details. "Maybe she wanted to—or had to—wait until Jack was dead, so he couldn't fight her for the letter and ownership. It sounds like these 'ladies' weren't exactly on the up-and-up. All those wild stories from the Internet, even if they're exaggerated, surely they're grounded in some speck of truth, don't you think?"

Jack moved to the table and rifled through his aunt's papers, trying to get a sense of the woman whose story they held. "We'll need the diary as proof, obviously, because my aunt's notes jump all over the place. I wonder what the hell Aunt Cee was trying to pull, lumping things together like this. I can only imagine what else we'll find when we read the real thing."

He cocked his head toward the table. "Anyway, back to this. I guess, though Anne and Mary had both slept with Rackham, they felt more loyalty to each other. This could've been Mary's last act of friendship, giving Anne her baby and the letter of marque."

When he paused, Lexy said, "This is so beyond anything I expected. Where do you think Anne's diary is? We have to find it and make sure we have as much of her first-hand account as possible."

"Right. We've gotta fill in some of these damn holes." His hand clenched. "And God help that thief if he got his hands on it."

He shook his head, the revelations clearly weighing on him. Without a word, he left the room, returned with two beers and handed one to Lexy.

After a deep pull, he said, "I feel like I'm missing something." He frowned at her. "I know I saw something else in this mess … if I can find it again. There's so much here, and none of it in order. Hang on."

Standing over the table, Jack sorted through his aunt's handwritten pages until he found what had barely sunk in upon first reading. His dazed voice broke the stillness. "Here it is … I knew I read something before." He held up a sheet filled with Claudine's distinctive script.

"Son of a bitch, Lex." His eyes bored into hers. "Anne and Jack had another child together, years before they were captured. It seems the genealogist missed that kid in his research." Fury radiated from him as he scowled. "What kind of researcher is this guy? He found all that info and traced us back to the 1700s, but he stopped there? What the fuck? How could he miss that Anne and Jack had another kid together, a kid they'd abandoned in Cuba? Why didn't he continue his search, make sure there wasn't more to find? God, don't you think he would've finished his fucking job?"

Lexy crossed the room and laid a hand on Jack's arm. "I'm sorry, Jack, I obviously can't answer that except to guess. Who knows why he stopped when he did. Maybe he found the diary and gave it to your aunt and thought that was sufficient. Hell, I don't know." She waved a hand through the air. "That seems unlikely, when the rest of his work looked so thorough. Maybe he really wasn't finished yet. I can't say."

She grabbed him by the shoulders with a not-so-gentle shake. "But I can say this. There's another branch of your family out there, so our work isn't done."

Jack waited a moment, staring into Lexy's eyes. She read fear and hesitancy in his gaze.

"You're right," he said. "I may be nuts to say this, but there's no point holding back now. Since we heard from Matt, my gut's been telling me that whoever's behind this craziness with the jewels is somehow linked to that thirty-five-year-old salvage attempt. After all, the only thing recovered back then were those jewels—said to be cursed, don't forget—and ever since you flew down to Eleuthera for them, mayhem has pretty much been the norm."

He took a deep breath and went on. "Am I way off base to think the salvor might be related to me and Aunt Cee? That he might be descended from Jack and Anne's first kid? And he's been looking for what he's considered his rightful treasure all along?"

He snorted. "Or do you think that's completely insane and I'm losing it?"

Lexy mulled over his words. "Well, I was headed in that direction myself. If only to brainstorm who could be behind the murders. But, shit." She strode to the table and flipped through Claudine's paperwork. "To think that someone related to you, even nominally, could do such awful things … that pretty much sucks." She looked back at him with concern. "It bears looking into, of course. Your aunt was able to find out all this about Jack and Anne and Mary. Why couldn't someone else find out the same?"

She picked up one of the sheets Jack had tossed onto the table. "Look at the rest of this. There's a note that says Anne, after being released, went back to Cuba and searched for, but never found, her first child. We don't know anything else. He or she could have grown up believing they'd been abandoned, unloved and God knows what else. That child could've gone on with their life, angry and bitter and stewing over the injustices they'd faced."

Jack's inscrutable gaze followed her as she retraced her steps and stood in front of him, one hand on her hip.

"I think that's where we go from here, Jack." A spark lightened her eyes to silver. "We track down the other side of your family tree and see what we find."

She tilted her head, wanting to lighten the weight of his unusual burden, and smirked at him. "So, are you up for it?"

Chapter 37

In lieu of words, Jack cupped the back of her head with his hand, angling it up. He leaned down and dropped a searing kiss on her lips. Lexy inhaled sharply before easing into the kiss, only to have him cut it off too quickly. She blinked and reached up to feel the burn that tingled her lips. *Wow.* Realizing how that must look, she dropped her hand and attempted to appear unaffected. *Fat chance. Wow.*

"Um, Jack ... does that mean you like my idea?" She hoped nonchalance would cover her reaction.

Jack let out a burst of laughter, then moved in for another fast, fiery kiss, pleased at her obvious enjoyment and discombobulation. "Yeah, Lex, I do like your idea." Then his teasing expression sobered, and he leaned back. "But I think we need to do something else first.

"I want to catch this guy. Now. Whoever he is. Set a trap, something that'll trip him up. Maybe make him try to steal the jewels or more files. Hell, maybe even both. We'll have to figure that out, but we have to catch him in the act."

Intent, he grasped her upper arms and said, "He won't know the police still have the stones. We can use that to our advantage." His grip tightened. "The police don't have any leads on the break-in, and they're still investigating the poison that killed my aunt. I can't see them getting

their heads outta their asses anytime soon. I want this guy behind bars."
He struggled to contain his anger and purposefully eased his hold.

"I'm with you. So let's think ...."

She took a step back, still feeling the aftershock of his kisses.
Needing the breathing space to clear her head, she moved around the
stacks of paper littering the floor. "We obviously have more files to go
through, but we found the preliminary substantiation for your aunt's
claims. Her summary refers to the letter Mary stole, but we still need to
find the original document, as well as Anne's diary. I think we can be
pretty confident Mrs. S. was searching for more than the jewels, more
than a way to clear Calico Jack's name. But no one else would know
that."

She tapped her fingers against her lips. "We spread the word that
we've found these two crucial documents which hold the key to 'so
much more.'" She air quoted at Jack. "People will naturally assume
we're talking about more jewels or treasure. That should draw out the
murderer. He wants the stones and whatever else he can get his hands
on. And after all, what could be more enticing than the promise of
riches?"

She raised an eyebrow at him. "So we tell people we've found
the clues to the rest of Calico Jack's loot." She warmed to the idea as she
walked around the room. "We say Mrs. S. had done all the research. Her
quest was to continue the search for the remaining jewels—which it was,
as far as everyone at the awards dinner is concerned—so no one should
realize we don't have any actual proof of the treasure's location. Or that
it most likely was lost at sea when the *Revenge* went down.

"And if the murderer is connected to the salvor and knows about
the shipwreck already, he'd still have to find out what we know. He'd
have to find out if we'd uncovered definitive evidence that the rest of
Jack's bounty was aboard the *Revenge* when it sank."

She paused. "Of course, we have to be realistic. Even though the
salvage team recovered only one set of jewels, it doesn't mean
everything else is on board, lost somewhere in the Caribbean. Almost
three hundred years have passed since the ship first went down. It
could've been salvaged or lost many times over, given how hurricanes

can move things around. God only knows where the *Revenge* is by now, and what treasure—if any—it might still hold."

"But," Jack said, "what if the thief stole the letter or the diary? Or hell, something more valuable that we don't know about?"

Lexy considered how to answer. "I think our plan holds water in any case. Look, he'd still have to find out what we know, right? He only grabbed a small portion of the files—which clearly also contain a lot of garbage—so he'd have to find out what else we uncovered. Either way, I think it'll work. Either way, he'll come after the jewels. Don't forget that."

Jack roamed around as he digested her idea. He stopped in front of her and asked, "How do we get the word out? And what kind of trap do we set? And where, exactly? And when?" He tossed the barrage of questions in her face, and she fielded them one by one.

Fingers ticking off, she began. "First, we decide where we want to lead the murderer … here? My shop? Or someplace else?" She tapped her fingers against her lips again, pondering. "I'm thinking the shop, since he's already been here. He'll know you've overhauled the security by now. Plus, the shop has a vault downstairs, in case we need it.

"I got it." She snapped her fingers. "We say something like the police returned the jewels, and we have them at the shop so I can authenticate them, and that you're dropping off the documents on some particular night so the shop can keep everything under lock and key. In light of your break-in here, that makes the most sense. We should tell the police, but I think we do that right before we're ready to put the plan in action. We'll need them in case anything goes wrong." She glanced at Jack and saw him nod.

"As for spreading the story, I'll make calls to some of the industry folks who were at the dinner, tell them what we've found out since then. You know … get the industry vibes a-buzzin', that sort of thing. I'm thinking it's likely the guy was at the dinner, right? I mean, from all the mystery novels I've read, if you can believe them, poison is a pretty personal crime. Wouldn't you think he'd've been there to watch his handiwork?"

Jack flinched at her comment, and she rushed to remove her foot from her mouth. "I'm so sorry, Jack. That was thoughtless. I meant it's possible he was there or had some kind of connection with the event or the JIC. If he's traveling in these circles, then spreading the word to my colleagues will hopefully trickle down to wherever that slimeball is."

Jack gave a terse nod. "And I'll talk to Charlie about Aunt Cee's friends. I hate to think it could be someone she considered close. On the other hand, if there's any chance this murderer is someone she knew, then Charlie might be able to help with that." His hand clenched as he said, "The next question is, when do we do this?"

For forty-five minutes Lexy and Jack hammered out the plan's logistics. The key would be tempting the murderer to react and having the police at the ready, should things turn ugly. They settled all the details except one: when they'd pull off their plan.

"Don't worry. I'm sure Christian will be okay with this. I wouldn't've offered the shop if I thought he'd have a problem with us using it. *Holy crap, I hope I can get Christian on board.* "Besides, it's the safest and most logical place."

She peeked at the time on her cell phone. "Damn, Jack. It's after midnight." She stood and gathered her belongings scattered around the room, then dumped everything into her bag. "I've got to get my tired butt to bed. I don't want to be late tomorrow—if I'm going to talk Christian into going along with our plan. Where'd my other shoe go?" she asked with a sweeping glance. "Oh, there it is." She pulled it from beneath a chair and bent to slip it on.

When she rose, Jack stood beside her. As it had since she first met him, his closeness unnerved her and set her skin humming. "Oh, hey. Uh, so I'm gonna get going. I'll give you a ring tomorrow after I get the okay from Christian. Cool?"

He ignored her and asked, "How're you getting home?"

"Mmm, I'll probably jump in a cab. I don't feel like dealing with the subways at this time of night." She stepped back, heading toward the door to Mrs. Stellery's suite and the main staircase. Jack followed.

"I'm going with you."

She stopped short. "What?"

"I'm going with you."

"Hey there, buster," she said, annoyed at his presumption. "Just because we kissed—granted they were a couple of really hot kisses— doesn't mean you get to come home with me. So no, I don't think so."

She turned again for the stairs, but stopped when she heard his burst of laughter. "Now what?"

He tried to contain his glee, partly succeeding. "I like the way your brain works, Lexy-girl." He chuckled again. "But that wasn't exactly what I had in mind. At least not for tonight," he added, winking. Seeing the confusion etched on her face, he said, "I'm going with you in the cab. To make sure you get in okay." He smiled as the realization hit her that she'd over-interpreted his offer. "Then I'm going to take that cab back here. So I can get a good night's sleep. I hope."

As she blushed a thousand shades of scarlet, he added, "Unless, of course, you'd rather I stay and give you a few more … what did you call them? 'Really hot kisses'?"

His whiskey eyes melted her, and she struggled to collect her cool. Giving it up for lost, she tried to bluster through with sarcasm. "Oh, ha, Jack. You're so very funny. But there's no need for you to shuttle me home. Thanks for the offer, though," she said over her shoulder as she sailed down the stairs. "Say good-night to Charles for me."

She'd made it through the front door and turned to pull it shut behind her when she collided with Jack's chest. "Oomph." She backed up a step. "Come on, this is really not necessary."

But he was already nudging her down to the street and locking up. "Lex, humor me, would ya? It's late, and after everything that's happened, I'd feel a whole hell of a lot better, okay?"

I'm a sucker. She gave a mental shrug and acquiesced.

They said little in the taxi, and pulled up in front of her apartment in good time, given the light traffic. Jack had the driver wait as he eyed the street and walked Lexy to the door. She took a deep breath of warm night air, trying to rid herself of the cab's scent of old sweat and deli sandwiches.

She let herself in and said, "Okay, you've done your good deed for the night." Then she smiled. "Now go get some sleep, and I'll touch base with you tomorrow after I talk with Christian. Thanks for keeping me company home."

"My good deed, huh?" He laughed quietly. "If that's my good deed, then what's this?"

He eased in, staring first at her eyes, then her lips. He fit his mouth to hers and kissed her, shooting electricity along her body. He drew her forward and deepened the kiss until she leaned into him, pressing her hand against his nape to bring him closer. A low "Mmmm" slipped out on a sigh, but she couldn't tell who it came from.

After a few moments, Jack shifted back and stared at her. His smile was gone, replaced by hungry desire. *Dangerous and potent.* The thought flickered through her brain. "Jack …." she began, but stopped to catch her breath.

Trying again, she said, "Jack, you need to go home." She shook her head as he began to protest, saying, "Now you've done your second good deed, except this one will probably keep me awake half the night." She meant to scold, but instead the words came out as a sort of compliment, which made him grin. "You're not spending the night." Which turned his grin to a scowl. "We both really need some sleep. And more importantly,"—she gave him a light shove against his chest—"we need to keep our heads on straight until this mess is cleared up." She watched him try to come up with a valid, logical argument. "You know I'm right."

He tilted his head toward her, still wearing a small frown. Instead of speaking, he leaned in once more. This time, though, his kiss was light as air, a stroke of lips that, despite their softness, left an imprint she would remember. He didn't touch her anywhere else, though she felt his heat everywhere. He pulled slowly back from the kiss, and she staggered into him, unwilling to break away.

"Christmas," she mumbled on a ragged breath, then bit her lower lip.

"I hope that gives you something to think about tonight. Crazy woman. So damn interested in overthinking things." He said it with a grin that doused the quick spurt of indignation she felt.

She smacked him on the arm. "Go home, already. Before I hit you again."

He laughed, dimples flashing, then retreated and ducked into the idling taxi. "Later, Lexy-girl. Sleep tight," he called.

"Yeah, you too," she replied. Then she sighed. "Son of a bitch … whew."

Turning, she closed up downstairs, trekked to her apartment and let herself in while dialing Claire. Despite the late hour she knew her friend would be awake writing. When she answered, Lexy proceeded to fill her in on the night's details. All of them.

Repeated "Are you out of your mind?"s came zinging over the line as Claire voiced her opinion of Lexy and Jack's plan. Followed by "You'd better freakin' call the cops, is what you better do!" and "You kissed him? What were you thinking?"

The comments set Lexy's teeth grinding. *Maybe this late-night chat wasn't the best idea.* Still, she had needed to talk with her friend.

"Okay, Claire, okay, I hear you. There's no use yelling anymore, at least not tonight. And yes, Jack and I will tell the cops, once I make sure my boss is okay with the plan and we have the timing and all the details squared away."

Done with that part of the conversation, she went on. "As for kissing him, well, he kissed me first, and there was nothing I could do but go with the flow." She wondered what Claire thought of her rationalization. "Plus, he's a fantastic damn kisser!"

Claire, even in her tizzy, couldn't miss the smug smile in Lexy's voice.

"I'm talking OMG and all that. The timing might not be the best in the world, but God, I really love a good kiss."

Claire cooled off enough to laugh with her friend and garner a few salient details. Soon after, the two said good-night.

Claire's final admonition to be careful echoed across the line.

*****

Time's running out. I know it is.

Chills crawled up his neck. *I've got to get my hands on the jewels. She's gotta have them sometime, but when? When the hell will the police release them? Shit! Those guys won't wait forever, and then what'll they do to me?*

Nervous sweat broke out, the scent sickening him.

I've got to get those stones!

Chapter 38

Thank God I have the most awesome, amazing boss in the world.

Lexy had repeated that sentiment several times to Christian earlier that morning. The idea had not been an easy sell to her boss—not that she'd thought it would—but she appreciated that he felt strongly enough about Claudine and finding out the truth that he agreed to use the boutique to set the trap. Provided the police were involved. After their conversation, Lexy spent a portion of the day making arrangements for the items they typically stored in-house to be removed for the duration of their plan.

She took a break at lunch and called Jack with the go-ahead.

Later that afternoon the two of them reached out to their contacts with the story they'd prepared. They began to spread the crumbs that they hoped would lure a killer.

Eager ears heard the tale: Claudine Stellery had discovered clues to the missing bounty from Calico Jack Rackham's ship. The police finished testing the jewels that had poisoned her, and a court order mandated they release them to her nephew, Jackson Hughes. A recent break-in had occurred at the Stellery residence; considering her long-standing relationship with the shop, Mr. Hughes elected to have both the gems and the documentation detailing the whereabouts of the remaining treasure safeguarded in the shop's high-security vault. All would be turned over to Lexy on Friday, for safekeeping until Monday morning, when Mr. Hughes would leave to track down the lost bounty somewhere in the Caribbean.

"Blah, blah, blah and et cetera, et cetera, et cetera," she reported to Jack later that Wednesday evening from the comfort of her couch. "That's the gist of it from my end. Very official and top-line, and peppered with juicy tidbits here and there, to hopefully whet that asshole's appetite. You wouldn't believe how nosy some of those guys were," she added. Then, thinking it over, she said, "Maybe you would. I'm sure you encountered some of the same on your end.

"Oh, and before I forget," she rushed to say, "get this ... remember that guy from Eleuthera? Evan Maxwell, one of the others bidding on the jewels?" She assumed Jack's grunt confirmed his recollection. "I've spoken to him a few times since your aunt died, trying to get information from him on the jewels, how he heard about them, their provenance, you know the drill. But no dice. Zippo info. It's like he heard about the auction and decided to head to the Bahamas on a fluke or something. Very odd. And whenever I spoke with him, he struck me as overly curious about how your aunt died.

"At first I thought it was morbid curiosity. Some people are like that. But he rang me again right before I left the shop tonight. I don't think he could've heard our news already, but his timing was way coincidental, which is hardly a good thing in my book." She paused for a sip of chilled Sauvignon Blanc and enjoyed the crisp, citrusy flavor that met her tongue. Its sharp, simple scent made her smile, despite the worrisome topic under discussion.

"So, I did a quick member search for him on a few of the jewelers and collectors databases we have access to, and guess what? Nada. Nothing. Zippo again. I even did a super-fast Google search, but damn, there was too much to go through and nothing that seemed relevant at first glance." Another swallow. "At any rate, I don't get that warm-fuzzy from him, you know? He might need a closer look." She drained her glass and carried it into the kitchen. "How did your calls go?"

Jack, at last allowed to speak, recapped his afternoon on the phone. She heard him wandering and wondered which room had been subjected to his pacing; if he felt anything like she did, he was anxious to get on with the show.

"I've got something to tell you."

This time when he spoke, it wasn't nerves she heard; excitement filled the line.

"I found the letter of marque and Anne's diary."

"Jack! You damn holdout! How could you keep quiet this whole time?" Lexy scolded. But, like flipping a switch, eagerness overrode her annoyance, and she said, "So what do they say? Is the letter legit? What about the diary? Does it substantiate everything in your aunt's summary?"

"Yeah, but it gets better. Aunt Cee also had someone do a translation. And before you can cut me off, yes, everything was written in English, but apparently there were lots of discrepancies and spelling differences back then. And Anne Bonny was only semiliterate, and that combo makes for challenging reading.

"The letter looks straightforward, granting the captain and crew of the *Revenge* a commission from the king of England to capture anyone traveling under Spanish colors. As long as Jack and the crew had the letter and the ships' passes to prove Spanish sovereignty, those ships and their treasure were fair game." He took a breath and shifted topics. "I skimmed the translation and matched some key passages—like the ones about Mary and swapping babies in prison—to the actual diary entries. Everything seems to jive."

Despite his words, Lexy heard traces of disbelief and amazement in Jack's voice.

"There's more. After Anne's rich and seriously tolerant father bought her way out of jail, she decided to walk the straight and narrow. She married an American guy, settled down as a farmer's wife. They didn't have kids of their own, but together they went to Cuba and searched for the child she and Rackham had abandoned."

Lexy could almost see Jack shaking his head.

"You believe that?" he said. "She gave up her firstborn years before, but even though she and Mary helped Jack to the hangman by stealing his commission, somewhere in her crazy ol' pirate heart, Anne never forgot about the kid. She also never found him."

"Him? Jack, they had a son?"

"Yeah. They named him Christopher."

The two were quiet for several moments. Lexy's mind raced back through time, imagining sad scenarios of a discarded little boy, absorbing the true lost fortunes of those gone long before her.

Jack's voice cut through the silence. "I have more of the diary to read, but so far it looks like I found the proof we needed."

After a pause, he said, "Along with the translation, I found more notes from Aunt Cee. You were right. She did intend to find out if we have other relatives still alive, out there somewhere. After her research proved Rackham was a legitimate privateer, she had two goals: find the rest of his treasure and find our lost family to share it with them." He half-laughed, half-sighed. "Pretty phenomenal woman, my aunt."

"I'll say. That she was."

Another brief, weighty silence enveloped them.

I really miss you, Mrs. S. I never should've doubted you. Lexy's eyes misted, and she sighed, relieved Jack couldn't see her weakness.

Then she coughed and spoke up, bringing them back to the original purpose of the conversation. They needed to finalize Friday's plans to transport the fake jewels and diary to Lexy's workplace for safekeeping. In actuality, the police still held the gems in evidence, and Jack would lock up the important papers they'd found in a safe deposit box at his aunt's bank. They'd use decoys of both items Friday afternoon, when Jack visited the shop.

After hashing out the few remaining issues with the dummy materials Jack would carry, Lexy segued into the trickiest aspect of their plan.

"So, Jack, did you talk to the police about all this yet?" A trace of trepidation flitted through her.

He heaved a sigh and said, "Yeah, I did late this afternoon. Basically, I got the shit handed to me from the detective working my aunt's case. I thought he was gonna blow a gasket, but he eventually calmed down. He was pissed as hell we're doing this, but since he really can't stop us …. The official take is that 'the police don't sanction any action such as we're undertaking' et cetera, et cetera. But after he finished cursing me out, he grudgingly agreed to send extra patrols past the shop this weekend. I guess being a Stellery relation has some perks."

Jack paused and let reality sink in. "You know that means we're pretty much on our own in this. Are you sure you're up for it, Lex? It could be incredibly dangerous. Be honest."

"Truthfully? Of course I am, and I also admit our little endeavor worries me. But I think we both understand the risks we're taking, and we have to finish this. For your aunt and for ourselves."

She fought revealing more to him. Now that they'd set their plan in motion, it felt a great deal more dicey. Not only had they put themselves on the line, they risked Christian's shop with a break-in and God knew what else. Lexy crossed her fingers and called on an old friend, bravado.

"Besides," she added with flourish, since she had good news to contribute, "when I spoke again with Christian about this, he decided to bring on a security guard for the weekend. So it'll be three of us, since he has a business trip tomorrow. The two of us and the guard. We'll be fine," she assured him, squeezing her crossed fingers tighter. "We have our own guard, the silent alarm is wired into the police and your detective will have extra patrols roaming the street. That's pretty much all we can ask for—and that the son of a bitch takes the bait."

Jack chuckled at her vehemence. Then they spent several minutes reworking the details for Friday night to include the added security guard.

"Alright, Lex. It sounds like we're pretty much covered. I guess tomorrow we let the gossip mill do its thing and hope word gets around." One more deep breath and a smothered curse came across. "Let me know if anything changes, yeah? If not, I'll call you Friday morning, and we go from there. Cool?"

"Cool by me. Chat to you Friday, if not before. Try not to stress too much," she teased, wanting to end on a lighter note.

She added a cheeky thought. "Here's a suggestion, something to keep you occupied until then. How about you think of what the two of us can do with all our free time when this nonsense is over? You can dream up some good ideas, can't you?" She laughed. "'Night now, Jack. Sleep tight and all."

She hung up with his halfhearted groan sounding in her ear.

Chapter 39

Thursday passed without incident. Lexy spent her time at the shop catching up on work and finalizing arrangements for securing the rest of the inventory. She realized vaguely that she hadn't experienced any more stalker-esque feelings. *God, I hope that's a good sign. But that reminds me, where the heck did I put my keycard for the shop? I'd better ask Stace if she's seen it anywhere. I know I had it when we ate lunch the other day.*

The thought fled as Friday's details crowded her brain. A quick call with Claire caught her up and reassured her friend that Jack had informed the police of their plans.

The pieces slowly came together.

Tension woke with Lexy Friday morning, like hangover breath that takes a good brushing to expunge. The potent scent and flavor of her extra-large Dunkin' Donuts coffee swept away some of her restless night, but worries lingered as she tried to concentrate on work.

Jack rang at noon. "Yo. I'll be there at five wit' da goods."

He attempted a cheesy New *Yawk* accent for levity. The accent sucked, but the levity worked, and a short chuckle sneaked out of Lexy as she swiveled around in her chair.

"Works for me, Jack. Everything here's as ready as it can be." She began a quick recap. "The guard will come in at four o'clock dressed in plain clothes. He'll be stationed in the anteroom of the vault downstairs. When you arrive, we'll lock up the dummy jewels and documents in the safe, and then I'll send you on your way to camp out in the alley behind the shop. I'll close up at six and head out with Stacey."

Her rings jingled against each other as she tapped through the rest of her list. "We'll go for a drink at the bar down the block so I can keep my eye on the front door. I really don't expect anything to happen that early, but I'd rather be prepared. Once it gets dark I'll sneak out and meet you in the alley, let's say eight forty-five for good measure. We'll let ourselves in the back door and then sit tight while we wait to see if our little story did the trick to lure the murderer."

She exhaled a quiet, deep breath. "All that cool by you?" A nervous twirl of her hair accompanied the lightly spoken words. "Any questions?"

"Nope. I'm all set, Lexy-girl. Got everything ready to go. Then, as you said, we play the waiting game. How about you? Nervous?"

"Not at all," she lied, and then paused. "Duh, of course I'm nervous, Jack." She stuck out her tongue even though he couldn't see her. "I just stuck my tongue out at you, by the way."

She heard him laugh and appreciated the sound. *Laughter really does help a lot. Thank goodness for small favors.* "But I'm pretending not to be. Makes me feel better." She smiled a bit. "Still, we've committed to this, and hopefully it'll soon be over. I spoke with a few other contacts yesterday, too," she added. "Sounds like the news is spreading quickly, as we'd hoped. The sooner we make this happen, the better."

"You got that right. Okay, guess there's nothing left to do for now. See you at five. I'll bring the sandwiches."

He clicked off to the sound of Lexy's laughter.

All went according to plan that evening.

Jack stopped by the shop and dropped off "da goods," as he insisted on calling the decoys. The security guard positioned himself in the room outside the vault, after familiarizing himself with the shop's layout.

The last employees headed out at six o'clock. Lexy locked up and walked to the bar down the street with Stacey in tow. She planted herself at a corner window with a view of the boutique's front door. Stacey, oblivious to the unfolding events, ordered the first round.

Lexy clinked glasses and gulped a Hoptical Illusion, another of her favorite beers. She kept one eye on Stacey, the other focused on the quiet shop.

There's nothing more I can do now. Everyone's in place and everything's ready to go.

She looked at Stacey and dredged up a smile. "Cheers."

Chapter 40

"What was that? Did you hear something?"

"Calm down, Jack. It's just the AC cycling on," Lexy whispered. "It's been running all night. How come you're hearing it now? Never mind," she said before he could reply. "Stop worrying. And stop driving me bonkers," she ordered in an undertone, staring at him through the gloom.

The two sat inches apart in the boutique's dim storeroom. Midnight had crept away, and the shop remained quiet—more or less—since they'd sneaked in around nine.

Lexy felt odd, sitting in the dark with Jack, so close she felt his heat sharing their space and smelled the subtle, spicy scent of his aftershave. Odd, because they were waiting for a violent criminal to strike. Odd, because her insides clutched in anticipation whenever Jack looked at her.

This is surreal. I can't wait for this night to be over. Provided everything goes according to plan. Please, God, let everything go smoothly. She tried to smile at Jack, but anxiety drew her face into a grimace.

The night passed slowly, intermingled with snippets of muted conversation. Except for their whispers, the shop stayed cathedral quiet.

Lexy heard nothing from the guard posted downstairs in the safe's outer room. *I hope to God he's awake.* Her brain ran rampant with worry.

Because the vault was housed in the windowless basement—a fact they'd well-advertised during the week—the only entry point was through the ground floor of the shop. Lexy and Jack huddled near the open storeroom door. They kept the stairs in view.

"Did you hear that?"

Lexy flashed her eyes to Jack. A low-pitched whine pulsed somewhere. They held their breath and listened for it to sound again.

Silence.

Moments later, Jack whispered. "I don't hear it anymore. Maybe it was nothing."

Quiet surrounded them again, and they waited.

Lexy wiggled to get her blood flowing, and thought about their plan. *Thank God Christian agreed to bring in an armed security guard. I'm more than happy to let him deal with the bad guy. As long as these buzzers work, we're in business.*

Lexy and the guard both held small signaling devices. She would use it to alert him when the criminal broke in and headed downstairs. *As soon as the guard knows the thief is on his way, it's only a matter of timing things so we catch him—or her—red-handed.*

She sighed. *Ugh. So much for easy-peasy. Not that I really believed it would be.* A lump settled in her throat. She swallowed hard against it. She reminded herself the silent alarm would trip, notifying the police, as soon as the criminal broke any threshold. *The cops'll be en route as soon as the alarm is triggered. The guard'll have the thief in custody by the time they arrive. See? Nothing to worry about, Lex.*

The internal conversation served her well. It helped steady her breathing when she started thinking too much about everything that could go wrong. *Let's not go there, right?* She stretched and shifted to alleviate the pressure on her bottom.

Another two hours crawled in silence. The sandwiches were long gone.

"Lex, you still awake?"

"Huh? Yeah, yeah, of course I'm awake." An insulted tone carried through her whisper. She scooted around, waking up her limbs, and tried to recall when she last had feeling in her butt. The night was dragging. "What about you? Drifting off at all?"

"Nah, I'm okay. Tired, but okay. I wonder how our friend downstairs is doing. And I hope this bastard shows his face soon. My ass hurts."

Lexy agreed with a soft chuckle.

She shut up immediately, held a finger to her lips. Jack stared at her, ears pricked, and waited for her to acknowledge the question in his eyes. She returned his look, but held steady.

Then he heard it, too.

A scratching sound near the front of the shop. A scratch that hadn't been there a moment earlier. Hadn't been there since they'd set up camp. Intent, straining, they leaned in to listen.

Quiet. Deep quiet.

Too quiet. Fear flashed in Lexy's eyes.

Breath-held quiet.

She turned to Jack. He knew it, too. Someone was in the boutique. She prayed the alarm had been activated, and the police really were on their way, sirens silent but lights flaring.

She inched out to see into the main room. Shafts of streetlight slipped past the gated windows. She couldn't tell how the person had entered. Yet there he stood, motionless, a deep shadow where no light penetrated.

And it looks like a he.

A tall figure, shrouded in black, loomed in the space. Lexy struggled to see his features, but she couldn't distinguish anything.

Her fingers itched on the signaler, but she held off. Sweat popped out as her tension skyrocketed. The thief had to go for the bait. Anything less would mean complete failure. Or worse.

Finally, the shadow stepped toward the stairway, moving softly, head turning to check every direction.

Jack and Lexy held their breath. She squeezed his hand, realizing only then that she'd gripped him.

Down the steps the darkness drifted.

She pressed the transmitter.

They waited, a beat, a lifetime. The time felt incomprehensible. The barest of sounds emanated from the basement. Lexy and Jack crept near the top of the steps, well aware that at least one armed individual remained close.

The seconds crawled. Still nothing happened.

A scraping sound came, brushed metal against metal, and a single creak of heavy resistance.

For a minute, everything remained silent.

A switch clicked. Light showered upward and blinded them. Something crashed. The sound echoed up the stairs. They heard the guard yell for the man to drop his weapon.

Scuffling sounds reached them.

"Let me go!"

A fist connected with a snap of bone and flesh. Another crash sounded.

"Get your hands off me!"

Momentarily paralyzed, they eavesdropped on the shuffling, grunting din of a fight. Curses rose from the depths. They heard the crunch of fists and the thud of a body hitting something solid. Finally, a satisfied call from the guard rang out.

"It's over, guys. I've got him."

Jack grabbed her before she could dash down the steps. "Lex, stay put until I check it out. The police should be here any minute, so please," he said, "wait here until I'm sure we're in the clear." She nodded mutely as her adrenaline rapidly drained away.

Jack crept down the steps. A moment later Lexy turned and saw police cruiser lights brightening the front windows.

The next minutes blurred together as she let the officers in and explained who she was and what had happened.

When she turned back she saw Jack leading the way from the basement. The guard followed him, dragging a scowling, angry man in zip ties.

Evan Maxwell.

"Son of a bitch!" flew out of her mouth.

She launched herself at him, socking him square in the jaw before Jack could stop her. "You bastard! How could you do this?" Fear, sadness, anger overwhelmed her and flowed out of every pore. "How could you pretend to be nice to me, pretend to help me, when all along you killed Mrs. Stellery? All along, you were after her jewels," she railed at him, disregarding his look of shock.

Jack grabbed her shoulders and pulled her to him in a fierce hug.

"How could you?" she spat, eyes full of derision.

Evan struggled against his bonds and spluttered, "What the hell are you talking about, Lexy? I didn't kill anyone! I didn't have anything to do with Claudine's death." He spun around as much as his restraints allowed, frantically sounding off to the police, to anyone who would listen. "What the hell is going on here?"

An officer stepped forward and relieved the guard of his captive. For the first time, Lexy noticed the gash on the guard's head and the stream of blood painting its way down his face.

"Oh my God, are you alright?" She rushed to help the woozy guard and tried to ignore Evan's cries of innocence.

"I swear on my life, Lexy, Jack, I didn't kill Claudine! I needed those jewels. My God, I have to get those stones," he cried.

Lexy looked at Jack and shook her head sadly as the police dragged Maxwell away.

With the murderer hauled off and her adrenaline evaporating, Lexy struggled through the officer's questions. She made sure the guard got taken away by an ambulance. The locksmith had come and gone, replacing the bolts Evan had all-too-easily bypassed. She made a mental note to find out how the keycard system had failed.

The vault was another story entirely. But after cleaning up the mess from the fight, she knew the rest could wait until morning.

She reset the silent alarm. The only thing left to do was go home.

Exhaustion swamped Lexy in the now-silent shop, and as she looked at Jack she knew he felt the same. Despite their relief that the night ended successfully, a dull sadness pervaded the air.

She flicked off the lights and walked straight into Jack's embrace, feeling him, absorbing his emotion. Claudine was still dead, though they'd caught her killer. The knowledge weighed on them, made heavier by Evan's denials. It hurt to think about.

They stood there in silence for a long while, holding each other up. It felt alright in the dark, with only the waning moon squinting in. Respectful, somehow.

"It's time to go home, Lex," Jack murmured into her ear. The whoosh of his breath warmed her to the core. "Let's get out of here."

She nodded, knowing where they were going without another word.

"I'd like to make sure everything is squared away downstairs first."

He nodded and followed her through the darkened shop. They went downstairs, where she hit the lights to illuminate the chamber. Lexy moved with ease in the small space, rechecking that nothing was out of place, that the vault was secured. The routine soothed her.

Satisfied at last, she doused the lights, grabbed his hand and headed for the staircase.

A crash of shattering glass broke the silence.

Chapter 41

Lexy jumped with a quiet gasp. Jack hauled her back into the room, away from the stairs. A sound of screeching metal carried down to them.

Someone else was breaking in.

And they weren't being subtle about it.

Which meant the intruder could be downstairs and in the vault's outer room in seconds. Two hearts pounded in the tiny room.

Jack scoured his mental image of the space, straining to recall anything he could use as a weapon. Blank, he turned to Lexy. In the darkness, he could barely see her. But the metal pipe she handed him felt like Excalibur.

He pushed her deeper into the room and positioned himself inside the doorway. Sweat beaded on his body and threatened his grip.

They waited, silent, scared.

A tread sounded on the steps moments later. Down, inexorably down. Heavy and determined.

Who the hell is out there?

Jack stiffened and held his breath. *We reset the silent alarm, so it should've been tripped again. The police should be on the way. God help us if they write it off as a false alarm because of the first break-in.*

Then silence.

The darkness of a shadow within a shadow hovered in the doorway.

Jack tensed.

The shadow moved in.

Jack struck at the intruder's midsection. A massive "whoomph" rushed out as he doubled over. He recovered and dove at Jack. The two of them fell to the ground in a tight struggle.

Jack's grip slipped, and the pole clattered away. He knew it rolled out of reach. He punched the man's stomach, then grabbed his face and shoved. Curses bounced off the walls.

From the back corner, Lexy could differentiate the men from the lighter black of the open doorway. But in the dark, she couldn't see where the metal rod had gone. She angled her way around them and reached for the light switch, flooding the small area.

She threw a hand over her eyes against the instant brightness. When she recovered, she saw Jack on top of the intruder, a knee to his back to hold him down. The intruder sprawled face-down on the floor and tried to buck Jack off.

Lexy ran for the rod, lifted it and slammed it down with a thud on the intruder's legs. He cried out in agony, then stilled.

"Jack, are you okay?" She stared at a cut oozing blood down his face.

At her words, the stranger kicked again, not speaking, desperate to throw his captor. Jack pulled him backward by his collar and knocked his face onto the floor.

The man lay quiet, beaten.

"Yeah, I'm alright," he huffed out. "You have anything to tie up this guy with?" He threw a swift glance around the room. "I really don't feel like sitting on him until the police arrive." He gave a little jab with his heel to the intruder's leg, satisfied when he heard him groan.

Lexy returned with cord from the upstairs storage room. "The police are on the way. I called, but they'd already responded to the alarm. I told them we were alright. They'll be here any minute." She eyed the motionless lump on the floor. "How do you want me to do this?"

After a few minutes of wrestling with the rope, Jack had the man's hands and feet tied. He gave an extra tug to check the knots' security, then muttered, "Now, let's see who the hell this asshole is."

Jack rolled his captive over. He staggered back, floored.

At his feet lay Peter Lambert. His friend. *Pete.*

A scowling, bloodied, raging Pete.

"Pete? What the fuck, man?" Jack looked as if a breeze could knock him over. "What the hell is going on?" He backed away.

Peter struggled against his bonds and snarled, "I came to get that damn diary, Jack! It's mine! Its secrets belong to me!" Venom spewed out with his raspy voice. "That, and those goddamn jewels! They're all mine, and I'll get my hands on them one way or another," he swore.

Jack shook his head, blank-faced. "What the hell are you talking about? How do you know about the diary? About tonight?" A harder shake this time.

A deep frown settled over Jack's face as anger supplanted confusion. "Why in hell do you think you have anything to do with this? Exactly what the fuck is going on here, Pete?"

Jack moved forward, but Lexy pulled him out of Pete's proximity with a firm hand on his arm. Jack scowled at her but backed away. "Tell me why you're here."

Pete edged onto his side and spat a wad of congealing blood in Jack's direction. He remained silent. Police sirens hummed, barely audible in the distance.

Pete divided a glance between Jack and Lexy, and then decided to talk. He jerked his head to flip a strand of ratty hair out of his eyes and cursed. "Those jewels, and every other piece of treasure that once belonged to Calico Jack, are mine! You and Stellery aren't the only two Rackham descendants … I'm his blood kin, too."

He pasted on a grim smile and said, "Say hello to your long-lost cousin, Jack-o."

Lexy stepped up when she saw Jack's jaw drop. "What do you mean, Peter? You're related to Calico Jack? You're *related* to Jack Hughes?"

"Damn straight I am," he roared. "And that diary proves it. The start of it, anyway. My ancestor is the kid that Rackham and Anne Bonny ditched in Cuba. Too bad they tried to dump their little problem way back when. Who knew it would come back to haunt their happy little family so many years later." He sneered.

Jack tried to form a coherent thought. *This is my friend, Pete. Hell, I thought of him as family long before this. And now ... he really is family?* Jack shuddered. *Now he's tied up on the floor for attempted burglary and God only knows what else.*

"Pete, if this is true, if you really are descended from Jack and Anne's first child ... how could you never have told me? Man, we were practically brothers! You live on my goddamn property! How could you not have said a word?" Disbelief and hurt warred for supremacy.

Pete laughed at him, straining against his bindings. "Jack-o, you're a goddamn fool," he bit out. "I've known who I am my whole life. But getting close to you, watching you and that crazy aunt of yours all these years, well, hell, that almost made up for all the shit my father went through."

He saw Jack's bewilderment and continued. "I grew up knowing my legacy. My father found Anne's diary. He was desperate for money and pawned it, but not before he learned the truth about Jack and Anne.

"Right from the start, when they abandoned their kid." Bitterness filled his words. "Ol' Christopher was old enough to understand what happened when his folks left him in Havana. He grew up fast and hard and with a hatred for those pirates. But he knew their bounty rightfully belonged to him, as the first-born son.

"Only he couldn't find the damn treasure!" Peter lunged once more against his ties, growing angrier, dark eyes wild around the room. Pushing with his legs, he sat up and leaned against the wall.

"Those fucking hurricanes! They wiped away all traces of the loot before Christopher could recover it. And ever since, *ever since*, my family's searched the Caribbean for any trace, with no luck.

"Until my father, thirty-five years ago."

Lexy inhaled sharply, and Jack started forward again. "Your father? Your father was the salvor who found the jewels on that shipwreck?"

"Damn straight! He searched his entire life for that wreckage. Finally he found it, but all he ever brought up were those goddamn cursed jewels. Only to have them stolen by that bastard Edwards! They were ours! Do you know what that did to my dad? Do you?"

He didn't wait for an answer. "It shattered him! I was a kid when it happened, but he was never the same after that. Not after that second hurricane came and washed away any chance he had of finding anything else." He shook his head, scowling. "He was a different man. Aimless, empty. One day he went out to the bar … and never came back."

When Peter paused, Lexy heard the sirens stop outside and she hurried to let the police in. The men had the room to themselves.

"Tell me, Pete. How far does this go?" Jack's hands clenched into fists as the silky, quiet words slipped out. "Are you responsible for everything that's happened since the gems were auctioned?" He took another step forward. "Are you?"

An evil laugh escaped Pete before his voice cracked into a rough cough. "Those stones belong to me, Jack-o! They're mine, and I had to get them. I'm not rich like your aunt, so I had to get my info any way I could. Our 'friendship' gave me access to all the inside info I needed about the search, courtesy of that old bitch." He leered at Jack, whose face contorted with rage. "You two were chock-full of helpful, juicy tidbits of information. Thanks ever so much."

Pete got off by taunting him and continued, unaware that Lexy had quietly led the police detective halfway down the stairs, where they listened out of sight. "I heard the rumors about the jewels being auctioned. When you told me that's why you were heading to Eleuthera, I knew I had to get there. Obviously I couldn't bid on the gems, but I figured I'd have it easy, stealing them from that guard. Too bad for him." He laughed, an eerie sound that hovered in the small room.

Peter's eyes flicked over Jack, flat and icy.

"But the stones had already been locked away. And damn me! I couldn't break into the vault before daylight! Then there was that fucking, last-minute change of your aunt's to helicopter the jewels from the airport. What a son of a bitch." A sinister, gleeful look lit his eyes.

God, he's enjoying this. That bastard! I hope like hell he has no idea the police are listening. Jack chewed the inside of his cheek to keep from interrupting Pete's confession. *Go ahead, you asshole. Dig your grave.*

"Do you know how hard it was to get my friend behind the stick of that 'copter? Then he went and died, trying to toss them like we planned. Fool." Pete tilted his head and frowned.

Jack wondered whether the frown was out of sadness that his friend had exploded over the Hudson. But Pete's words disabused him of that idea.

"You see, Jack-o, how mad that made me. So fuckin' mad that I could've killed your aunt!" He stared with sick intent at Jack.

"Oh wait, I did kill her."

At the harshly uttered words, Jack dove and viciously punched Pete, snapping his head against the wall. Lexy and the detective sprinted down the remaining steps and tore Jack away before he could continue the pummeling. Pete laughed, a crazy, keening sound, while blood spurted from his nose and lip.

Lexy wrapped her arms around Jack from behind. She pulled him backward, hugging him tightly. "Let it go, Jack. There's nothing more you can do. We can't bring Claudine back."

He gripped her arms with his right hand and let himself be drawn back. His eyes followed as the officer dragged Peter Lambert away.

Chapter 42

For the second time early that morning, Lexy and Jack cleaned up the shop and sat through a police debriefing. So many questions remained. Lexy and Jack wondered if they'd ever find the answers.

They would have to wait until the police finished their investigation before they could learn exactly how Pete transferred the poison to the jewels. The cops had already interrogated the security guard from the awards dinner. He claimed a man had paid him for a chance to look at the gems, nothing more. Though he'd remained in the room with the man, the guard admitted the emeralds were out of his eyesight, behind the open lid of the case. The police expected Pete's testimony would shed more light on his actions.

After hearing him rant, Lexy and Jack guessed Peter's sense of vengeance was so great, he believed he could poison Claudine and retrieve the stones after the police had finished with them. Complete egotism at its worst.

On their second visit the police offered new information about Evan Maxwell. Before he lawyered up, he had rambled on about gambling debts around the Caribbean and falling in with "the wrong sort of people."

"Apparently," the detective said to Lexy, "that whole auction thing had been a ruse on his part. He never intended to buy the jewels, only to scope out the place. Lambert's offing the guard disrupted Maxwell's plans to steal the stones. After he couldn't get his hands on them in the Bahamas, he followed you around Manhattan, waiting for you to have the gems so he could steal them. He figured Hughes would turn them over to you for appraisal after the police returned them. Maxwell figured you˙were an easier target. He broke into your apartment and lifted your pass card for the shop."

As the detective's words penetrated Lexy's muddled brain, she shivered. "God, that asshole. I knew something felt off about him. But at least a few other things make sense now. And see, I knew it! I knew I was being followed." She turned triumphantly to Jack, then realized how silly she sounded. "At least I can say 'I told you so' to Claire and Stacey …."

She thanked the officers for their update. They returned to the precinct with their newest prisoner.

Before Lexy and Jack could leave, though, she needed to make two calls: Claire and Christian. After reassurances that she and Jack, the shop and everything else were more or less alright, she hung up.

"You know, Jack, despite all this, I think Christian likes having me in the shop watching over things. He travels a lot himself. I wonder if I could parlay that into something mutually beneficial … like a partnership?"

She let the question hang in the air as she glanced his way. "But let's not worry about that now. It's time to blow this popsicle stand."

A pale sun hovered in the eastern sky when at last they left the boutique.

On the desolate street, Lexy recalled a niggling question and asked, "If Peter knew the wreck had been re-sunk, or whatever you call it, thirty-five years ago with the rest of the treasure still intact, then why did he think the diary contained secrets, clues to its location? Why did he want the journal, too?" Her gray eyes bored into his amber ones, wanting answers she knew he didn't have.

"I don't know what to tell you, Lex. I still haven't read all of the original diary. Maybe there's something important I haven't found yet."

He turned his head slowly this way and that, taking in their surroundings. Breathing in the crisp morning air.

"Half my life, I thought of that guy as my friend, but now? I don't think I could tell you a single true thing about him." He hung his head a moment. "I can't believe how much he hated us."

He rubbed his eyes with the heels of his palms. "Hell, I don't even think he'd care Aunt Cee planned to find him *and* the rest of the treasure and share it among the families." Sad eyes flicked her way. "I think he was too far gone for anything I could've said."

Lexy stepped forward and pressed a soft, lingering kiss on his lips. Then she punched him in the shoulder.

"You're right, Jack. He *was* too far gone. I'd tell you not to beat yourself up over him, but it wouldn't do any good. So I'll say this: At least now we know what happened to Claudine. And we know the truth about Rackham, Anne and Mary, and even something about the other crazy-ass relations you have out there—though, God, I kind of hope Peter is the last of them."

Jack chuckled slightly, and she smiled.

"Don't forget," Lexy said, "we also know there's treasure still out there somewhere, waiting for the right guys to come along and suss it out."

She cocked her head at him, and the morning sun shimmered in her eyes, turning them silver. "I happen to have a contact or two down in the Caribbean, you know." She smiled. "I think Matt might be amenable to a small side gig, don't you? Besides, right about now, I'm thinking the two of us could use a vacation."

Jack shook with a full-bodied laugh, and his tension began to ease. "You're damn right, woman. I'm getting a little booty fever." He wiggled his eyebrows at her. "But I've got something else in mind. C'mon, Lexy-girl, time to get the hell outta here. Let's grab a taxi to the townhouse."

He moved next to her, draped his arm across her shoulders and snugged her close. She settled in, feeling the fit and liking it.

"No way, buster." She winked. "My place is closer."

She turned him toward the river, and they walked away with the sun warming their backs.

www.ingramcontent.com/pod-product-compliance
Lightning Source LLC
Chambersburg PA
CBHW060408180626
46817CB00007B/2547

* 9 7 8 0 9 9 6 6 0 0 2 1 7 *